Dreadful Outcomes

The Wickesborough Chronicles

By David Heckman

Table of Contents:

Introduction and Acknowledgements:

Without the encouragement of several people this work would have remained in a desk drawer gathering the tears of my despair.

First off, I have to thank Mike Welte, who gave my efforts the time, corrections and editing needed. His eye for style, punctuation and spelling filled the gaps in my education in English from Emerson.

Thanks also to John McCann, who encouraged me over coffee and BLTs at Foxy's. Thanks as well to Darleen Richter for the superb cover.

Wickesborough does not exist; it is an amalgam of places that do exist in western Pennsylvania. The rest of Pennsylvania is well chronicled by the likes of John O'Hara, John Updike and James Michener, I was lucky to find a section that wasn't already visited by far better writers.

The Dreadful Outcomes in The Wickesborough Chronicles are all true, either experienced by me or told to me by people I trust. It only remained for me to change a few names and locations to avoid litigation. It goes without saying that every name was changed to protect the guilty.

D.G. Heckman

Cannibals, Not Zombies

It was a coal dark night in downtown Wickesborough and the only light was the glow from WCVR's broadcast studio window. The station boasted that it was the Clarion Valley's "Hometown Radio" and management thought that having their studio in a storefront on Main Street in Wickesborough would drive the point home. In the morning and afternoon it attracted a spattering of interest from passers-by, but at night it overlooked the desolate streetscape that was Wickesborough after dark.

The DJ, Ozzy Mandis, nee Byron Mandlstein, was behind the mic for his graveyard talk shift. He was a radio nomad, working at AM talkers across the country. His biggest market thus far had been Seattle, but the station there had been bought and automated, so now he was in Wickesborough waiting for something better to come along. Ozzy had a following among the local insomniacs, drunks and other nocturnal creatures, but none of them were likely to wander downtown to peer in his window on a night like this.

It was just as well, he had some plans for later, with a special fan, if the coast was clear.

"Good evening Night Owls… You're tuned to WCVR the voice of the greater Clarion Valley and you're listening to Night Terrors, the show that covers and uncovers all the weirdness and spookiness going on in Wickesborough County… I'm Ozzy Mandis, the Night Crawler, up late like you. Tell me what's keeping you up tonight. What's on your mind? Go ahead caller… Dave…. From Blanket Hill...

"Hi Oz… First off, I love your show… Especially…

"Thanks Dave… What's keeping you up?"

"Right… You know how people always call in about weird stuff in Wickesborough."

"That's why we call the show The Night Terrors… with Ozzy Mandis. Remember? What's on your mind?"

"I was in a bar the other night…"

"What a coincidence, a lot of our listeners are in bars right now… How about a big Night Terrors shout-out to the gang at the 422 Tavern… where Thursday is ladies night and draft beer is just fifty cents."

"Yeah… Well I heard this guy talking about cannibals."

"OK… Like Donner party cannibals, missionaries in big pots cannibals, or reanimated ghouls after brains?"

"Neither…"

"That's too bad 'cause I could have helped you out with the ghouls… A hollow point in the head and no more ghoul."

"Exactly how is that supposed to work? Isn't a lack of brain waves…?"

"Best not to question life's mysteries Dave… just give'em a tap… and move on."

"I suppose… But these guys weren't stumbling ghouls; they were more like you and me…"

"Speak for yourself Dave… Did this guy claim to be a cannibal?"

"That's what I been trying to say…"

"So the other night, you met a person, in a bar, who said he was a cannibal? It wasn't the Clarion Marina was it?"

"No, do cannibals usually hang out there?"

"Uh … No Dave… Practical jokers yes, but I don't think you'll find a cannibal."

"It wasn't just him… He had, like maybe, twenty friends."

"All cannibals?"

"I guess… I didn't ask everyone."

"What did the other customers make of it?"

"Not much, it was after hours and I was the only one there, excepting the bartender and bar-back… and the cannibals."

Ozzy knew he was in for a long night.

"The Night Terrors Show" was on the radio when Brad Randal saw the headlights ahead. He had just turned down the road leading to his deer stand. It wasn't a stand really; just a tree he could climb that overlooked a salt lick.

It wasn't really a road either, just a worn down track into the woods and it wasn't really deer season either, but the less said about that the better.

Brad could see a group of people standing around. He counted twenty or so, clustered around about a dozen cars, laughing and carousing. They were having a grand time, drinking, eating and making noise.

A crowd of noisy people wouldn't enhance his chances of bagging some out of season venison; no deer would come within a mile of here tonight. They were pulled off the road and Brad thought about it, but decided to turn around; no reason to climb a tree if the deer weren't going to show up.

He'd go home and surprise the wife instead. At least that was the plan, until he backed into a ditch and buried his rear wheels in some mud. He was up to his pumpkin and getting no traction no matter how hard he gunned it. It looked like it would take an hour of digging and rocking back and forth before he got unstuck.

He'd just begun the first round of ineffectual rocking when a girl appeared at his window.

"Hey… You stuck?"

Brad was about to make a snarky reply when he took a second look. She was a slender brunette with long lank hair, the kind of girl he favored, even though he was married to Doris, a sweet, dumb, short-haired, chubby, dishwater blonde. Doris was kind of the reason he was out here. Aside from the sheer pleasure of being away from her, Doris had a new recipe for venison meatloaf that she wanted to try.

The girl at the window was wearing a denim mini- dress with snaps closing the front, the kind of dress Brad imagined he could get her out of with a quick tug. Then he thought about Doris, and the trouble he was asking for, and expelled the thought from his mind.

"You need some help?"

"I would be most grateful."

She leaned in the window and took in the cab of his truck; she saw his deer rifle while Brad peeked down her slightly less than discreet neckline.

'I would hit that,' Brad thought, but remembered his wife at home and resolved to be good.

"You're a hunter?" "Yeah…"

"A little early for deer season isn't it?"

"Not if you have a taste for venison."

"Amen… When I want venison, I have to have it." "You ever want anything other than venison?"

She rolled her eyes. It wasn't much of a double entendre, but she'd caught his drift. Hell, a little flirting couldn't hurt, he wasn't dead. Smoke from a barbeque wafted by and Brad remembered he was hungry.

"Whatever it is you're cooking sure smells good."

"Yeah… It ain't venison, but it'll do."

"I'll bet… Would you mind driving my truck while I push it out of this mud?"

"How about I get Chet and Oscar to push it out of the mud, while you drive and I stand around and drink a beer?"

"Even better."

"I'm Melissa, by the way," she said as she led him to the party. "You look like you could use a beer too."

'Maybe the night wasn't going to be a total washout after all,' Brad thought, 'although if Doris gets wind of this…'

Ozzy was bathed in red light as he worked the board. Basically, he ran commercials, answered the phone and talked about whatever the listeners called in with.

Tonight, Dave was talking about cannibals; it was as good a subject as any.

"We're back… Ozzy Mandis here… The show is called Night Terrors and Dave is on the line talking about zombies…"

"Cannibals actually… They were very specific… They are cannibals not zombies…"

"Explain…"

"Well the guy I talked to made a good point, zombies are the undead and he was very much alive…"

"He just eats people."

"Exactly."

"Did he say how he comes by people to eat? It's not like they have people cutlets on sale at Hill's Market …"

"He said they ate people no one would miss... He called it culling the herd."

"He said herd?"

"Yeah… He meant people no one would miss … You know marginal folks."

"That's kind of scary Dave… any idea… any idea how he knows who's marginal?"

"Oh … homeless guys, runaways, folks with domestic problems... Sometimes they take requests…Wives who don't want their husbands anymore… That sort of thing… You know how sometimes you just wish someone would go away…"

"Yeah, I kind of feel that way now."

"Well, Chet makes it happen."

"Do a lot of people use his service?"

"Well, it didn't look like he missed many meals."

The party was going strong when Brad got his beer; Melissa introduced him to Chet, and Chet introduced him to a bunch of other people whose names he instantly forgot. He watched a knot of people swaying to someone's choice of eccentric music and sucked down beer. The beer tasted particularly good tonight.

Melissa swayed along with the other revellers, while Brad sipped beer and watched. He didn't like to dance in public; he thought it made him look like a dork. Melissa didn't mind though, her denim skirt had ridden up to mid- thigh and the neckline was suddenly open a couple more snaps, hinting at perky breasts. She put her arms around him and began riding up and down his thigh.

He grabbed her by the waist and pulled her into him, this was almost good enough to risk getting in trouble with Doris. She kept grinding on him until the song ended. They made their way to the beer cooler and Brad was handed another tall boy and a sandwich. Chet was tending the smoker and slicing meat.

"It's late to be picnicking. What are you guys, a bunch of vampires?"

"Nah, vampires only drink blood."

"You sure picked an isolated spot … Why are you out here?"

"The authorities don't exactly approve of what's on the menu."

"I knew it … You're poachers."

"Well sort of… Mr. Out-of-season-venison hunter… There's no season for…"

"No, no, no… It's okay; I don't know why fish and game makes such a big deal about taking out of season deer… It's not like we are going to run out of them…"

"I know… and culling keeps the herd healthy."

Brad bit into his sandwich, it had a flavor he'd never tasted before, but was strangely familiar anyway. He would have called it "epicurean déjà vu" if he subscribed to Gourmet Magazine, but Brad's idea of sophisticated dining consisted of having Swiss instead of American on his cheeseburger at TGIF.

"This is delicious," he said with his mouth full. "You guys have a way with venison."

"Not really… that isn't venison."

"Then its pork… tastes like pork."

"We call it 'long pig'."

Brad was feeling warm, so Melissa helped him off with his shirt. She ran her hands up and down his chest then reached around and grabbed his butt.

"You have a nice firm ass," she said. "Nice and meaty."

"Can't drive a ten inch spike with a tack hammer."

Melissa laughed, rolled her eyes and rubbed his penis through his jeans. Brad liked the way the evening was going so far, maybe he would take a chance on Doris finding out. Somebody changed the radio to Ozzy and The Night Terrors.

Ozzy looked at his watch, he wanted Dave to wrap up his rant about cannibals so he could sign off. The overnight guy, "Rockin" Jon Stoney, was coming in early so Ozzy could hook up with a cute little blonde.

Ozzy met her when he was doing station promotion at a gun show; her husband was shopping for firearms and she was bored. When she caught him admiring how well her butt filled out her jeans, she introduced herself. He autographed some WCVR promo crap for her and she said she was a big fan, a really big fan. Ozzy liked a girl with some meat on her, so he made it clear he was interested.

She let Ozzy know the interest was mutual.

Her husband was browsing through nearby tables of guns, but that didn't seem to matter. She suggested they meet up some night when her hubby was out. Ozzy didn't like the odds. While dating her had a pleasant, guaranteed upside, betting that her husband and his new gun wouldn't interrupt them was a wager with a potentially lethal downside. He wasn't going to take the chance for a piece of white-trash trim unless he was sure the coast was one hundred percent clear.

It didn't seem to matter much now, with Dave on his endless cannibal rant; he might be on the air for hours. Ozzy prayed that he would run dry, but Dave was becoming more voluble on the subject of cannibals.

"Before the break Dave was just finishing telling us about his encounter with some local cannibals…"

"They aren't really local… they're like one of those hippie tribes… except they look normal… they go from town to town picking off strays and eating them. It's not a full time thing either… more like a road trip. They got jobs and things to do, just like everybody."

"Did they mention kuru?"

"No they didn't, Ozzy… What's kuru?"

"A disease you get from eating people… It makes you insane."

"I would have thought being a cannibal already qualified you as insane."

"Good point… Are your cannibal pals going to be at the bar tonight?"

"We ain't really friends… I only met them the other night…"

"Okay, your acquaintances … Did they mention where they'd be tonight?"

"No… He did say they were on the road after tonight… I don't think they want to attract attention."

"Okay… So, can you warn our listeners where they might get swarmed by a bunch of ghouls?"

"Oh they don't swarm… they throw a bag over your head and whack you with a hammer… At least that's what happened to the bar-back."

"They killed someone right in front of you?"

"Oh yeah… right after he brought up a case of Miller Lites."

"Did the bartender say anything?"

"No… He'd already brought up the Buds and Iron Cities so he was pretty much done for the evening."

"And they ate him?"

"I guess so… not there in the bar, but what else would they do with a dead bar-back?"

The party was winding down for everybody but Brad. Melissa, Chet and a couple of their friends were making a fuss over him. By now though, it was getting a little old and Brad was feeling woozy. He'd only had three beers all night and beer never hit him like this before, but he sure felt it this evening.

Melissa sat him down and rubbed his neck, it felt nice, but it also made him sleepy. Brad wanted to get home.

"I don't feel so good… Do you think your friends could help me get my truck out?"

"Sure… But don't leave… The party is just getting started."

"I think I'd better be going."

"Please stay… My friends want to have you for dinner."

"I appreciate it, but I better be getting along."

Brad headed back to his truck, Melissa, Chet and some other guys tagged along to help get it out of the ditch; one was gnawing on something crispy and barbequed that almost resembled a foot. Brad stumbled and had to steady himself. Melissa suggested he take a nap before driving home. His head was swirling, but Brad was insistent.

"No… My wife would kill me if I don't get home by morning."

"Oh Brad… I don't think Doris will care."

Brad looked at Melissa quizzically. He wondered how she knew Doris and why everyone else was laughing. There was irony in her voice, but he didn't get the joke. His head was spinning and he really needed to sit down or he'd pass out. He sat on the tailgate of his truck and stared back at the people laughing at him. He was sure he'd be okay in a few minutes.

Brad never got those minutes. The blackness came down with the canvas bag that was slipped over his head. The drugs they'd given him made it impossible to resist.

He was confused and disoriented, but only briefly, soon he was feeling nothing, nothing at all.

Ozzy buzzed in his relief, while Dave continued to ramble on about cannibals. Ozzy was convinced he was being pranked. Ramrod Rick Riser was a friendly rival at a station in Butler and Dave was probably a plant of his. He must have heard about Ozzy's date and sent Dave to try and cock block him. It was time to shut Dave down.

His replacement gave him the high sign and it was time for Dave to go.

"You know Oz… I heard that "Silence of the Lambs" was based on a true story, but I never believed it… until now. It was like I was talking to that Hannibal guy except he wasn't in jail and he talked normal…"

"Dave…"

"Yes Ozzy…"

"You know cannibals are deeply troubled people, don't you Dave?"

"Yeah… but they're creepy and weird like your show."

"Do you think you and Ramrod Rick should be making fun of these troubled souls?"

"Who's Ramrod Rick?"

"Thanks for calling Dave… Well that's all the time we have for tonight. Thanks for listening to Night Terrors. "Rockin" Jon Stoney and the Overnight Thunder is next up on WCVR…"

The station's ID jingle played and they hit the network news and weather feed on time. So far so good, Rockin' Jon Stoney slid behind the mic and Ozzy could officially split.

"How was the show?"

"Okay… One guy went on and on…"

"About cannibals… I heard part of it driving in… wild stuff… A chick named Doris is waiting for you in the lobby. "

"My date."

"Sweet… Oh and a guy named Chet left a message for you on the station voicemail… he said the coast is one hundred percent clear."

Waiting for Andy

The rain was coming down in a thin grey gruel, a windless, cold mist that soaked to the skin without rising to the level of a shower. It ran down the walls of the houses in Wickesborough and stained their Kittanning brick walls with soot it washed from the air. Johnston Avenue was quiet, everyone was inside, their porch gliders silent and still. The residents drank their coffee at warm, dry, kitchen tables and counted themselves lucky. The soaking made the street shine like a ribbon of jet, so shiny it reflected a cop in yellow raingear tapping on the windshield of Groverton's car.

"Rise and shine, asshole."

The aging red Cadillac was familiar to Wickesborough PD. It belonged to Cyrus Groverton, a lowlife the police were having trouble convincing that they didn't want him around.

Groverton liked to sleep it off on Johnston Avenue.

He wasn't exactly homeless, but he wasn't exactly welcome at the address he gave in Butler, so Johnston

Avenue was as good a place as any to recuperate. The cops didn't care for that, so they'd started giving him tickets while he was passed out in his car, just to make the point.

Groverton got the point and cranked the wheezy Caddy for all it was worth. The last time this had happened, Groverton had mouthed off and the cop had inflicted some gratuitous dings in his car door with his nightclub.

"I'm moving, officer."

The Caddy pulled away, headed for the brickyard where Groverton conducted his business.

A shambling, diminutive figure watched Groverton from the shadowy cover of an alley across the street. It was Andy Woodhouse, and this morning he was careful to recede into the gray half-light of the morning drizzle. They would run him in for truancy if the cop saw him, so he stood perfectly still and became invisible while rain dripped down his neck.

Andy was soaked to the skin by the time Groverton left for his place of business. Andy followed; he had some business to conduct as well.

Groverton sold counterfeit jeans to local kids in the brickyard. The brickyard was abandoned like everything else in Wickesborough, and abandoned so long ago that even the bricks were gone—usually the last thing looted from industrial wreck sites. Groverton parked behind an abandoned office, as far up the yard as his Caddy would go. There he was hidden from the cops, but convenient for his clientele.

His clientele didn't care the jeans were fakes; it added some dazzle to their drab lives. Groverton earned enough to stay drunk, full of KFC and occasionally throw a twenty and a pair of jeans at local girls for sex. The girls didn't consider themselves whores yet—that revelation was still to come.

The cold drizzle saturated the clay beds and a stream of brick-colored slurry ran down the center of the driveway. It ran swift most of the way, but eddied in pools near Groverton's car. The slick clay made it rough going for Andy as he made his way to where the car was parked.

He had some heavy scissors hanging from a lanyard around his neck. They banged painfully against his concave chest with every step. They were serious shears, eighteen inches long and solid steel. Andy was after some jeans and the shears would come in handy when it came time to make alterations. He would watch, statue still, in the derelict yard and waiting until the time was right.

Andy watched a young girl, prettier than she knew, performing the foreplay Groverton demanded for his jeans. She was oblivious of Andy's presence as she did what she had to for some jeans. Andy saw her skinny white buttocks when she lay across the back seat to consummate the transaction. Groverton's own flabby flanks were dimpled with cellulite and dappled with scabs, but he pushed against the girl with a youthful enthusiasm.

It was over quickly, too soon for Groverton, but not soon enough for the girl who was anxious to get her barter and be gone.

"I should make you do me again."

"Can't... I got school... I need the jeans."

"Hold your horses…"

"I got to go."

The girl rummaged around in the rag pile that was her clothing and pulled out a pack of Marlboros.

Groverton was inclined to let her linger until he was ready for another round—he couldn't have cared less about the girl or her life, until she fired up a smoke amidst their post coital-clutter. Groverton hated smoking, particularly in his car. He threw the girl some jeans and kicked her out.

Naked in the rain, she hobbled toward Johnston Avenue, pulling on clothing as she went.

"Go… You whore."

Groverton took a draught off a handy bottle and lay down in his bed of sordid nuptials. Satisfied with his day so far, he went to sleep.

Andy watched their antics with interest. He was an adolescent boy, though his size and shape concealed the hormonal storm going on in his body. The girl, Milan Kumnacker, went to Andy's school; if she knew Andy Woodhouse she ignored him. He wasn't the sort of people she or her family associated with. Even whores have their standards.

Andy was small and deformed a difficult birth for a mother who smoked and drank her way through pregnancy. By the time she took cognizance of her condition it was too late to shed her poisoned foetus.

As a final insult, the forceps were mishandled during his delivery and Andy was left with a withered arm, a foot that dragged and a football-shaped head that tilted down and to the side.

Andy's appearance made folks stare at him at a distance and look away when he drew near. He had quasi-Asiatic-features that suggested Down's syndrome, and made him look exotic enough to be a magnet for the cruelty of children. His dragging foot prompted his peers to call him Igor when adults weren't around. There was a patch of psoriasis on his head which he picked constantly despite the objections of onlookers.

Almost nothing about him pleased anyone. His mother ignored him and none of her lovers showed any interest in him or claimed paternity. Her parents died mourning their dissipated daughter and their misshapen grandson.

Andy was hard of hearing and was thought to be visually impaired because no one imagined he could see through eyes that squinted so badly. He could see fine, but nobody cared to investigate. They did exchange sympathetic looks over the boy's condition and wondered how any mother could neglect a child so completely. Invariably, her dissolute life was recalled, and they turned away.

In the used clothes his mother never washed, he drifted through the town. Andy reminded folks that their town was a place where the flotsam of humanity washed up, people like Andy, and Groverton.

Andy despised his tormentors and well-wishers equally. The anger lurked just beneath his placid exterior and threatened to erupt at any time. He exploded, once, after he was caught doing questionable things with stray pets, which earned him the attention of local authorities. Their response was as effective as it could be without actually doing something; they assigned a cop, Braxton Dunkel, to be the At-Risk-Children's Task Force in his spare time. Andy never exploded again. He learned to moderate his anger and the Task Force was deemed a great success.

None of that was on Andy's mind today; he was after some jeans of his own. He didn't think the jeans would make him popular; he wanted them because everyone else did. Groverton was snoring away and Andy decided the time had come to steal some jeans. Breaking into the trunk would be easy, the latch didn't work and

Andy had seen the Groverton pop it by slamming his meaty hand on the lid. Andy gave it a shot. The trunk lid floated languidly upward on its hydraulics revealing the cavern of denim treasures within. There were all kinds of jeans, of many brands and different sizes. Andy had just grabbed a few off the top when Groverton's hand came down on his neck. Andy was surprised that Groverton had revived so quickly, and Groverton was surprised to find he had the local retard in his grip.

"Let me go faggot," screamed Andy as he squirmed in Groverton's grip.

"What the fuck are you doing, you little fuck?"

Groverton tossed Andy a few feet and considered his next move. The two combatants sized each other up across six feet of muddy runoff.

What Groverton thought of Andy, if he thought of him at all, was that he was a harmless spaz other kids bullied. He was going to let Andy off with a warning, until he noticed the shears and decided it was the better part of discretion to fetch the ax handle he kept for protection. As he made for his car, he slipped and fell into a pool of silty water. The sight of the fat man wallowing in the mud made Andy laugh, and the laughter made Groverton furious.

"I'm going to fuck you up, you little prick," Groverton bellowed at Andy as he made haste retrieving the ax handle. Groverton made good time to the safety of his back seat, but Andy made better and caught Groverton looking the other way. Andy's heavy shears caved in Groverton's temple. After repeated strokes, it was clear Groverton wouldn't bother Andy any more.

Andy gathered his loot and took it to a dilapidated garage on an alley near the latest apartment his mother had rented. It had mostly collapsed sometime in the last century, but a fortuitous convergence of building materials and gravity kept it from falling down completely. It smelled of termites, mouse piss and dry rot—in fact it smelled like the town smelled, just a little more concentrated by enclosure.

An old man, Nathan Howard, actually owned the garage, but left Andy alone and had no curiosity about what he did there. He knew Andy's mother left him alone most days while she recovered from nights of debauchery and cocktail waitressing, but he was too preoccupied with his own dying, which hovered not far over the horizon, to care.

He kept one treasure, a fancy car, in the garage. It hadn't moved in years, was covered in dust and had a flat tire, but as long as Andy didn't mess with it, they were fine. The old man thought there was a kind of a contract between them—as long as Andy didn't bother his car, he didn't bother Andy.

The garage was spacious enough for both, so the arrangement worked out fine, even if Andy was unaware of it. Nathan regarded Andy as an unpaid watchman who kept other kids from using his garage to do drugs or engage in other immoral pastimes. Andy might be lame, deaf and blind, but at least he didn't start fires or leave smut lying around.

The town was full of elderly singles like Nathan, busy with dying, and rootless teenagers, too blinded by youth to realize they were doing the same. The widows and widowers locked themselves away in their paid-off houses and retreated to the rooms they actually used as they lost their battle with time.

Spare bedrooms for relatives who never visited and front rooms that never accommodated guests were abandoned until only essential rooms were occupied. The rest of their houses and yards were cast off and left for ghosts and the feral children of unknown neighbors to explore and claim.

It was the nocturnal ramblings of children that caused Nathan the most worry. On sultry evenings, long after most people were asleep under damp sheets, the kids would meet seeking the mischief they defined as fun.

It terrified Nathan. He heard their muted voices making plans, the older ones hanging off cars, the younger ones scurrying down alleys, worrying latches, searching and exploring everything that came under their gaze. Sometimes they prowled through the homes of the elderly, for what purpose no one, including the prowlers, knew. Sometimes, Nathan called the police and, in the process, became known as the neighborhood prick, a bitter old killjoy with an overactive imagination. Most of the prowls were harmless, according to the indifferent cops.

"Nothing but youthful hijinks," they said, and started ignoring his calls.

Nathan disagreed. He saw sinister shapes out of the corner of his failing eyes and wondered if he was alone. By now, he hardly ever left his kitchen or the easy chair in the rec room where he slept through his TV shows. Sometimes a creaking floor board would awaken him and he'd search the darkness for an unwelcome visitor.

His dusty gray garage was the sort of place the prowling kids were looking for, an abandoned outbuilding where they could pursue the hobbies of youth: sex, drugs and the music of acceptable rebellion. It offered perfect access to the vulnerable back of his house and a door with a decrepit lock any child could slip. Nathan knew it was only a matter of time before the teenagers moved in and added this nuisance to his other ailments.

Today, he did an uncharacteristic thing; he peered through the dirty window in the garage at his beloved old car. He saw Andy was cutting some jeans up with large scissors. There was something disquieting about the shears, but the old man wasn't sure why. He'd seen them before, but couldn't remember where; he wondered how Andy had gotten them.

Nathan was going out today. A church group periodically rounded up isolated seniors and bused them to a Wal*mart outside of Pittsburgh. There they'd buy cheap trash that would be thrown away by their survivors. When their chaperons decided they'd spent enough of their remainder on such trivia, they were rounded up again and returned home. The chaperons felt good about themselves and much uplifted.

Andy was happy when the old people left; from experience he knew he would be undisturbed all day.

Andy sat on the garage floor in a tailor's squat, or as close as he could get to one, given his distorted leg. He was trimming jeans from Groverton's trunk that were too long with the huge shears The jeans were ragged and uneven by the time he finished but he didn't care, the hems would be ground down to a gray fringe after he dragged them under his feet for a few days.

Andy found the shears while prowling through the house of an ancient seamstress who lived nearby. Andy would wander the house's shadowy interior when the only illumination was from street lights. Her home was full of the fabric, mannequins and machinery she'd used in her trade before she retired. It was scary and creepy. He felt the adrenaline rush of fear, fear of being caught and fear of the unknown as he lurked in the darkness. He was the monster in his own horror movie, but the cool dark half- light was reality not fiction.

He liked to stand quietly in the old lady's house and listen as it creaked and groaned, like a living thing in the last throes of existence. Sometimes he'd listen to the old lady's raspy breathing as she slept the unquiet sleep of the elderly. Her birdlike head lay on a lacy pillow, her frail body groaning and creaking like her house. He was sorry the old lady had to go; her house and its accumulation of her lifetime had given him many thrills.

The last time he saw her he was standing at the top of the stairs just off her bedroom door. He was standing very still listening, just listening, when she woke from a troubling dream and saw something new in her house of sixty years. She walked over very deliberately and looked at Andy not believing he was real. She examined him, unsure if he was a left over fragment of a dream or a new horror from this world, and then, unbelieving, touched him to see if he was real.

The shears lay on a bolt of thick fabric, splayed open and ready to do their job. They were heavy, sharp and tight, the edges ground at an angle that made short work of anything that had the audacity to be too long. Andy loved them at first sight. There was a casual violence to them, they sheared cleanly every time and could glide through the heaviest canvas or the sheerest silk with equal ease. They had the pleasant indestructible heft of iron when Andy held them in his hand.

The house smelled of death the night Andy took the shears, but it didn't bother him. The lady lay silent, at peace, for once. A month later, Realtors hired a crew of Mexicans to clear the house of a lifetime of memories and painted the inside from a palate of fashionable colors. The next time Andy went exploring, the smell was gone along with the effluvia he loved.

The old lady was just a residue of memories now, floating in his imagination like the dust motes swirling in the pool of light he sat in. It was a chilly light, courtesy of the garage's lone window, filtered through half rain and half mist and barely adequate for the haphazard tailoring he was doing. Andy didn't care; he hacked away, unconcerned, deconstructing his jeans.

At first, he was unaware he was being watched and when he did notice, he didn't react. Three local boys, the Berrigan boys, no better or worse than their contemporaries, were looking for new territory, a place to do whatever they wanted to do. They didn't care what Andy thought, and nothing he could do would stop them.

A local girl, Renay Dobler, tagged along at an age when most girls were wary of being alone with groups of young men. She got her name from a popular song her parents liked. They thought it sounded sophisticated, even continental. Unfortunately they misspelled the name on her birth certificate, so anyone who saw her name written out knew she sprang from uneducated hillbilly stock.

Nature had not been generous in its other gifts to her; she was mousy girl with sallow skin and a narrow face, which was unfortunately enhanced by buck teeth. The boys tolerated her because she was developing the attributes of a woman. They liked seeing her naked and, when she obliged; she got their approval and acceptance. The boys had notions about sex that they got from porn and older boys, but, for now, looking would have to do.

Renay loved putting on a show, as she called it, and felt the shiver of a thrill when the boys looked at her. If she had the vocabulary she would have said she was empowered by the control she exerted on the young males staring at her crotch. Nothing in her brief life compared to the sensation it gave her, and she didn't care what her father or female peers thought. Instead, she laid back and bathed in the feeling of being the center of attention.

She couldn't compete with the funny, pretty, nasty girls that the boys flocked around at school. Her father had promised her braces, which she dreamed would transform her from the put upon duckling to the graceful swan of her imagination. In the back of her mind she knew he was a poor man and prone to making promises he couldn't keep, but that bitter cup lay in a distant future that would never be. Today she was special, here in Nathans's garage she was getting the attention she craved.

She was anxious for the show to begin and wore a short little summer dress and her most grown-up panties, completely inappropriate for the tomboy activities her father foolishly believed she was engaged in. This time, she would get completely naked instead of just hiking up her dress and reclining while the boys stared. Naked like the girls in the magazines the boys drooled over.

The boys were looking for a place where they could drink beers while Renay provided entertainment. The old man's garage was perfect, and Andy's prior claim wasn't much of an obstacle. They kicked his pile of jeans into a corner and threatened him with the same if he didn't show them respect.

"Get out."

"I was here…"

"Didn't anyone tell you not to play with scissors?" One of the boys examined the shears and threw them with some force at the garage wall. The whole garage shook from the impact.

"Get lost gimp."

Andy kowtowed to their superior strength. He skulked back to his disordered pile of jeans and began gathering them up.

"Geez… it's just Andy," Renay said. "He's almost blind and he can't hear much. Leave him alone.

Renay was impatient with the boy's stupid dominance rituals. From her point of view, the only reason to be in this filthy garage was to get naked and glory in the boys' attention, not watch them pick on another boy. She also had protective feelings for Andy; they were both outcasts and victims of bullies. She did a short-but-effective striptease that froze the boys in mid assault and diverted their attention from Andy and back on her.

Her party had begun at last.

The boys stood motionless and silent. Her breasts were only beginning to bud on her freckled chest and pale pubic hair was just sprouting on her genitalia, but she beguiled them as completely as any pin-up queen. She savored the moment as they stared. Andy stared too until one of the boys cuffed him and told him to look away.

"He can't see, right?"

Renay shook her head at the leering boys; her nakedness lent her an air of adult authority.

"He doesn't know what's going on here, he's practically retarded."

They pushed Andy into the corner where he wouldn't disturb them and Renay continued her show. She enjoyed the fascination of her audience and reclined on the back seat of the old man's car. The boys watched, their excitement mounted and they began pouring beer down her compliant throat.

That was okay with Renay—beer was how she dealt with life anyhow—but this time she drank far more than she'd ever managed to sneak out of the refrigerator at home. She'd starved herself the night before, reasoning a skinnier body would please the boys, but they didn't care, and the alcohol on an empty stomach just got into her bloodstream faster. Any residual inhibitions Renay had were dissolved by the beer, her boundaries were shredded and she became a toy in a boy's game.

The boys overcame her resistance with superior strength and ignored her pleadings to stop. She said no emphatically, every time, but by now she was blaming herself for what was happening. She had taken her clothes off and allowed them to get this far, and even if she didn't want it to go any farther, it was too late. In her beer-addled brain, she'd forfeited the right to say no and the boys had their way.

They took her again and again in the ways they learned from dirty magazines and internet porn. She was intoxicated to a point past caring and felt the weight of their bodies come down. They did things to her she had never heard of, let alone fantasized about. Finally it became a great big tedious, humiliating bore. Eventually she drank enough beer to pass out. Then they did things to her they would have been ashamed of if she had been awake.

She awoke with the smell of musk on her and the Berrigans gone. They left in a hurry, leaving her on the car's ruined upholstery, pausing only to steal some of Andy's uncut jeans. She wept at her disgrace, for the hopelessness of justice and the unlikelihood of revenge. She cried until she noticed Andy, poor forlorn Andy. Poor sightless Andy was looking at her.

Her shame had a witness, although that wasn't her first thought. She saw an outcast, as damaged and lost as herself, staring at her from what remained of his cache of jeans. Her heart went out to a fellow victim, he'd done nothing to provoke the boys but they stripped him of his possessions and dignity all the same. In her head, she took responsibility for his plight, since she'd told the boys to find a place for her to put on a show. Her first thought was to comfort him.

She didn't understand Andy, but she got up on wobbly legs and crouched beside him, still as naked as she'd been with the boys. Like a stray puppy, he'd won her heart and she comforted him, reading hurt and sorrow into his expression. She pushed a stray wisp of hair from his face and wrapped her arms around him, trying to soothe his hurt feelings.

The smell of sex floated off her and filled Andy's nostrils. Andy was odd looking and stunted, but he had instincts and desires in abundance. He was aroused and he started responding the way a teenage boy would, even a boy as misshapen and half made up as Andy. He didn't feel he needed comforting; he was a boy and wanted a boy's portion.

She patted his head, oblivious to the effect she was having on him; Andy licked her neck and tasted her sweat as she held him close. Her arms enveloped him, but his hands were free to do mischief, he fumbled around and started rubbing Renay's thigh. Soon, Renay noticed and objected. True, three boys had done what Andy wanted to do, but Renay had decided that enough was enough.

"Stop it! Stop it! Stop it!" she screamed, adding a flurry of slaps and punches for emphasis. Andy just grunted and jumped on her.

They wrestled in the garage dust, he tried to pin her shoulders to the earth so he could have her, while she fought his presumption. Boiling over with rage, she fought and fought fiercely, landing a righteous kick that sent Andy flying. They stared at each other across the garage panting like animals. She hated him now. She was bigger and stronger than Andy, but he had the shears. She screamed and called him terrible names, so he shoved the shears into her chest.

The pain was intense. Renay couldn't scream, but she gasped as the shears penetrated, gasped again, then gasped some more and tried to make a sound but the air dribbled out in bloody bubbles. The blades had punctured her lungs and collapsed them; they never drew another breath. She expired quietly on the floor with a confused, surprised look on her face, aspirating blood, bleeding out on Andy's jeans.

Andy stared at the mess she had become and knew that he had to hide her body. The old man would be back soon and Andy didn't want him to know what had gone on. The brickyard was a good a place to dump Renay, but there was the matter of getting a gangly, bloody, naked dead girl there without being noticed. Andy looked around; all he had were some jeans and the shears. They would have to do.

The shears cut through Renay's flesh and sinew with little more effort than the fabric they were designed for. Eventually she was in small enough pieces for Andy to stuff her into some extra-large jeans. He tied the legs and waist closed and Renay was a compact, hideous package, ready for transport.

The drizzle was a blessing for Andy. It kept most of the people on Johnston Avenue indoors as Andy dragged Renay in her denim shroud to Groverton's car. The rain covered his tracks by washing away what oozed from his parcel.

Despite the cold rain that ran down his collar, Andy was sweating by the time he slogged up to the brickyard; even drained of blood Renay was a lot to carry. The trunk yielded to Andy's touch and Renay mutely joined what was left of Groverton's livelihood.

No one missed Renay immediately. Her father worked nights and her mother had disappeared long ago. He trusted her latch-key savvy, but eventually he tumbled to the fact that something was wrong. Renay was no social butterfly, but he called a couple of parents of kids she did socialize with. No one had seen her.

He filed a missing persons report with the police and they waited an additional 72 hours before they put it on the wire. They were reassuring and helpful, but no one responded. The town had a history of runaway kids, so the police weren't that concerned about the child of one more luckless loser.

In the days following her disappearance, Renay's father discovered the guilt that accompanies the loss of a child. He didn't know anything about raising a girl. Renay always seemed so mature, grown up enough to take care of herself, but now his easy going relationship with her started looking like parental neglect.

He had no idea who she hung out with or how she spent her days. His knowledge of his daughter's day began when he fixed her breakfast before school and ended with tucking her in at night before he left for work. The police were his first, last and only stop before despair overtook him. No investigation was ever mounted, no bulletins or Amber alerts went out, and there were no milk carton portraits for his daughter. It was as if Renay never existed, and her passing was little noticed or remarked upon.

He had no idea where to begin looking, so he wandered around Wickesborough showing people her picture and asking if they had seen her. People told him by look and gesture to be a better parent next time and left him to his hopeless search.

At school, Renay's absence was noticed but ignored; she, like Groverton, had simply disappeared. Andy wore a pair of the jeans to class and the stench of dried blood alerted the kids that something bad had happened.

Milan Kumnacker saw Andy dispatch Groverton when she returned to retrieve her cigarettes. Her boyfriend, Leno, saw Andy dragging something into the brickyard.

They said nothing. Whatever happened to her would rebound on whoever spoke up, and almost no one cared what had happened to Renay anyway. The only people who missed her were the boys. They asked Andy where she was and he said he didn't know. The boys had no reason to doubt Andy, so they took the jeans he hadn't mangled and left.

Officer Dunkel, the At-Risk Children's Task Force, did take action. Even before Renay's disappearance the Berrigan boys had caught his attention and he decided they were at risk. He suspected them of petty crimes they hadn't committed, and kept an eye on them to see if he could catch them at something. Unfortunately, he wasn't watching them on the day they raped Renay, but he did confiscate the jeans they took from Andy. The jeans went in a box under his desk in case anyone reported them stolen. He never connected them to Groverton, Renay, or Andy.

It was Milan that finally led the police to Renay. She was pregnant and rather than admit she was a whore, and a not very smart one at that, she said Groverton had raped her, which, in the legal sense he had. The police looked in the brickyard and discovered Groverton's car. Groverton and Renay were side by side in the trunk on top of more jeans, next to the shears.

The state police sent a unit to investigate and collect forensic evidence, which effectively shut out the local cops. The jeans in Groverton's trunk were placed in evidence and someone remembered that Dunkel had collected some jeans from the boys. Renay's blood was on the jeans and her autopsy showed her wounds were consistent with the shears. The boys admitted to rape, but denied committing murder. The prosecutor was sure they had done both.

He had a strong case. Groverton had a bruise that matched the scissors' handle, the boys' semen was all over Renay, and a fingerprint from the boy who tossed the shears in the garage was found. A conviction for multiple homicides and sexual assault was a cinch.

Andy's prints were also on the shears, but they were explained away. It was decided Andy was too weak and "mentally deficient" to have gotten the better of Groverton and the girl. They accepted his explanation that jeans were the only thing he cut with them.

The Berrigans had long antecedents in the Clarion Valley and their friends and relations figured in Wickesborough legends and ghost stories, none of which involved violent crime. That was the substance of their defense, but the boys fit the evidence and looked guilty; so they pled guilty to lesser counts to avoid the death penalty and were sent away.

At first, Renay's father believed the boys' confession, but doubt soon cracked his certainty. He started following Andy around town, trying to get him to tell him something, until Rosemary, Andy's mother, got a restraining order. Even after the boys went to prison, people pointed fingers at him as the father who allowed his daughter to fall in with the bad crowd that killed her.

They blamed him, and he agreed. He took to wandering around town in an unfit state of mind, scorned by decent folks and held up as a bad example. Later, he turned up dead in Saxonburg, some said he died of regret, others said it was booze.

Nathan Howard had his suspicions about Andy, but kept quiet, even though he knew Renay's father from church. He had no proof of anything he suspected and nothing he knew would have saved the father. Saying something would have gotten him involved, being involved had unforeseeable consequences, and the consequences might have unacceptable outcomes. He was, after all, the neighborhood crank who the police ignored.

He'd seen footprints leading from his garage on the rainy day after a church outing to Wal*Mart. Andy dragged his right foot when he walked and that was apparent in footprints he saw. He saw puddles of blood in those foot prints before the rain washed it away. He saw where Andy dragged something on the slog back to Groverton's car. He saw the mess made on the upholstery of his car and he saw the blood soaked into the concrete floor where Renay bled out. He saw enough to make some assumptions.

He remembered where he saw the shears before as well. He'd seen them hanging around Andy's neck and before that on a bolt of fabric in the house of his friend, Violet. She was a friend from their mutual youth, when he was younger than Andy and she was a golden girl that he desired across an impossible chasm of a five-year age difference.

Nothing ever happened between them, but she remained a fond unattainable infatuation from his past. He retired from the military and she became a seamstress spinster. Their age difference shrank to insignificance as toil and faded hopes withered their lives.

When he returned to Wickesborough, he made a point of checking up on Violet and making sure she was well. Over the years, she never failed to remind him of her seniority but, in fact, he still saw her as the girl she was sixty years before. At least until the awful day he discovered her lying dead at the foot of her stairs. There was no denying her age then, or the decrepitude of the husk that had once been Violet Martin.

He never realized how small she was, or how gray her hair was, until it was fanned out in a black/burgundy halo of blood on the floor. Her skin was like transparent crepe stretched across the frame of her fine boned skull. He remembered how it once glowed with youth and how freckles appeared across her nose in the first blush of summer. They'd never shared a single intimate caress in all their years, but he still loved her and it broke his heart.

"She probably lost her balance and struck her head on the newel post," the police told him.

"That's ridiculous… She wasn't doddering or anything like that."

"Mr. Howard… Elderly people fall… There is no reason to suspect foul play."

"But she was as healthy as me."

The cops listened patiently to the man they remembered was a neighborhood crank, prone to exaggeration and dismissed him as an old man denying his own mortality. They never took him seriously.

She'd told him a troubling, recurring dream, about a creature that came to her during the night. It was like a goblin, twisted and stunted, that had an odd shaped head and Asiatic features. He dragged a foot when he prowled around, he didn't seem to notice how much noise he made. The creature stared at her as she slept, waiting for God knows what. At first, she thought he was part of a nightmare, but lately she had come to suspect he was real.

Nathan knew where Violet's nightmare had come from. Andy was still in town, and, though older, still went on nocturnal prowls. The allure of dark, nearly abandoned, buildings had stayed with him, even after the police interrupted a couple of his nocturnal jaunts. To them, Andy was just a local simpleton, and they released him with a warning.

Andy's trespassing was different from the rest; it was solitary and had a sinister purpose. He returned the cruelty he'd received to the weak and vulnerable he found in Wickesborough. Old people sometimes died after his visits, but not at an alarming rate, there were many old and infirm people in Wickesborough and no one connected their passing to Andy.

Nathan had a collection of wheezes, aches and chills he knew would eventually carry him to the grave. He didn't care, this world held no pleasures for him. His future was clearer than the broth he ate with every meal. He knew that every time he went to bed it was possible that he would never awake. That was fine with him, when his time came he would walk into the light without regret.

In the meantime he had one thing left he wanted to do if he got the chance. Every night he made sure his back door was unlocked and settled in to watch some TV. In his silent, dark house he waited, waited with his gun across his lap, waiting for Andy.

The Chair

No one knew exactly how long the old oak had been growing there, but it was a mature tree when the first white settlers slaughtered the previous inhabitants and founded Wickesborough. The tree was strong and healthy, with a generous canopy that shaded the square surrounding it.

It had to go. Wickesborough was a prosperous town, the seat of the eponymous county and required a public building befitting its dignity. The tree was in the way of progress.

There was sentiment in town against its felling. The residents were attached to it; the old tree had been in the center of town since before Wickesborough had a center, or was even a town. Their settlement on the Clarion River had flourished under its boughs until there was no doubt that Wickesborough was as permanent a fixture as the tree.

Cutting it down was severing a connection to Wickesborough's frontier history. The tree's demise, though, was mostly un-mourned by residents of a delicate sensibility, since it was known locally as "Hanging Oak."

In 1756, a Colonel Armstrong had eliminated the Indians living around the tree during the French and Indian War. The Indians, known as Captain Jacob's Band, had made numerous raids on white settlements during the French and Indian War, killing more than their fair share. Captain Jacob and a number of his henchmen were dispatched by being strung up on a bough of the oak.

Having proven its value for such duty, the oak served as a convenient place to dispatch miscreants who had earned the locals' ire.

In 1834, Pennsylvania ended public executions, objecting more to the "public" aspect of the penalty than the "execution" part. By then, most locals had learned to stop settling their disagreements with pistols and knives, but any who hadn't would pay for their folly on a gibbet designed for the purpose, enclosed within the new courthouse.

The bad and unlucky continued to step off into eternity at declining intervals in the courthouse, until 1913 when the state took over the role of executioner. From then on, a first-degree murder conviction earned you a one way trip to the State Correctional Institution in Rockview and a seat in "Old Smokey," as the new electric chair was nicknamed. The folks in Wickesborough didn't miss the death house; Wickesborough was, by now, a model of decorum and had not used its services for years.

The gibbet gathered dust while local officials waited to see if the folks in Harrisburg would change their minds. By the '40s, it was obvious they were serious about taking over the death penalty business, so the mayor and borough council hired a local carpenter to tear the thing down. The carpenter knew a thing or two about wood and took the lumber the gibbet was constructed from as partial payment. He would make chairs out of it.

The carpenter, Audley Bauser, had lived his entire life in Wickesborough and was an artist at joinery. His furniture was known for its sturdiness and craftsmanship, so there would be no shortage of customers. The pedigree of the wood made the chairs even more desirable to aficionados of local history.

Audley met the demand by mixing in oak from less infamous sources. Still, every buyer knew that at least part of their chair came from the Wickesborough gibbet.

One chair, in particular, caught everyone's attention. While planing a rough bit of lumber into usable board, Audley discovered a musket ball encapsulated in the wood. It had some wadding wrapped around it and a fragment of rough woven fabric was embedded behind that. It wasn't much of a leap to speculate that the bullet had passed through an unfortunate during Armstrong's expedition and lodged in the tree.

The age of the ammunition was right and fierce fighting was said to have taken place around the tree, so the tale was plausible. At any rate, the ball had found its way into the tree, and over the years, the tree had healed and grown new wood around its injury.

Bauser set aside the piece of wood and saved it for a special chair. He made that chair right, with one-hundred percent gibbet wood, putting all the care he could put into its joinery. The piece with the bullet fragment became the top rail of the chair's back; the bullet was clearly visible, a little left of center just above where the splat joined it, about heart level if an average man was sitting in it.

Bauser applied several coats of varnish to protect his masterpiece and invited interested parties to inspect the finished work. He anticipated selling it for double his normal asking price, more if the bidding got serious, so he set the reserve price accordingly.

Local worthies walked around the chair as it hung drying in Audley's shed and agreed it was a fine chair, furniture anyone would be proud to possess. They also agreed that something so well-crafted and connected to the town's history would be a priceless family heirloom. What they couldn't agree on was the opening bid. For lack of a buyer, the disappointed carpenter kept the chair in his shop.

He died in his shop a few days later, seated, in the famous chair, slumped over his desk. There was nothing unusual about his passing, he was up in years and taking nitroglycerin pills for his heart, so no one made any connections with the chair and his death.

There was no shortage of interest in the chair when Bauser's estate was probated, and the bidding was vigorous. The mayor eventually took it home for a little more than twice what he would have paid before Bauser died—nothing does more for an artist's career than his untimely demise. His Honor placed his special chair at his dining room table along with three less special chairs he'd bought earlier. In it he presided over family meals like a patriarch of old.

Or, he did until he choked to death on a bit of trout he inhaled about a week later. Again no one associated the chair with a curse, until the owner of Holabaugh's Restaurant bought the dining room set, put it in his establishment and started running up the body count.

A subtle pattern began to emerge, no one pitched over dead at the restaurant, but every couple of weeks the police would drop by to make discreet inquiries about customers who ate their last meals there.

It was the wait staff that put the thing together and began steering their best tipping customers away from the "fatal chair." The manager was as clueless as managers usually are, and enjoyed the increase in memorial dinners the lethal furniture provided.

Unfortunately, a disgruntled employee leaked the "death chair" story to The Wickesborough County Herald Examiner, Press Telegraph, Clarion and Evening Bulletin and Holabaugh's business dropped off precipitously. The manager did his best, removing the chair to his office where it sat unused until his business went bankrupt. The manager may have been a victim of the cursed chair himself, he apparently fell off it and broke his neck, while trying to hang himself.

There was no rush to acquire the infamous chair after that. It was a local legend by now, and no one wanted to destroy a piece of history– however dangerous– but no one wanted to acquire a chair that you would only let creditors and in-laws sit in. So it sat, gathering dust in the abandoned restaurant which never reopened. It became, in local lore, "The death chair in the diner of doom."

The derelict building became a magnet for teenagers and other ne'er-do-wells, some of whom decided to test their courage and fate by sitting in the chair. An unknown number paid for it in mishaps common to their sort and after a while, even the town's drunkest braggarts became wary of the chair.

Scoffing at the supernatural in the convivial atmosphere of the 422 tavern on a comfortable bar stool was one thing, to actually sit in the chair that was reputed to have sent more souls to glory than Pittsburgh Phil Strauss was quite another.

Years passed and the derelict eatery was looted of its valuables. The furnishings got scattered around Wickesborough, owned by new people that didn't know their provenance and didn't care. The "death chair" got painted by some folks who owned an antique shop and sold to a yuppie couple in Elderton who thought Wickesborough County's rural ambiance would be good for children. They lost their fortune when the stock market crashed and then died when their U-Haul trailer jack-knifed on the Clarion River Bridge.

The chair disappeared after that. It is presumed to be in the Wickesborough area, but no unusual deaths have been linked to furniture. Most people now think the legend of the "death chair" is just that, a legend conjured up by a string of coincidences and the overactive imaginations of people long since gone.

Old timers are still wary though, and always look behind them for a telltale piece of lead in the chair's back whenever a deadbeat borrower or a brother-in-law asks them to have a seat.

Whatever Happened to Tracy Harris

Wickesborough is a crossroads town where the mountains and the Clarion conspire to force the passage of men through choke points in their thoroughfares.

Choke points, by their nature, crowd people together, some by choice and some by chance. People who have never heard of Wickesborough meet there and move on, or not. A few people linger and leave their mark on the locals and are recalled fondly, or not.

Sometimes the marks are private, known to a few and quickly forgotten. They are mixed, swirled and combined in unusual blends, some pleasant, some not so. The encounters are mostly mundane, but you never know what you're going to pull out once you put your hand in the hat.

"I am a psychopath," he said. "Don't worry. I am not a sexual sadist, but it will hurt. I will do what I want and you will comply. I don't care about your pain or you, what happens to you or anything you care about. I will use you in whatever way I care to; if you resist it will go badly for you. You will be as degraded and humiliated more than you thought possible. When I am done with you, I will leave and never think about you again. And that will be the best day of your life."

His words were calm and soothing meant to seduce her into untroubled submission and compliance. He was relying on her shock and disbelief to reject the facts of what he was saying. Outwardly, at least, she was going along with it.

She sat across the table where an untouched carafe of wine sat evaporating off the heat of her excitement. She wanted to scream. Curiosity had kicked open a gate of hell and she had walked through it.

He was new in town. She had run into him while shopping. Well put together articulate men are rare in Wickesborough, so when he asked if he could sit with her while she drank her awful French roast coffee, she said yes. Coffee had gone well, so, against her better judgment, she gave him her number. A week later he called.

She dressed appropriately for a first date, the first date in some time. She didn't want to give him the impression that she was desperate, although she was, or indifferent, which she wasn't. In the mirror stood a slender woman with qualities a man should appreciate. Large brown intelligent eyes, aquiline nose and sensuous lips stared back at her. It was a face to break hearts and launch ships.

She had a coltish figure with perky breasts, a term she hated, and the silhouette that would do justice to a woman twenty years younger.

She slipped on lingerie she'd bought some time ago, but never had the occasion to wear. A black sheer bra and equally sheer thong, that had just enough filigree and lace to obscure the money makers, but was revealing all the same. She had no expectations, but as the boy scouts say, be prepared.

She put on a simple white blouse; it was loose with a large collar. She undid one more button than she normally would. Peek-a-boo titties was a game men enjoyed. Depending on how the evening went, it could be either the PG or R version when show time came around.

She wore a skirt with a slit up the thigh, so when she sat down it revealed a generous expanse of leg, while remaining discreet enough to be decorous.

She ran her hands up her sheer silk hosiery. There were no wrinkles; she just liked feeling them against her hand. She trembled a little when she imagined his hand doing the same. A moment's indecision about her shoes ended when put on her best come-fuck-me pumps; they made her ass look great and her legs terrific. She liked her legs, and knew that men did too.

She was new in town as well. She had arrived at the Butler Coach Bus Terminal and thought Wickesborough would be a good place to get away and stay awhile. It had a bulletin board with rentals, services and jobs on it, no internet tomfoolery in The Butler Coach Company waiting room; although even in Wickesborough nobody used the word "tomfoolery". She selected a furnished one bedroom apartment, prices were so low she could afford a house, but she didn't need the bother. Later she would shop at a Bed, Bath and Beyond for necessities.

Her previous life had been spent wandering, from town to town, city to city, across the country, so she had mastered the vagabond existence. Once she had lived in major cities, later she lived in regional hubs where local powerbrokers strode like colossuses across their circumscribed territories. Over the years she'd known quite a few men like that, a few of whom she might have married, but never did. Now she was in Wickesborough.

When she was younger, men had been easy. Her looks and personality had delivered them in quantity and she had all she needed to keep her satisfied. They came and went, most never got close enough to learn her secret, that she was careful to keep hidden. When she felt like someone might be catching on, that was the end as far as she was concerned, and she vanished without a trace. Always, she kept moving; terrified someone would find the secret she was hiding.

He arrived for their date on time; he wore a nice suit and drove a nice car. When she was younger, that was enough to get her into the back seat, but now she was more finished, schooled in the refined game between men and woman. He waited while she futzed away the requisite amount of time, fixing things that were fine, wondering about what she forgot and touching up her lip stick.

He was patient and uncomplaining, two things in his favor. It had been a while since a man had danced attendance on her, she would overlook a lot of gaucherie to make the evening turn out the way she wanted. He kissed her without permission; she liked that. The evening had just taken an exciting, dangerous turn.

As she got older, when her supply of eager men began to wane, she started circulating hotel bars looking for the companionship she needed. She was competing with younger and younger woman and she stood out as an older woman among a sea of fresh faces. Although she applied all the feminine wiles available to her, the men she attracted became less acceptable and of less utility. By now she had gone from sporadic dry spells, to a needy desperation for relationship, and she hoped this man would be her supply for the near future.

He'd made reservations at a restaurant connected to a hotel she'd never heard of, she was unfamiliar with the area and outside her new-in-town comfort zone. It made her uneasy, but he was in control, a quality she liked in a man. It was located somewhere outside Pittsburgh near the campus. Mostly empty, because it was still early. It had dark décor, white linen and polished stemware. The tables sat in their own pools of light. It wasn't the most flattering look, but it had the effect of turning each table into an island of light at center stage, isolated in its own pool of light. It shouted expensive and discreet. He would be getting a command performance from her over dinner, and probably more later on.

He slid her chair in and she leaned forward enough to reveal some bra strap and a hint of what lay beyond. He focused on her eyes, but took in her femininity peripherally, a perfect gentleman. Her plans for the evening were already way past hand holding and a romantic walk along the riverwalk, and they hadn't yet had the Chardonnay.

She had a twinge of melancholia over what would be the outcome of this evening of bright promise and hopeful beginnings. She knew what she was and what she wanted. He was a man, just a man, and would try, try hard, but his best would not be good enough to satisfy her. She would have to look to her own devices once he had finished with her, she would have regrets but the secret would safe. That was her shame and fear, the terror that someone would learn her secret. She couldn't go on with the charade; she would release this one and go her way. He would wonder as she fumbled some inadequate excuse and walked away.

"I will need you to do some particular things you will find unsettling."

His words shook her from her reverie, and altered her perspective. This was new. She was a modern woman with modern experiences and she had experienced what men had to offer in the way of distraction. Willingly and unwillingly, singly and in pairs, she learned what actions, openings and surfaces of her body provided the correct friction for an interested partner. Used and sometimes humiliated by members of both sexes, she had serviced and satisfied and above all thrived in that submissive role.

The man before her promised to go beyond that and she was inclined to let him, until the fear and remorseless self-loathing came back. She put down her napkin while he took a sip of wine.

"I think I better leave… so you can have the best day of your life."

She watched his eyes narrow and his lips become set. His hand moved with breathtaking speed, grabbing her by the hair. It was useless to resist, she was dragged from her seat across the floor as her legs spavined and splayed. He pulled her up so that her feet dangled in the air, the come-fuck-me's she had taken so long to select were kicked into different parts of the restaurant.

He pulled her skirt up and her panties down and the room submerged into a sullen quiet. Exposed, her crotch winked at a couple at another table as they burrowed into the menu. Her date was whipped into frenzy by her struggling, as she expected, now he was beyond control and meant to do her then and there. He put one arm around her waist and reached into her blouse. He feigned unhooking her bra. Eventually, it was torn from her and tossed across the table. He exposed her naked breasts while he roughly fondled them, worrying her nipples with his thumb and index finger until she cried.

No one noticed, or at least none of the staff or customers seemed surprised, or much interested. No one was inclined to help her either; involved indifference was the rule of the day here. He refused her pathetic modesty as she tried to cover her nakedness. Finally, he dragged her by her hair through the restaurant to collect her possessions, shoes, panties and the like and then out to an alley where he made use of her mouth.

He offered her to a passerby. "Take the whore…Use her."

The pedestrian was more intimidated than she was, too scared to comply, but afraid of what would happen if he refused.

She gagged her way through it. His car became her prison.

"Get in the trunk."

"I'll scream.

"I'll tape your mouth shut…and when I rip it off your lips will come with it."

She got in the trunk and he slammed it. It was a rental with an emergency release on the inside. He didn't know it but she did.

The energetic abuse continued in his hotel room. Nothing was left un-penetrated, no demand left undone, nothing foul left unperformed. She was on her knees waiting for him to inflict the next humiliation on her when he collapsed in a heap. He lay sprawled and exhausted; she waited submissively until her patience wore thin.

"Is that all?"

She twerked her butt, attempting to inspire his interest.

"Go away, I am done with you."

He struggled. His intent was to sit up, but it was beyond his ken.

"Done, where are the friends you want me to do? Don't you want to humiliate me in front of them? Show them what a whore bag I am. Come on, give them a show, you went to college with them."

She assumed the second-most conventional pose of a porn seductress.

"They'd like some of this."

He wondered where this iteration of erotic fiction came from; he hadn't suggested anything like that.

"I'm done, so you can go."

"I'm not nearly degraded enough. Call me a slut, call me a cum bucket."

His fear rose in him as he saw a red hot madness rising in previously doe-like eyes, but an equally powerful tide of fatigue was carrying him away.

"I've had enough. I don't care what you want.

It was beginning to dawn on him that he had bitten off more than he could chew.

She studied him; the Rohypnol she had slipped into his Chardonnay was doing its job. She retrieved a syringe from her purse and gave him an extra jolt in the neck; he would be down until she administered Romazicon. He was new at this, a hatchling not even fully fledged. She suspected she might have been his first attempt at a kill. He was so young, so innocent; she regretted she was ending his career so soon. Still a girl had to do what she had to do, so she went to work.

She stripped off his clothes and rolled him onto his face. Cable ties cuffed his little toes and little fingers together, then she tied them both together behind his back. The effect achieved resembled a giant plucked turkey, trussed up and ready for the oven.

She super glued his mouth closed and put a long cable tie around his neck, tight enough to be uncomfortable, and super glued it to his back. If he struggled, the cable tie would cinch down and he would strangle himself. He wouldn't be going anywhere, and he wouldn't be screaming for help, nothing and no one would keep her from getting what she needed.

She used the rest of the super glue to repair a nail she broke during the rough and tumble.

In his car she found duct tape, rope, a plastic drop cloth and bleach. Like a good Boy Scout, he had come prepared, like a good psychopath he'd lied about not being a sexual sadist. She wondered what the forensics guys would make of "The Vic" having a receipt for the stuff "The Perp" used to dispose of him.

Hours from now he would find himself back in his trunk, or at least parts of him would be, still alive, but unable to pull the emergency latch she'd noticed. She thrilled when she imagined the terror he would feel before the flames got to him.

She needed to buy some gas.

A neighbor boy had molested her when she was a child. To keep her quiet he threatened her parents, her sister, her friends, her pets, her grandparents—anyone he thought she cared about. One day, just to make the point, he had cut open a stray kitten and made her watch. He laughed, but she was fascinated. The tiny cat squirmed in agony; its uncomprehending eyes stared at her, and aroused her.

Later when he raped her, she had an orgasm and the die was set, a masochistic mind was imprinted on her, but she became a predator. At least that's what she told herself, it always felt rooted deeper than that, something primal in her animal brain that needed blood. Nothing felt as right to her as when she stood over her prey, covered in the victim's blood.

The neighbor boy died too quickly for her tastes, and he had whimpered pitifully. She remembered with a wry smile, him begging for mercy, and her denying it to him, like she would later, to so many others. The boy had taught her to savor the humiliation and pain, but shorted her education when it came to the limits of other people's endurance.

This night's partner would awaken soon. His eyes would open and he'd see her, naked and smiling. There would be no blood or transfer evidence on her clothes.

Slowly he would begin to comprehend what was happening and stare into her eyes with the terror she so enjoyed.

There would be an uproar and terror throughout Wickesborough about the serial killer loose in the county, and then there would be nothing. No one knew her, no one would remember her, when she left no one would care, like so much water under the Clarion River bridge. She wondered if, in all the places she had lived, anyone would remember or ask whatever happened to Tracy Harris.

She laid out a razor sharp fileting knife she'd bought at Bed, Bath and Beyond. She would be satisfied and her secret would be safe, for now. She was ready to begin.

Dead Ringers

There are two motels in Wickesborough to accommodate visitors and locals who might need a night away from a spouse. One is up on 28 and the other is by the Clarion River. The clerks don't ask questions or volunteer answers at either one.

Charles Deutsch was an overnight visitor, he needed a room and their availability was his only question. He had run his car off Branch Valley Road looking for Mt. Lazarus Cemetery where he planned to visit the family plot, so he needed a place to stay.

Ordinarily, he wouldn't have visited Wickesborough, he had no family left there, but his business in Pittsburgh was done and his discount flight required a weekend layover. There was nothing waiting for him at home except conflict with the wife, so he decided to spend some time amidst the sepulchers of distant relatives. He was an unsentimental man, but he had time to kill.

His ancestors had settled in and around Wickesborough during the 1700's after fleeing a German village on a popular invasion route. The graveyard was packed with generations of his Himmeldeutsch predecessors who led quiet lives in greater Wickesborough. It was a tradition continued to this day by anonymous second and third cousins many degrees removed. It would have been his fate too, except his parents got fed up, dropped the Himmel from their last name and scattered to the edge of the continent.

He had been back on family pilgrimages as a kid; he remembered indulgent grandparents and being introduced to obscurely related relatives. This trip was prompted by curiosity to see if Wickesborough lived up to his memories, but, unfortunately, those memories didn't include the switchback on Branch Valley Road. He took it faster than he should have, and woke up in an ambulance with paramedics hovering over him.

"Sir... Can you hear me? Are you having any trouble?"

"I'm fine... I just feel a little woozy...

"Sir we'd like to transport you to county…"

"No, I feel fine," he said, failing to mention the headache and blurred vision he was experiencing. His indulgence in cultural tourism had cost him the deductible on his rental car insurance and his mobility until he got a replacement vehicle, he didn't feel like adding medical expenses to the bill. The paramedics were insistent, but they couldn't force him to take their advice, so they left after a tow truck arrived. Himmeldeutsch towing was stenciled on the door.

"Hi… You need a tow?"

"Yes… Are you a Himmeldeutsch?"

"John Himmeldeutsch."

"We might be related… My great grandfather had the same name."

"Was he from here?" "Yeah…"

"Himmeldeutsch is a fairly common name in Wickesborough; throw a rock and you'll probably hit someone related to you."

They made easy conversation as John drove. There was something about John Himmeldeutsch, an easy friendliness that put Charles at ease. Charles decided it was the difference between the manners of small town folk and the rude city dwellers he was used to.

Charles watched the half remembered town go by; prompting feelings of deja vu which he figured were caused either by having seen the same scenery from his parent's car years before or the effects of a concussion he probably should have let a doctor examine him for. They went down Johnston Avenue, past the courthouse and towards the Clarion River Bridge. It was a truss bridge of three spans with two piers resting on Appalachian bed rock, a local landmark that dominated the scenery around it.

They drove through a business district consisting of store fronts with white washed windows, but the only commercial activity in evidence were signs of realtors offering the same property for rent.

John turned right before the entrance to the bridge and stopped at a tan building by an old rail road right of way. It was the Clarion Princess Motel, a newly renovated hotel adjacent to an abandoned rail depot.

The Princess, nee Hotel Clarion, was a building three stories high, constructed out of Kittanning yellow bricks, abandoned and fallen into disrepair after trains stopped going to Wickesborough. An instructor of hotel and restaurant management at Indiana U. ran it as a hobby with student interns and government grants.

It had few amenities and the renovation ended at the first floor, Deutsch looked around on the second floor, it was a warren of dusty corridors clogged with roll-away beds and other hotel effluvia. Having exhausted the amusement value of the Clarion Princess, Charles gave the desk clerk his cell phone number and asked him to call whenever the car rental company showed up with his new ride.

Despite a headache, he went out to explore Wickesborough. He went up one side of Market Street and down the other, the prospects being as bleak on one side as the other. The Main Street Diner on the corner of Main and Market Streets was still in business with a lunch counter and some booths along the wall, Charles decided he was hungry and stopped in.

The woman pouring coffee, Ruth, looked familiar, but he couldn't place the face, he attributed it to the fact she was probably a distant relative. He wondered if he had stumbled into a Himmeldeutsch family reunion.

"Excuse me… Have we ever met? Are we cousins?"

She smiled and gave him a look that said she thought he was out of his mind. Wickesborough was a town where people kept their opinions to themselves as long as you didn't look them in the face. She thought it was the strangest pick-up line she'd ever heard, after all if she wanted to date a relative she had abundant opportunities to do so in Wickesborough.

He ate watching the foot traffic on Main Street and saw lots of faces he thought he recognized. Men and women, children and adults all seemed familiar; it felt comfortable, like home. Charles had an uneasy feeling he was having an emotional reaction caused by the accident. He paid up and left the restaurant.

A few minutes of window shopping down that boulevard of failed dreams showed Main Street was as devoid of commercial ventures as Market Street. There was a bored radio engineer in one store front manning the console for WCVR, the Clarion Valley's Hometown Radio Station, or so a banner said. Charles watched for a minute or so, but the engineer never looked up.

The Butler Coach Company had a waiting room around the corner, where customers could buy a ticket to Butler and catch a ride if a bus stopped. The waiting room was as bleak as the rest of commercial Wickesborough; it resembled a cross between Edward Hopper's Nighthawks and Theatre Guild production of "No Exit". Even at high noon it seemed like three in the morning, but still it was a way for carless folk to get out of town.

He arrived at the intersection of Water Street and the Clarion River Bridge. He had never crossed the bridge that he recalled and curiosity momentarily caused him to wonder what might be on the other side. Crossing it in the rental car that he was sure was waiting for him at the Princess would be even better, so he headed to his motel with hope in his soul.

Across the street from the Princess there were park benches on a grassy strip above the river bank that looked inviting. Charles decided to spend a few minutes watching the water roll by, hoping it would ease his throbbing head.

A solitary old man was sitting by the river bank casting a line into the middle of the stream; Charles had a dim memory of doing the same thing years ago along a river that was as wide as the ocean and as deep as the sea.

Charles realized, with a start, that this was the place where his grandfather had taught him to fish. The river, so wide in memory had been shrunk by his growing up. He stared at the lone angler and imagined himself as a toddler, hanging on the old man's words of riverside wisdom and catfish lore.

The sun was going down and the man reeled in his line, picked up his bucket and headed up the bank towards Water Road. Charles watched him leave, not intently or directly, that would be impolite, not to mention threatening anywhere but Wickesborough. He couldn't help noticing how much the man reminded him of his Grandfather. He called out to him and the old man stopped and smiled, he was a dead ringer.

"I couldn't help but noticing how familiar you look... Do I know you?'

"I don't know... Do you?"

The old man gave Charles a wry smile.

"Hi, my name is Charles Deutsch... Originally Himmeldeutsch... Have we met?

"I don't think so, but in Wickesborough I run into folks I think I know all the time."

He grabbed Charles' hand and shook it vigorously but gently. His hand engulfed Charles' hand, their differences in size was like that of a child to an adult. It brought back memories.

"Pleased to meet you Mr. Originally Himmeldeutsch... I'm George Cunningham... I guess we've officially met now."

He smiled again and bade Charles adieu and walked down Water Road into the gathering gloom. Charles watched him until he disappeared; he had the same name as his other grandfather and the same large hands.

Back at the motel there was no car waiting and no message from the rental company, just an unhelpful desk clerk without information. Charles tried the Pittsburgh number for the company, but the office was closed, so he tried the 800 number in the phone book. Various representatives were unable to help him much without an ID number, a confirmation number or an account number.

All those numbers were conveniently located on paper work he'd left in the glove compartment of his wrecked car. His credit card number finally rang some cherries somewhere and that operator took his cell number and promised to call him when she got to the bottom of the mix up.

After that fiasco, he thought about his wife.

Although he doubted she'd be concerned, she might be wondering where he was and he owed her the courtesy of a call. She'd probably give him Hell for wasting money on gas to drive to Wickesborough. The accident and motel stay would either make her suspicious, or convince her he was even more of a screw up than she thought.

He steeled himself for a harangue but got her voice mail instead. He left a business like message with all his numbers to call if she needed to get in touch. It was the middle of the day back there, so he wondered if she was visiting a "friend". He shook off his own suspicions and closed the call with an "I love you".

The next morning he went to breakfast. His fishing acquaintance was talking to the waitress Ruth, they broke it up when they saw him and she came by to take his order. He asked her if she could give him directions to John Himmeldeutsch's garage and she gave him another funny look. It was about a quarter mile south on Water Road behind Holabaugh's Diner off Equerry Road. It was an easy walk, she said.

Charles started out for the garage, but not before seeing more people he thought he knew. A man that looked exactly like a favorite high-school history teacher loitered near a pay phone. Deutsch smiled, only Wickesborough would still have a pay phone.

He wondered if his old teacher was still alive. Not likely, he thought, the man he knew was in his fifties then, thirty years before. He caught a glimpse of a woman who bore an astonishing resemblance to Emily, an old girlfriend from Emerson College. They'd broken up ugly and never spoke again; he'd heard that she had committed suicide. A mutual friend claimed she was depressed after aborting his child. The woman he married was prettier and a better wife, but he'd never felt the emotional bond with her that he'd had with Emily.

Charles saw a double for his old scout master, Mr. Hill, who looked as old as Hill did when he finally gave up being a scout master. He must have seen a dozen look-a-likes from his past and it began to worry him. Why were the only people he recognized from his distant past? Why were there no look-a-likes of his boss, cousins or contemporary friends?

The folks he saw were uniformly long absent from his life and probably... dead. He must be having some kind of hallucinations, he thought, perhaps he'd been more damaged by the accident than he realized. He'd heard of people that suffered head trauma and felt all right, only to die a few days later. He'd have John take him to the infirmary after he got his paperwork out of his car.

Holabaugh's Diner was easy to find, he saw it the second he turned south on Water Road, a two story sign towered over the one story building. The diner had closed a while ago and things didn't look any more promising down Equerry Road. There were several small industrial looking buildings decaying peacefully, but no apparent garage or impound lot. Then, exactly as Ruth had described, past the restaurant he came upon a small building, some open air grease pits and a sign on a loose hinged door that read Himmeldeutsch.

The place was past decaying and well along to collapsing. It hadn't been occupied in years. Charles wondered what it all meant, the faces of dead acquaintances mingled with equally dead relatives in his mind while he thrashed it out. The man who towed him out of the ditch came from a place that looked like it had last opened in 1935. His logical mind rebelled; it played the Twilight Zone theme back in his head to the obedient laughter of an invisible audience. The relief didn't last long, a curtain of blackness suddenly came down and he fainted dead away.

John Himmeldeutsch was standing over him when he came around, there was a pillow under his head and he was lying on a sofa in some kind of commercial waiting room that was intended to mimic a parlour.

"You okay Mr. Deutsch?"

"I guess so... What am I doing here?"

"Ruth called me. She wondered why anyone would want directions to a garage that closed eighty years ago... Put two and two together and realized you meant Himmeldeutsch Towing."

"Thanks for coming to get me... Where am I?"

"Himmeldeutsch Mortuary."

"A mortuary... Why?"

"Well besides being a tow truck driver and impound lot owner... I am also the proprietor and funeral director of Himmeldeutsch Mortuary."

His beat up rental was in the lot behind the funeral home and Charles retrieved his paper work. John drove him back to the Princess. Again, no car was waiting, no messages for him or suggestions from the dour desk clerk. Charles was determined to get something out of him so he asked him what there was to do in town.

"Nothing," the clerk replied, barely acknowledging Charles' presence.

"What was on the other side of the Clarion River Bridge?"

"Nothing."

"Why build a bridge then," asked Charles?

"I don't know… Maybe to get to the other side?"

Charles was, by now, beyond exasperated and concerned that his wife hadn't returned his call. She may be seeing someone behind his back, but they were still married and he expected a return call. He left a blistering message on her voice mail, got his paper work together and prepared to do battle with the rental company.

This time he got through promptly and an apologetic service rep explained somebody had canceled his replacement car. He was mollified when the rep waved the insurance deductible and promised to get him back to Pittsburgh in time for his flight home even if the rep had to drive him herself.

"Why was the car canceled?"

"We received an accident report on your vehicle and whoever took it was under the impression the driver was deceased."

That shook him; Wickesborough was getting just a little too eerie for his taste.

He left the Princess and sat on the same bench he sat on yesterday and before long George Cunningham sat down and asked him if he cared to "drop a bobber". The expression was one his grandfather used on holiday phone calls and was his way of reminding him that the fish were waiting. By now Charles accepted that uncanny coincidences were a matter of course in Wickesborough.

"Thanks, but the Clarion Princess doesn't let guests cook fish in their rooms."

"That's the way it is these days," the old man sighed. "It used to be that the chef at the hotel would prepare the game and fish guests brought in. The Clarion valley was famous for its hunting and fishing, as far back as when the Seneca were running the place. I guess those days are gone."

Charles felt at ease enough to question the man about Wickesborough. He told him that the commercial heart of the town had decamped to a strip along 422 that bypassed Wickesborough to the south; it was where the locals shopped and socialized. If you looked down river you could barely see the modern looking bridge that carried the highway across the Clarion to the interstate. Charles asked him about the Clarion River Bridge.

"It was bypassed like the town," George said. "But it never had much in the way of traffic even in its heyday."

George couldn't recall the last time he actually crossed the bridge, but he remembered it connected to roads that went through dying towns half as prosperous as Wickesborough.

"It's a pretty enough bridge… It would look good on a post card if anyone bothered to make a post card of Wickesborough, but it doesn't go anywhere. It's like a deceptive promise that tempts the gullible and disappoints the curious."

That statement filled Charles with foreboding.

"The desk clerk said it was simply a way to get out of town."

"He's pretty much right."

They talked about fishing and the town's history until the old man left to catch his supper. Charles suddenly felt ill and his headache came back with a vengeance. He welcomed the excuse to return to his room and lay down.

It felt like someone was jabbing him in the head with a sharp stick. It didn't help that there was no message from the rental place desk telling him when they were coming to pick him up. He was furious and became even more so when the extension he had for the helpful service rep turned out to be non-existent. He left a message for his wife asking her for help and thinking better of his previous message, apologized for being rude and closed again with, "I love you".

Looking around he realized he was alone; the desk clerk was on one of his endless breaks. The clerk was another odd bird in Wickesborough's aviary, although he didn't resemble any dead relatives or acquaintances, his name, David Grant, was familiar to Charles. He wracked his brain but drew a blank; he put the search on hold when he noticed he had a message from his wife on his cell phone.

He listened with growing distress. She was crying and pleading with who ever had her husband's cell phone to stop calling her. She had received three messages from his phone since he died, all saying he loved her, and she begged whoever was making the calls to respect her grief and stop the cruel joke. He immediately called back and heard her say hello.

She seemed not to be able to hear him and kept asking "Who is this? Who is this?"

Somewhere in the back of Charles' mind something dreadful clicked. He said "I love you" and hung up the phone. She may have heard that because the last words she said were "Charles... Is that you...? Charles?"

The desk clerk passed him as he left the motel and Charles recognized him this time. They had been in school together for one year back in high school; David Grant had disappeared one day and never returned. The young man before him was the same David Grant he'd known then, no older, no younger, exactly as Charles remembered him when he vanished that golden summer, years ago.

Charles Deutsch left the hotel and began to walk. He walked briskly. He was getting out of Wickesborough one way or the other. The Butler Coach Company had buses leaving every hour, but the bridge beckoned to him; he had to see what was on the other side. He headed toward the Clarion River and the bridge. He would cross it and see for himself what was on the other side.

He dug in and started running as fast as he could.

He'd never run so hard, his legs ate up the ground between himself and the bridge. He was running like a teenager, but the bridge seemed to be getting further and further away. He kept running anyway; he had to cross it if he was ever getting out of Wickesborough.

The attendant, Clark Morley, topped off his coffee with a little Irish and took a satisfying drink. He slid the casket into the hearse and slammed the door, he was glad to be rid of this client. Postmortem spasms were one thing, but this guy almost walked off the embalming table. Although he'd worked in the morgue for many years, these jerky unpredictable movements by the deceased still bothered him, it was like they didn't realize they were dead.

The client, Charles Deutsch, had died in an automobile accident a few days before, his death being as unremarkable as his life. He had roots in the area and was on his way to pay his respects to relatives in Mt. Lazarus Cemetery when he died. The funeral director asked the family if they wanted to bury him in Wickesborough, but the widow insisted he be shipped back, she wanted him home.

Clark was driving the body to Pittsburgh airport himself; it was an easy drive across the Clarion River Bridge, down to route 422 and out of town. Charles Deutsch was going home.

Indian Lights

A few miles outside of Wickesborough is a town called Blanket Hill. "Town" is a charitable description of the place. It's a collection of houses by a wide spot in the road under the loom of the eponymous hill. Its geographic center is Truman's store at the intersection of Rabbit Run Road and Kittanning Trail, a source of victuals and sundries for the dank, gloomy valley.

Long before John Updike was heard of, Rabbit Run flowed through the valley draining, eventually, into Buttermilk Creek, the Clarion, and onto the Allegheny, Ohio, Mississippi Rivers and thence the Gulf of Mexico.

It's a modest stream, but with ambitions.

Rabbit Run is parallel to the deeply rutted road which bears its name for part of the way. It goes from Brick Church to Elderton and conspires with the creek to make that rough bit of highway a charming drive, provided you don't care about your car's suspension, tires or oil pan. It intersects the Kittanning Pike which runs up the hill and disappears into a tangle of brush, hairpin turns and switchbacks to emerge near someplace called Kittanning, but, the trail isn't by a creek, so it isn't charming and it doesn't go anywhere but Kittanning, so it's rarely traveled.

Because Rabbit Run bursts its banks every spring, the houses of Blanket Hill are set back in the woods above the flood plain and, consequently, are hard to see from the road. A traveler might miss Blanket Hill entirely if he wasn't paying attention. Except for Truman's Store, a passerby might assume that the valley was uninhabited and devoid of interest. The latter part would be true, little has happened of interest in Blanket Hill during its last two hundred and fifty years, which suits all its citizens, spectral, mortal, or otherwise.

The residents prefer those monotonous expanses of time that account for most of its history and regard outsiders as a source of trouble.

The last event of interest around Blanket Hill concerns outsiders and involves how the hill got its name. During the French and Indian War, a Colonel Armstrong was dispatched by the governor of the Pennsylvania Colony to subdue troublesome Indians from the Clarion Valley who were raiding frontier settlements.

By "subdue", the governor meant exterminate, and by "raiding", it was understood that the Indians had tortured, slaughtered and kidnapped men, women and children who had believed that the governor had a clear title to the land they were sold.

Armstrong rode out with six hundred men and attacked an Indian town along the Clarion River. Unfortunately, it was mostly full of women and children at the time. Armstrong did manage to kill a Captain Jacob and some hapless Lenapes, but the main culprits, Shingas and his Mingo warriors, were off on another of their innumerable raids, and escaped.

It was a near thing though, as the absent warriors returned with their scalps and hostages, they discovered Armstrong's hidden horses by the as-yet-unnamed Blanket Hill. The Mingos slaughtered the pickets and stampeded the horses by waving blankets at them. The horses scattered far and wide, beyond any reasonable hope of retrieval.

When Armstrong's crew arrived shortly thereafter, they found the horse holders dead, scalped or otherwise mutilated and a hill covered with blankets, but no horses. Satisfied with the exchange of atrocities, Armstrong named the place Blanket Hill before he began the long walk home.

Despite that auspicious start, Blanket Hill never prospered. It was clear cut—before that term was invented —and had grown back into a tangle of impenetrable secondary growth. There were a few acres of arable bottom land along the creek but not enough to make a living. The people who settled there subsisted on game they hunted or fish they caught in the nameless brooks and streams tributary to Rabbit Run. Some families let a few hogs run wild and fatten up on the bountiful mast of acorns the woods provided, and then ate their pork and bacon during lean winter months.

Time passed slowly in Blanket Hill and nothing much changed over the years. Some of the young men went away, some to war, some returning, some not. Young girls married and had babies or not. Some succumbed to the blandishments of fleshpots like Pittsburgh or Cleveland, and some just went away. Blanket Hill never varied much except that the graveyard got bigger. A soul that left in 1760 would have recognized the place if he returned in 1960, although he might have wondered why amenities like electricity and telephones were still unavailable.

Jordan was a common name in the vicinity, the family having punched out descendants every generation since the paterfamilias arrived from Scotland. He had carried a musket in the service of Armstrong's company and liked Blanket Hill because it reminded him of his dreary homeland. He homesteaded the otherwise unappealing valley, and settled in for uneventful generations to come.

While it was a common observation by the urbane sophisticates of Wickesborough that residents of Blanket Hill were "ignorant, inbred crackers," the Jordans, at least, were exceptions. They took mates from as far away as Allentown, of Catholic, Irish and even Baptist stock. The one thing you could say about Jordan men was they liked girls from out of town.

The Jordans had spread far and wide since arriving in Blanket Hill, but even when prospects there seemed most unpromising, when the chances there were bleakest, at least one of the clan remained rooted in the rocky loam under the loom of Blanket Hill.

Rodger Jordan had deep roots in Blanket Hill. He was the grandson of a man who left for the opportunities in Philadelphia during the 1920s–but his father–Rodger's great- grandfather continued living in Blanket Hill well into great old age and provided a connection to the place.

Rodger's grandfather never really severed his ties to the old homestead, so every summer Rodger joined his grandparents on their annual pilgrimage to visit family in Blanket Hill.

These jaunts were a great adventure for Rodger, a suburban kid in the 1950s. While his indulgent grandfather reconnected with friends from his youth, Rodger got to wander the woods free of supervision. Everyone around there knew who he was and ignored him as he wandered across their properties, exploring what interested a boy not yet a man.

It was the year of the flu, and Rodger had contracted a pretty severe case of it, with a raging fever, pneumonia and a lingering malaise. His parents were terrified, fearing the real possibility their only son might be carried away by the disease. When the time came for the annual visit to Blanket Hill, Rodger's health was still fragile and it looked like he would miss the trip this time.

Rodger was determined to go; he loved the time he spent in Blanket Hill and begged his parents to let him go. He persisted all spring and eventually his exhausted parents saw the wisdom of allowing him to go.

His adventures around Blanket Hill were tame, even by the standards of that gentler time, but worthy of a Daniel Boone by the standards of his home town outside Philadelphia.

Mostly he hiked along the nameless creeks that wandered into the Clarion. He always carried a .22 caliber revolver to deal with any snakes he might come across. Nobody asked how likely it was an untrained marksman would hit a rattler if he encountered one. For generations, Jordans had been going into the woods and, it was understood, they always went armed.

At night he would have dinner, watch fuzzy television from Pittsburgh with his great grand-parents and talk to them about adventures they were well acquainted with from their own vanished youth. He was still sickly.

His temperature percolated a few points above normal; he was frequently short of breath and had persistent night sweats. The local doctor couldn't find much wrong with him except he was a kid incompletely recovered from the flu; moderation and rest were his prescription.

At night, he would lie down in the camp bed his grandmother made up for him on the sleeping porch and listen to the silence of the night in the country. Some nights, the quiet was broken by bugs buzzing around the street light down at Truman's, sometimes by mysterious sounds in the surrounding forest or someone driving down Rabbit Run Road, but mostly it was quiet.

When the forest was its quietest and he was just about to drift off, sometimes he saw lights in the trees. It was a single file of lights, in the trees above Rabbit Run that moved downstream, towards the Clarion. They were beyond the resolvable distance of his vision, so he was never quite able to make out what they were.

The lights defied logical explanation. They were far more mysterious than the noises he heard, which he could associate with the mundane activities of nocturnal critters. He was mildly curious about the lights and expected some unexciting explanation from his elders.

When he asked his grandfather, the answer provoked more questions. The old man told him they were Indian lights and looked at Rodger quizzically, but said no more.

One day, on a branch of Beaver Dam Creek, he encountered a man in a tie, fishing from the front seat of an old Desoto. The car was parked on a turnout near a bridge; the driver had simply opened the door and dropped a line into the creek. The man recognized Rodger as a Jordan—Rodger bore a strong family resemblance to every Jordan that ever lived—and proceeded to explain how they were related.

His name was Harriger, Mr. Harriger, and his family had been in Blanket Hill as long as the Jordans. He said he was retired and spent his spare time fishing. The rest of his day was spent attending to his ailing wife and watching what little bits of the world passed by while he sat on his front porch glider.

Rodger listened as the old man unspooled a lifetime of memories while pursuing the rainbows, catfish or whatever else jumped on his hook. Harriger was a fount of local knowledge, liked to talk, and Rodger listened well.

Harriger had an excellent memory and supplemented his recollections with stories from his grandparent's past, told to him sixty years before—and some he made up. He had piled up an impressive collection of memories and lore he had hoped to unload on his grand- children, but being childless, he imparted them instead to Rodger.

By now, Rodger's time in Blanket Hill was close to an end. He would be returning to Philadelphia soon and his thoughts drifted to the upcoming school year. Harriger noticed that he was distracted and asked about it.

"Just thinking about school."

Harriger nodded and concentrated on an imperceptible hit on the line.

"It starts up after Labor Day."

Harriger set the hook with an abrupt pull with his rod, netted the catfish, and dropped him in a tub of fresh water.

"School is good, no future without it," said Harriger, watching the fish adjust to its temporary, galvanized home. "Can't learn a useful thing in Blanket Hill," he continued.

Rodger considered that. He'd learned a lot from the old man, none of which was useful.

"I don't know... Things are interesting here... Like the Indian lights."

"Indian lights," scoffed Harriger. "Where'd you hear about that superstitious nonsense?"

"From Grandpa Jordan... And I saw them... What are they?"

"Well, according to some, the Indians used to make a kind of lantern out of birch bark, tallow and a bit of yarn when they traveled by night."

"But there aren't any Indians in Blanket Hill...Armstrong killed them all..."

"So they say..."

"Come on... So who's wandering around at night with the lights..."

"Old timers used to say it was Indians coming for the souls of Armstrong's party... And any they catch are in for a bad time... It's all a bunch of hokum as far as I can see."

Rodger was silent. He wanted to hear more, but the headache that had been bothering him began aching intensely. It was a residual symptom of the flu, but today, the dull, familiar ache had yielded to an insistent knifing throb. He went pale, his eyes became dull and anyone could see Rodger was in distress.

Harriger noticed and asked what was wrong.

Rodger tried to slough off his concern but by now all he wanted was to be was in his bed under thick blankets. His head was spinning, the mid-day sunlight hurt his eyes and, when a well of black ink appeared at his feet, he gratefully stepped in.

Harriger drove the unconscious boy home and the doctor was summoned. In those days doctors came to your house when the situation warranted. They laid Rodger out on the davenport in the front room, in part to facilitate his care and, in part, from generations of experience with people dying at home. It was easier to remove a body from a downstairs room near the front door than an upstairs back bedroom.

An endangered child brings out the secret fears of all parents and soon Blanket Hill was on alert and making inquiries, usually with an attendant casserole. The doctor's diagnosis was as unsettling as it was nonspecific, Rodger had encephalitis, probably brought on by the flu, but no one could say for certain.

Rodger rested uneasily. There were horrible bouts of night terrors that shattered the dark, his screams piercing the silent humid evening along Rabbit Run. Sometimes he would babble incoherently between screams; rarely was anything lucid uttered. Sometimes, he would sit up and stare terrified into space at nothing in particular. When questioned about it later, he offered no explanation; he had no recollection of anything.

One night he tried to bolt out the door and was restrained, prompting a struggle on the parlor floor. His distressed grandparents paced frantically during these episodes worrying about what to do and blaming themselves for Rodger's plight.

For several days, Rodger lay in a state of semi- delirium. He was doused with the miracle drug of the day – penicillin–even though his encephalitis was probably viral and antibiotics are useless against viruses. They treated his symptoms: if he got chills they warmed him; if he was thirsty they pushed ginger ale or orange juice down his throat; the drapes were drawn to shield his eyes from the sunlight. He took respite after the sun had set, sitting by a window, wrapped in an afghan, and staring into the darkness.

A few days later, he felt better and, at his insistence, went back to the sleeping porch to recuperate. He was able to have visitors and Harriger dropped by. They talked about going fishing along the creek where they met, but neither believed that was likely to happen again.

Rodger couldn't remember much of what he had dreamed. All he could recall was running down a path in the woods with hands reaching out to catch him and pull him into the circle of anguished souls surrounded by the Indian lights.

Harriger regretted saying anything about the Indian lights. Most of what he told him was nonsense he'd made up on a whim. The tale had taken hold in Rodger's mind and manifested in his imagination as an Indian war party. Harriger knew something about these matters. Before his retirement he had been a Professor of Abnormal Psych at the school of psychology at Clark University. He knew that Rodger was emotionally exhausted and didn't have the strength to resist anymore, not even in his dreams.

Rodger was not recovering; he had settled into insensate melancholy and become resigned to his fate. The boy believed that specters from the French and Indian War were coming to carry him away. He believed in it powerfully enough to accept a coup de grace from some phantasmagorical Mingo warrior and let the illness take him away.

Harriger looked at the boy and saw the shadow of death upon him. He explained to Rodger that the Indian lights were just a bit of local folklore that he had embellished. Rodger looked at Harriger with cold lifeless eyes, either not hearing, or not caring. He exhaled a raspy breath. Harriger decided then to wait up with Rodger until he went to sleep and perhaps plant subconscious suggestions that would shake his conviction in the reality of his dream world.

They talked for a while about life, things in Blanket Hill and fishing until Rodger drifted into his unquiet sleep and dreamt. To anyone watching him, his sleep was fitful, no different from other nights, but the dreamscape Rodger was experiencing was different.

This time, his dream was much clearer. He saw Indian warriors plainly. They wore buckskin breeches and gingham shirts, their faces were painted red or blue and their hair was slicked with bear grease. They were intent on pulling him into a circle where a man, more dead than alive, was tied to a stake enduring the ordeal that they inflicted on their most worthy captives.

Occasionally, the victim would revive and insult his tormentor's killing technique, whereupon the frenzy of the torture would increase. They hacked at him with tomahawks and clubs until he was a gory mess. He was beaten with enthusiastic cruelty that stopped just short of killing him, for now. Rodger knew it would continue until the captive died, then the Indians would select a new victim and begin again.

Rodger couldn't look away. The scene was illuminated by the Indian lights Harriger had described. The painted men who held them kept coercing him inexorably into the light, towards the stake and the dying prisoner. He was grabbed by many hands and physically shoved to the center. Rodger resisted, knowing if he submitted it was his finish: he would be the man on the stake.

The nightmare felt as real as anything Rodger had ever experienced. He tried to wake up; he tried to remember it was a dream. Nothing he did broke the hold of the nightmare. He finally relaxed and let the hands carry him into the circle, if only so the dream would end.

Suddenly, Harriger was next to him, fighting his way through the Indians. Harriger was whirling, slashing and stabbing with the clasp knife he kept in his pocket to clean fish he caught. He was fighting like a man half his age with a terrible madness in his eyes, but he was taking as well as inflicting damage. Blood flowed freely down his forehead from a tomahawk wound in his scalp, staining his crisp suit. A knife cut carved a gash across the orbits of his eyes making the flesh draw back and revealed the eyes in their sockets. It made Harriger look like something from a horror movie.

Rodger took strength from the old man's vigorous resistance, but he could see it was only a matter of time before Harriger would be overwhelmed. The Indians closed in until Rodger and Harriger were fighting back to back, striking out and keeping the Indians at bay. Then Harriger took a blow and went down.

Rodger tried to help him up, but Harriger pushed him away. Rodger gave him the .22 caliber revolver from his belt. Jordan men had been going into the woods for years and, it was understood, they always went armed, even in their dreams. The momentum of the push carried Rodger away from the Indians and immediate danger.

Shots rang out and even in his dream Rodger smelled the cordite and the gun oil cooking off the hot barrel.

He came to on the sleeping porch, his fever broken. He tried to force himself into the dream to rescue Harriger, but all he could do was collapse on his cot. Harriger would be fine he thought, it was, after all, just a dream.

The next morning Rodger felt better than he had in months. Harriger was gone and Rodger assumed he'd left to try his luck down by the creek. His grandparents were relieved he felt better, but now that he was well enough to travel, they insisted he check into a hospital. An ambulance drove him to Pittsburgh that evening.

That was the last of Blanket Hill for Rodger for a long, long time. School, girls and athletics occupied his mind for the next few summers. His great-grand-parents were convinced to sell the house in Blanket Hill and move into an assisted-living facility, or as they were called in those days, a "rest home." They died within a week of each other, regretting that they'd left Blanket Hill. They had lived so long no one came to their funeral.

The rest of the Jordans lived out their lives in the greater Philadelphia area. Rodger eventually joined the navy, retired, and moved to Florida, his adventures in Blanket Hill a memory and a family joke. After the laughter stopped, he insisted that his encounter with Shingas' war party along Rabbit Run was the most vivid dream he'd ever had, more lifelike than his memory of real events.

His parents had inherited the long-lived genes of their ancestors but, in due time, they passed away. They asked that their ashes be spread around Blanket Hill, and Rodger was given the chore.

Blanket Hill, which had defeated change for so long, was in the process of doing the same to a failed golf course surrounded by unsalable condos. Truman's Store was still there, but it was now called Rascal's Emporium and it sold imported cheeses from Wisconsin and vile coffee from Seattle, catering to the non-existent residents of Rabbit Dell Country Club. Residents of Blanket Hill would shop at Wal*Mart now until the Trumans came to their senses. The Jordan family home had become a bed and breakfast run by a man and woman with desperate eyes, worried about their investment.

From the looks of things Blanket Hill would be back to normal in a few years.

Rodger thought better of dumping ashes on the old homestead since the current owners already thought the place was cursed. Every place else in Blanket Hill was unappealing or unavailable for disposal of the cremains, so he drove up the Kittanning Pike and down a fire trail to the place he first encountered Harriger.

He was astounded to find the old Desoto rusting away in the brush just feet from where he'd first seen it. He dumped the ashes into the water, hoping his parents would be satisfied with a water-borne tour of Blanket Hill, the Clarion, the Allegheny and, eventually, the ocean. He was sitting on the running board of Harriger's car meditating on the passage of time and transience of human life when a uniformed member of the Pennsylvania State Fish and Game Department, asked him what he was doing.

The game warden disapproved of scattering potentially toxic remains in a watershed and wrote him a ticket, asking him how he knew about the place. Rodger told him how he met the owner of the car at this very place years before. The warden asked if it was around the time Harriger died. Rodger told him he hadn't seen him since the summer after the Hong Kong Flu, but Harriger was still alive at that time.

"It was around Labor Day," the warden said. "Harriger was up here and somebody beat the life out of him."

"Did they catch the guy?"

"No... The old-timers used to talk about it when I was a rookie... It was brutal. He was butchered like a pig."

"What do you mean?"

"It was like somebody went after him with a hatchet... There was a pretty sizable manhunt going for a while, but it petered out after a couple of months... Folks were pretty nervous that a homicidal maniac was running loose... A guy down in Pittsburgh eventually confessed, but nobody bought it."

Rodger thought back to the last time he'd seen Harriger.

"The Indian lights," he said out loud.

"How'd you know about that? The guy from Pittsburgh talked about them but nobody knew what he was talking about."

"Harriger told me."

The game warden took him in for questioning at the Wickesborough County sheriff's station. The memory of an old-timer, Burton Himmeldeutsch, and a search of forty- year-old ambulance company records provided Rodger with an alibi and he was released.

The warden drove him back to his car by Harriger's Desoto and stuck around to follow him out. The sun had sunk behind Blanket Hill casting the creek into gloom, in a few minutes blackness rolled up the valley like an inky tide. Rodger took a last look at Harriger's car. It had been driven into a ditch, the front end crumpled, the frame bent. Saplings and some fair-sized trees had grown up through the wreck, Rodger walked around it, picturing Harriger fishing from the front seat, while the impatient game warden picked his nose and watched.

He kicked something in the brush and bent down to examine it. It was the .22 he had carried in the woods.

Jordan men had been going into the woods for years and, it was understood, they always went armed. Rusted to useless scrap after years out in the brush, Rodger remembered when it was working and new.

Bored and impatient, the game warden gestured for him to get into his car, but when Rodger tried to start it he discovered he'd left the dome light on and drained the battery. The warden had to check in back at the ranger station, but he called Rodger a wrecker to give him a jump start. The woods were closing in now as they do at sunset. Rodger felt the loneliness descend with the shadows as he watched the warden pull away. He sat in his car and followed the taillights as they disappeared into the trees. He may have dozed, but he woke up soon enough to see two lights coming down the fire trail towards him.

He got out of his car to greet the tow truck when he noticed a third light, a fourth, then a fifth and finally, many lights, moving in single file, moving downstream, moving towards him. They were beyond the resolvable distance of his vision, so he couldn't make out what was behind those lights, but he had a good guess. Something dark had slipped into this world from the next and it was coming for him. A long delayed reckoning was about to come due.

He stuck the useless bit of rusted revolver in his belt and faced whatever it was coming his way. He hoped he was dreaming.

Back Seat Driver

Despite first impressions, not all residents of Wickesborough are clueless yokels. Some of the most clueless were from the sophisticated environs of New York and Oil City. Dolts they may be, but they hail from different locales and venues, all stumbling around the county waiting to tumble into snares and traps their urbane experience has ill equipped them to avoid.

The locals have learned with Darwinian certainty that you don't ask too many questions or poke an unfamiliar sleeping dog. That way lays disaster and Wickesboroughians know how far out of control things can get before you realize you're doomed.

This catastrophe began with an impetuous disregard for the minefields that flank even innocuous activities in Wickesborough, Although crime is always perilous, crime was how Milan, Bosco and Leno chose to demonstrate their rebellious side, in this case by stealing a beat up old car to torch after a brief joy ride—without bothering to look in the back seat.

"Who's there?"

The voice came out of the landfill piled in the back seat of a large American car, of, indeterminate vintage and indifferent maintenance. Bosco and Leno were scared out of their wits, but didn't show it, Milan wasn't scared, but made a point of giving the impression that she was.

Bosco was driving but his attention was focused on finding where the mystery voice in the car had come from, instead of the sinuous contortions of Branch Valley road. Milan grabbed the steering wheel and prevented a disaster.

"What was that?"

"I'm guessing the ride you guys stole had someone napping in the back seat," she replied.

Milan was an uncommon name in Wickesborough County, so unusual; she usually didn't bother with her last name, Kumnacker. She was conceived on her parents honeymoon in Italy, they were in Florence, but in the States the name Florence carried associations with the best oil to fry chicken in. They went with Milan.

"No problem... She's a drunk with a crazy kid... We'll kick her out when we get to 422."

"Is that you, Bosco?"

"Mrs. Woodhouse?"

Milan stared at Bosco as if to drink in his stupidity.

"She knows who you are... I'd say we have a problem now."

The state university in Indiana Pennsylvania had two distinctions: being confused with the University of Indiana in Bloomington Indiana and being situated in the home town of Jimmy Stewart. It had recently acquired a third, providing Wickesborough County with arrogant and loud students and instructors, who believed that they could deal with anything life threw at them with an iPhone and a Prime account with Amazon.

Of course, the instructors and students were manipulative, full of contempt for others, convinced of their superiority and quick to anger when they didn't get their way. They quickly hooked up with feral locals of similar character and unleashed themselves on Wickesborough before anyone cried havoc.

Leno and Milan were gown and Bosco added town savor to the trio.

Rosemary Woodhouse emerged from a generous stratum of effluvia and eyed her kidnappers.

"What the Hell are you doing, Bosco?"

"It's all right Mrs. Woodhouse; we're just taking you home."

"The Hell you are."

"We're taking you back to Recluse Lane."

Recluse Lane was an undedicated road, a track actually, along a sand bar in the Clarion where the riper eccentrics of Wickesborough resided in trailers and lean-tos. The name was a bit of a misnomer. The residents had no problem mingling when they are where they aren't wanted, they just don't want to have anything to do with their neighbors.

Once every twenty-five years or so, the spring thaw would raise the Clarion enough to wash neighborhood away.

"I haven't lived there since my Andy disappeared."

The disappeared Andy, Rosemary Woodhouse's son, raised the eyebrows of Milan, Bosco and Leno. They knew him and his murderous reputation. Leno and Milan were actual witnesses to one of his crimes, a matter of some distinction since the others hadn't survived this long. He had practically run a clinic, a sort of Future Psychopaths of America club, for the guileless innocents he molested. They filled a wing at the State Correctional Institution in Rockview with his acolytes. Since his disappearance, the life expectancy of Wickesborough's elderly had risen five years. Mrs. Woodhouse doted on him.

"Well… where do you live now?"

"In this fucking car… The car you stole… my car… I'm gonna call the cops."

Crime and its penalties were abstracts to Milan and Leno; they'd dodged the wrath both of their victims and the police so far. Not so Bosco, he'd taken the rap, as the criminal vernacular has it, for a misdemeanor committed as a juvenile, with the same Milan and Leno.

Bosco was in love with Milan at the time, and Leno was his best friend, so he did what he felt was the noble thing and took responsibility.

Six months in a county lock-up disabused him of that fantasy and made him cynical about the nobility of sacrifice. That Leno and Milan had hooked up while he was in jail, helped. While Milan and Leno were grateful to Bosco they had come to regard him as a third wheel and hoped he'd move on.

To be candid, Milan was hoping both Leno and Bosco would both move on, she was seeing a variety of other men who had expanded her horizons beyond high school boys. She believed— actually knew–she could do better, but before that, emollients had to be spread on the surface of her current dilemma.

"There's no need for the cops Mrs. Woodhouse."

"Who the fuck are you, Missy?"

"I'm a friend of Bosco's… And Leno."

Bosco was immediately alert. Any police involvement would go worse for him. He had a record, Leno didn't, Milan had fingered him and Leno, but she had remained anonymous, at least until Leno folded during interrogation.

"We saw you in the back."

Bosco began improvising desperately.

"I thought we should take you to a hospital."

"Where, in Kittanning? … I thought you were taking me to Recluse Lane?"

Rosemary looked around, saw the gas can and rags, and drew the obvious conclusion.

"You were going to torch my car—and if I hadn't woken up, I would have been in it."

Milan, Bosco and Leno exchanged glances; Rosemary had them dead to rights. Bosco and Leno looked guilty; Milan was the picture of innocence.

"Mrs. Woodhouse… can't we work something out? It's all a misunderstanding."

"A misunderstanding… If I overlook car theft, kidnapping, arson and maybe... considering the forethought, the gas cans and rags… depraved indifference… That's a lot of misunderstanding to overlook."

"I know... we could compensate you for the inconvenience."

Milan's father was an attorney.

"Compensate me… You want to buy me off."

"Well, no harm, no foul."

Leno pitched that gem of NBA legal scholarship. It was all his parents had passed on to him.

"You want to slip me a few bucks… Probably max out your ATM card and tell me to get lost."

"We can get more money tomorrow."

"Along with a restraining order and a threatening letter explaining what extortion is… You people figure you can do anything to anyone… especially poor people."

Rosemary had them there; it was a fundamental assumption of theirs.

"What about Bosco here… He's broker than I am… Who's going to pick up his part of the tab?"

That triggered an exchange of glances and silence until Milan picked up the negotiation.

"Tell us what you want and we'll get it."

"Right now I want some Newports… And a Slim Jim."

Bosco steered into Jensen's Sunoco on 422; Officer Braxton Dunkel was inside talking to Reverend Conrad and Olstee Pettigrew, a reporter. Seeing three pillars of the community's moral elite batting the breeze in a filling station, Rosemary, naturally, headed towards them shouting that she had been kidnapped.

They stared at her, wondering who would kidnap a drunken homeless person. Rosemary was well known to local and county authorities as a ranting lunatic and they chalked it up to delirium tremens or wood alcohol. Leno and Milan headed her off and pointed her to the counter where the smokes and sausage snacks were waiting.

They hustled her back into the car, where Bosco just prevented her from lighting up around the gas cans.

"That was close…"

"Yeah if the gas had gone up…"

"I meant if Officer Dunkel had listened to her…"

Milan knew him from his capacity as the Wickesborough At-Risk-Kids Task Force and his frequent interrogations of troubled young girls he suspected of being on a path of promiscuity and juvenile crime.

"You've got to kill her."

Leno and Bosco exchanged another round of glances. They would have wondered if she was using the singular or plural 'you' if they had paid attention in English class.

"Not me."

Bosco pre-emptively took himself out of the equation. Milan rolled her eyes and saw Leno wasn't sold on the idea either. Mrs. Woodhouse continued smoking in her nest of flammable effluvia, with cans of gasoline conveniently nearby.

"All we have to do is get her intoxicated… She'll drop a cigarette and… poof, no witness, no problem."

"But it would be murder."

"Only technically… Remember how many people died when Andy was around?"

Milan and Leno left to buy vodka and weed for Mrs. Woodhouse; Bosco remained behind to keep her from wandering off or prematurely immolating herself.

"You know she likes you."

"How's that Mrs. Woodhouse?"

"Ah call me Rosemary… the girl, Milan, likes you… the guy she's with just annoys her."

"You really think so Rose?"

"Rosemary… Yeah, you give her an excuse and she'll dump… what's his name?"

"Leno…"

"She knows he's a lox… I'm a woman, I know… She likes you."

"Yeah but Leno… He's going to college."

"He's going to Emerson… I like you Bosco… My son Andy liked you…

Those words chilled Bosco's blood. People Andy liked usually had life changing experiences—the bad kind.

"Where is Andy these days?"

"They killed him… I think they killed him…"

"But they never found a body?"

"No, my poor boy is lost out there…Where no one will ever find him… So here's the plan… when Jack and Jill come tumbling down the hill…"

"Who, what?"

"Never mind… when Leno and what's her name return…"

"Milan."

"Right… Milan… You wander off and call the police. I'll say that Leno kidnapped me and you and the girl were innocent pawns… Oh, and pick me up some Doritos.

Bosco didn't have much time to consider the plan, Milan and Leno had returned from their errand sooner than expected. Wickesborough was the intoxicant hub for the tri-county area, so it didn't take long to shop, compare and buy what was needed to put Rosemary in a coma. While Milan and Leno administered Rosemary's last happy hour, Bosco drifted away back to Jensen's for corn chips, and to rat out his friends.

"So where's Bosco going?"

Milan was alert to any unexplained absences by her crew.

"I sent him to get some Doritos… I thought Leno might like some too."

"You should have said something… We could have gotten them."

"Now that you mention it…"

Milan left to get Mrs. Woodhouse her super absorbent, extra-large tampons which Leno absolutely refused to buy. He was instructed to watch Rosemary, by which Milan meant he should keep getting her liquored up.

"That girl is two timing you."

"Drink your vodka, Mrs. Woodhouse."

"You wouldn't have some Clamato up there?"

"No… What do you mean two timing?"

"I guess Worcestershire sauce and celery is out of the question? Two timing means she's fucking around on you."

"Yes, I mean no Worcestershire or celery… I have grapefruit juice… Who is she two timing me with…? Bosco?"

"Grapefruit juice gives me gas… Yeah Bosco… for starters."

'How about vodka, Snappy Tom and Oxycontin?

"Bosco, really…? For starters?"

"That'll do… Yes starters… They call her the recruiter for the Wickesborough Navy."

"Why?"

"She's always looking for more seamen."

"No… That isn't true… The recruiters only show up on career day."

"Think about it."

Leno thought about it.

"I'll kill her!"

"Well that would be easier than killing different guys each week. She's looking for the man of her dreams."

"Bosco?"

"I said she was looking for the man of her dreams, not a circus worker."

"How will I know him when he shows up?"

"She could be looking for degenerate Italian playboys, but they're kind of hard to find in Wickesborough. This isn't that hard… She's cheating on you with a bunch of guys… Start with Bosco and go from there."

Leno started the car and went after Bosco. He caught up to him on his way back from Jensen's, tried to run him down, but missed. Bosco was unaware of why he was being attacked, but was happy to drag Leno from the car and start pummeling him. Milan caught up to her brawling suitors and tried to separate them, but got pulled into the fight.

Reverend Conrad ran over from Jensen's to break up the fight between two members of his Methodist Youth Outreach. Olstee rushed over to get the lead story for tomorrows <u>Wickesborough County Herald Examiner, Press Telegraph, Clarion and Evening Bulletin</u>.

Wickesborough had gone through a phase of media consolidation just before the advent of radio.

Meanwhile Rosemary relaxed, leaned back, fired up a Newport and watched the fun. She watched until an ember of menthol flavored tobacco tumbled into her untidy nest and set the car on fire.

Leno, Bosco and Milan were too close to see the spectacular pyrotechnics when the gas cans exploded, but they were far enough away to survive, minus their eyebrows and hair. The bald, smoldering trio exchanged accusations and recriminations in front of the reporter, the Reverend, and even Officer Dunkel when he finally showed up.

The fire department eventually showed up and sprayed foam on the still smoking vehicle, Reverend Conrad said a prayer, a rather conditional one, for the soul of Rosemary Woodhouse with a reference to Foxe's Book of Martyrs and the manner of her passing.

Dunkel arrested the also still smoking trio of conspirators and charged them with everything: murder, kidnapping, car theft and anything else the commonwealth had declared illegal since 1689. He even invoked the Lindberg Law, saying they confessed to him of driving Rosemary to Ohio and back.

Andy Woodhouse and his mother watched the events from the shadows, munching on Doritos.

"Those two are the last ones that saw you dragging that Renay girl to the brickyard?"

"Yeah, I think…"

"Your pals in Rockview will take care of them?"

"Yeah…too bad about Bosco."

"Who cares? Once they're dead there's no one to connect you to Renay Dobler."

"Do I still have to hide?"

"Yes… for a while."

"Where?"

"Somewhere far away…

"Where Mom?"

"As far as the Butler Coach Company will take you."

The Boy Next Door

Walsh lived in a housing development in a borough immediately south of Wickesborough, named West Wickesborough by directionally-challenged founders.

The tract, Homewood Estates, was the dream of a local developer who believed he could persuade Pittsburgh commuters that West Wickesborough's rural charms were worth an extra hour's drive. His dream turned out to be an over-leveraged nightmare which died, like so many others, when gas prices spiked, the housing market collapsed and the economy imploded. The developer exchanged his dream for a bullet in the head, courtesy of a gun he'd bought with cash.

Walsh bought his home when the market bottomed.

He had a good job, so while others sweated out the recession, Walsh enjoyed a brand new home in a somewhat deserted neighborhood.

He was middle aged, single, and set in his ways. He no longer expected to plight his troth with a woman, so a solitary existence suited him fine. Nothing made him happier than to close his front door and know that nothing would disturb him.

The neighborhood wasn't completely empty; the development was kept about one third filled, stocked with renters and real estate bottom feeders. The heirs and receivers of the bankrupt developer saw to it that unsold homes were rented, vacant homes maintained, and the area patrolled by private security to discourage squatters. The illusion of an active community percolated up and down the avenues of Homewood Estates, illusionary because the residents had nothing to do with each other and might as well have lived on other planets.

Homewood Drive was the name of the particular loop Walsh lived on, and was well populated with pairs of young women from the nearby university in Indiana. There were also some divorcees, a smattering of families with workaholic husbands who were never around, and single women who snapped up a housing bargain when they saw one. What the neighborhood lacked was men.

Walsh suspected, but couldn't prove, that the owners of Homewood Estates discriminated against male college students and other down-and-outers with a first month's rent in hand, but slim prospects after that. That was fine with him; it kept down testosterone-fueled bad behavior. Walsh called it his "Bachelor's Paradise."

There was a ripple in the continuum when the house next door sold and Walsh braced for the novelty of new people. When the neighbors, the Benoits, turned out to be a man, his wife and their son instead of giggling co-eds, he was pleased. Walsh still appreciated the charms of young women, but the hours they kept conflicted with his own.

Although he worked from home, Walsh was expected to be online from early morning until eight at night for clients, on both coasts, who needed help setting up their digital routers. Young women being picked up and dropped off by young men on Japanese motorcycles at all hours would have tested his patience.

Like everyone, Walsh had a sequence of rituals he went through every morning, one was to walk a brisk mile every day at about dawn. It served to keep him acquainted with his neighbors as they went about their morning chores and dull the suspicion he had that he was becoming a hermit. He also liked to pretend, that when the time came when he might enjoy a woman's company, he'd know enough to pounce on an unsuspecting, if willing victim.

Walsh considered himself the neighborhood watchman, and kept an eye out during his morning exercise, but never saw anything that threatened the serene, unvarying rhythms of Homewood. Life continued as it had in the past and promised to do so in the future.

He waved at everyone he saw on his morning rounds, whether they returned the courtesy or not. The departing husbands eyed him suspiciously, their wives indifferently, the co-eds innocently and the divorcees acquisitively. The odd cougar watched him curiously, or dismissively, since he was age appropriate as a spouse but much older than their preferred sexual demographic. All in all, his morning constitutional generated dividends, which in Walsh's mind he was saving for a later day.

The Benoits always returned his wave since he had made it a point to introduce and explain himself to them. They took his hint about quiet after nine and seemed intent on ignoring him as well as he ignored them. Although Maeve Benoit, the wife, was as indifferent about him as he was of her, Walsh sensed Ben Benoit, her husband, was the jealous type. He carefully avoided any sort of casual encounters with Mrs. Benoit that weren't chaperoned. He didn't want Mr. Benoit entertaining any suspicions which, imaginary or not, inevitably led to gunplay in this part of the country.

He needn't have worried; Mr. Benoit and his wife Maeve were dull, chilly people, cut off from the same emotions he was. That was fine; Walsh needed no more than basic relations with his neighbors. The boy, Arthur, was a different story; he had imperfectly absorbed the family tradition of maintaining emotional distance, so he was more curious than appropriate, and prone to asking direct questions.

As refreshing as that was, considering the monotony attendant with life in West Wickesborough, Walsh wondered if he was inclined to poke around in other people's houses after dark. The kids in Wickesborough were notorious for such hijinks and he wondered if Arthur had caught that bug. Walsh decided to keep an eye on him and drop anonymous tips to the authorities if he did anything out of line.

For Walsh, the Benoits turned out to be perfect neighbors, and his life continued to uncoil in its unremarkable way. Arthur was well behaved, at least as far as he could tell, and his other neighbors continued living lives of quiet monotony.

The utter sameness of it all never bothered Walsh, but perhaps he felt it more acutely because he lived alone and never went anywhere. Maybe his neighbors led wildly eccentric lives outside of West Wickesborough, maybe they sky dived or wrestled bears on weekends, but everything Walsh witnessed on his daily excursions was excruciatingly mundane. To call it a routine was to underestimate the repetitiveness. Every day was so identical it was unnatural, as unvarying as the actions of a robot, it was almost non-human.

When school let out, Arthur spent more time at home in his bedroom over the garage. Walsh could see into the bedroom from a window in his office and watched him. He sat at the computer at all hours, never bothering to draw the drapes, endlessly typing away. At first, Walsh drew his own shades to avoid invading Arthur's privacy, but he missed the light and, since Arthur didn't care, Walsh stopped bothering.

Walsh spent most of his day by that window and every time he glanced over he saw Arthur doing something at the computer. Video gaming, he guessed, with an internal "harrumph."

'The biggest time waster ever invented,' he thought, although it did keep Arthur off the street and out of trouble.

After a while Walsh stopped looking that way, Arthur and his activities became part of the scenery, as unchanging and unremarkable as everything else in West Wickesborough. The only time he noticed Arthur anymore was when he went to bed, and saw him illuminated by the glow of the monitor, typing away.

One morning, the routine subtly changed and Walsh barely noticed. Arthur was not at his desk and his parents were nowhere to be found, not that Walsh searched very hard. After a couple of days, he started picking up their mail and newspaper to discourage burglars. Oddly, they got exactly the same mail every day; that struck Walsh as unusual although the same thing applied to him. He ignored that mystery as well and concentrated on where the Benoits had gone. He concluded, eventually, that they must be on vacation, the most benign of any explanation for their disappearance.

It was during his next morning walk that Walsh noticed the unusual; things were different on Homewood Drive. At first it was simple things, a car in a driveway instead of a garage, a newspaper on a lawn instead of a porch, simple things yes, but a break from the daily, identical pattern he was familiar with. Walsh was relieved, at least the problem wasn't in his own head, and his neighbors were human after all.

A couple of days later he realized that his neighbors had begun acting strangely. He was on the return stretch of his walk when he saw the couple he always saw saying good bye in the driveway at this time. It was a scene he'd seen a hundred times before: He waved, the man ignored him and the wife waved back. The man drove away and the wife picked up the paper and went back into the house, there was nothing unusual about it at all except that they were both quite naked.

The woman waved as Walsh walked by, completely nonchalant about her nakedness. Walsh waved back assuming that maybe they were nudists, or swingers, or in some kind of hippie cult, he knew of people that did that sort of thing. He disapproved, but as long as they kept their house up, it wasn't any of his business.

The same thing happened a few days in a row and his curiosity got the better of him. He stopped and introduced himself while carefully keeping his eyes above her shoulders. They chatted amicably enough until he brought up her lack of clothing, at which point she asked him what he was talking about. She thought she was dressed perfectly well for the weather and what was he, "some kind of pervert?" Walsh mumbled an apology about being more sensitive to the cold than most and walked away, convinced that she was an uninhibited nut case.

By now he was seeing other things that didn't make much sense; a young girl on a scooter kept passing him as he made his rounds. At first he thought she had gone on an errand and was returning, then he assumed she had forgotten something, by the eighth time he realized she was just endlessly circling the block. At one point, it seemed to Walsh's that she was hit by the van that always made deliveries at this time, but she emerged on the other side unscratched and continued her endless circling.

One house had a car parked on its roof. He watched as the driver calmly got out and removed the groceries from the back seat then went inside by a second floor window.

People he knew, or at least recognized, had gained weight or become rail thin; a woman plummeted out of the sky, but walked away uninjured. By the time he finished his rounds, Walsh was doubting his sanity, but at home everything seemed normal enough so he relaxed. Back in his office he looked out the window and saw Arthur busily typing away. At least that was reassuring.

His relief was short lived because when he brought the Benoits their mail, Maeve was walking on stilts in their living room. While Ben thanked him profusely, it was in a language he took to be Japanese. Arthur ushered him out explaining that his parents were tired after their trip and they would be fine in the morning. Considering what he'd seen that morning, Walsh was ready to accept the explanation, except that as Arthur was making it, Maeve stumbled into the ceiling fan and was decapitated.

Arthur's explanation, that this was a common occurrence whenever stilt walkers came into close proximity with ceilings fans, rang a little hollow to Walsh. He offered to call the paramedics, but Arthur insisted that all would be well in the morning. As his father picked up Maeve's head and placed it in a closet, Arthur slammed the door in Walsh's face.

Walsh called the police when he got home.

The call to 911 reached a voicemail box that told Walsh to have a nice day, put him on hold, and then asked him what his language preference was. Thirty-five selections later he got to English and then listened to a loop of Jingle Cats greatest hits. Possibilities raced through Walsh's head. Maybe he had unknowingly taken some hallucinogenic mushrooms, or maybe it was a CIA mind control experiment. Perhaps he'd run afoul of some satanic cult? Were these signs of the end times? Had he been kidnapped by aliens and put on a different planet?

Whatever, Walsh determined to get out of town as quickly as possible.

He went into the garage and started his car, but his garage no longer had a door. Walsh knew that was strange. He remembered getting the car into the garage through the door. He looked behind him to see if he had backed in, but there was no door on that wall either. He went back into his house without bothering to turn off the car, ran out the front door and began walking.

It was dark by now. The comforting familiarity of his neighborhood had been transformed into a mad carnival. The naked couple was walking back and forth between their car and their house. The scooter girl continued her endless journey, people plummeted out of trees, men the size of Jabba the Hut were talking to cats, and co-eds on bicycles were crashing into burning houses. Walsh put his head down and walked on, not bothering to return the wave of a divorcee who was planting kitchen utensils in her rose bed.

He turned left at the first intersection and left at the next, the way he knew led out of West Wickesborough. He walked a long time, longer than he remembered the trip taking, but he kept at it. Dawn was streaking long shadows across his path when he finally paused; he was standing in front of his own house.

It seemed normal from the outside; at least the garage door was back. The rest of the neighborhood was quiet now and also back to normal; the early morning rituals he knew would be starting soon.

Exhausted, Walsh went into his house and flopped on the couch. He was more tired than he knew and fell into a deep sleep, made all the deeper by the carbon monoxide that filled his house from the car he'd left running in the garage.

When he awoke, he was surprised, as anyone might be who had inhaled so much automotive exhaust, but for a different reason. His head rested on the desk in Arthur's bedroom, but his body was nowhere to be seen. He knew this because his eyes could scan the full arc of the room without moving his head which was also a surprise.

Arthur was typing, as usual, and didn't seem bothered by Walsh's disembodied head. Walsh was trying not to panic but his situation had a lot of disadvantages and potential dangers that Arthur might not immediately consider.

"Excuse me…"

Arthur was startled by his voice, but never stopped typing.

"That's odd I haven't run you."

"I beg your pardon?"

Walsh was suddenly aware that he wasn't actually hearing Arthur but he was somehow communicating with him via his keyboard.

"I'm still writing commands for you… I haven't actually run your program yet."

"Arthur, stop this right now… It's gotten out of hand and if you don't put me back with my body… Or whatever the Hell it is you've done to me... You'll be in real trouble mister."

"How are you doing that? Are you running in the background?"

"Arthur, I'm here on your desk."

"It's like you're talking."

Walsh paused for a second. To talk you needed at least rudimentary lungs to force air through a larynx, both of which he was currently lacking. He decided to ignore that issue and just deal with Arthur.

"I am talking… to you."

"But you have to be alive to do that, not just an app."

Walsh gave that some thought, maybe this was some sort of Tibetan afterlife. Maybe he was experiencing, the Bardo of being in an electronic device.

"Did I die?"

"No you were running fine… Too fine, I thought you needed some new code."

"I run on code?"

"Technically it's all you are… You're an avatar for the firewall that's supposed to keep Homestead safe."

"Homestead?"

"Yeah… We created a sim game… Sorry simulation game… and named it after Homewood Estates… Sort of… Homewood/Homestead… Get it… Cool huh?

"Arthur... I am not an avatar; I'm your next door neighbor."

"Relax... I'm an avatar too. I'm Arthur Benoit…I'm in Mr. Wexler's computer science class at Wickesborough High."

"Go Ravens," Walsh blurted out.

"Ravens Rule"

Walsh realized he had stumbled into a circle of Hell unknown to Dante, the one where an adult tries to get a straight answer out of a teenager.

"We are not avatars. You're Arthur, I'm Walsh, I am not a firewall."

"Well... not a very good one. Some guys over at Indiana hacked you, and Homewood started acting all weird."

This made sense, all the nudity and the absurdity of behavior had a sophomoric feel only geeks could appreciate. Walsh sensed he was getting nowhere and decided to humor Arthur.

"Then hurry up and get Homewood back to normal."

"Not so fast... Mr. W. made the rules so tight Homewood wasn't any fun... So we're making some changes."

"Fun... It's chaos..."

"Only if you live there."

"You don't live here?"

"You don't live there either... You are a program... You don't have any say in this... When we reboot, it'll be like old Homewood never existed."

"Arthur, if I didn't live in Homewood, why would I have a house there?"

"It's all a figment of a computer programmer's imagination."

"What about my family, my job, my history... I vacationed in Florida last year... I kept the receipts for tax purposes."

"What's your last name?"

Walsh was stumped. He had no body so he didn't have his wallet and couldn't produce his driver's license. He was over at the Benoits so his high school year book wasn't nearby, it was a real dilemma. He had no proof he could produce that he had ever existed, so he carefully considered his next question.

"If I am an avatar, who am I based on?"

"You aren't based on anyone... We copied your code from an existing firewall. The guy who wrote it was Walsh."

"If I don't exist how can I talk to you?"

"We don't know?"

"Can you ask around?"

"Mr. Wexlar is on leave, his wife ran off with the softball coach."

"What do you think?"

"Jeremy thinks you might be an artificial life form like Data on the old Star Trek show and Aleese thinks it has something to do with some kind of matrix thing. Try doing something we didn't program you to do."

"I can't do anything... I don't have a body."

Walsh realized it was like arguing with the DMV, apparently talking wasn't proof enough he was alive. He had to juggle while reciting "The Shooting of Dan McGrew" to prove to these future government workers that he existed in the real world.

"Right, Duh... Damian wants to run you in safe mode. Maybe that will get your body back."

There was no perceptible change, but Walsh was suddenly back in his living room, on his couch, his head resting in its usual spot on his shoulders. He immediately went next door and began beating the living daylights out of Arthur, who was, as usual, typing away at his computer. As usual Mr. Benoit called the police and Walsh was arrested, but, as usual, not before Maeve Benoit winked at him from the shelf where her head was resting. Mr. Benoit, as usual, took a pot shot at him as they led him away.

Walsh had a nagging feeling he was forgetting something, but everything was normal, exactly as he remembered it, exactly as it had always been in boring old Homewood. As the cops, as usual, dragged him away, Maeve's headless body broke out of the house and stilt walked across the lawn. The naked couple was in their driveway exchanging pleasantries and in the distance several homes were burning with a hearty, cherry red glow, as co-eds on bicycles rode into them. Nothing ever changed on Homewood Drive.

And in California, a man was on hold for hours waiting to get help with his router.

Cemetery Moon

Autumn is the favored season in Wickesborough. Summer tends to draw humidity off the Clarion River and makes for enervating days and the sultry evenings. Winter is bleak with its bare trees and fallow fields under windblown snow that imperfectly smooths out the stubble. Spring brings green rebirth, but at the price of allergies and weeks of soaking rains.

The fall, however, has cool dry sunny days. Nature is at it its apex of fruition and the lengthening nights are mitigated by the explosion of color when the frost hits the maples and beeches. Between Labor Day and Thanksgiving, the apex and nadir of the season, Wickesborough residents enjoy the pleasant weather and celebrate their good fortune.

For the kids in town the turn of seasons is an ambivalent time. It is the end of summer vacation and the beginning of the school year, the long Christmas recess a distant promise. Halloween provides mid-season relief from the grind and lets the teenagers indulge in some shenanigans. By long tradition, on the full moon nearest Halloween, what they call the Cemetery Moon, upper class men from the local high school fill naive freshman with tales of ghosts, zombies and ghouls, then have them rummage around Mt. Lazarus Cemetery looking for items planted amidst the graves of their ancestors.

Mt. Lazarus is an old fashioned graveyard with stately mature trees and neat landscaping. The older sections have rows of ornately carved sandstone markers popular with folks that make rubbings of old tombstones. The newer sections have the massive granite headstones, obelisks and mausoleums that became popular with the deceased during the second half of the nineteenth century.

Lately, flat, laser carved black granite stones have become the rage, if that's the appropriate word to described grave marker fashion.

Wickesborough is not a particularly superstitious place, but the town has a long history and acquired a sizable amount of lore over the course of it. Some of the lore is gruesome, some of it is true, and all of it is embellished for maximum effect. So, although they scoff at the supernatural, the citizens of Wickesborough tend to be a bit skittish about whistling as they walk by the graveyard.

Particularly since the cemetery's residents may not be totally at rest.

The cemetery, by virtue of its age and monopoly on local internments, became the default final resting place of the town's miscreants, some of whom have unfinished business among the living.

The late Eleanor Barley is a case in point. The eldest of three spinsters, she led a blameless life in the mid eighteen hundreds, but had the misfortune to live to a great age, entertain eccentric views on organized religion, and brew remedies from herbs she gathered in the forest.

She was a hopeless romantic, she brewed a love philter, she claimed, that only worked when the right people came together. In what was locally a rite of passage, young romantics would drink her philtre hoping to find their true love, but the outcomes were decidedly mixed.

Her great delight was to introduce young people to each other, and watch as the limerence grew. It kept her and her two sisters in the chips for a couple of generations.

Not everyone was charmed by Eleanor and her fascination with young love, by the time the Pure Food and Drug Act caught up with her most of the town considered her a witch.

Soon after her passing, it was claimed, she was taking post mortem strolls around Mount Lazarus and that clinched it. Since then, Eleanor has had a place in Wickesborough ghost lore even though, on most nights, she rests as quietly as her less controversial neighbors.

Still, it was said, she ruled the night of the Cemetery Moon, and you provoked her at your peril.

On the night of Cemetery Moon, underclassmen went to specific graves to bring back the plastic bones and skulls the seniors and juniors had salted around the cemetery, this was understood. The more sadistic upper class men took the opportunity to lurk in the shadows and jump out at unwary girls and boys, taking what satisfaction their unalloyed fear and soiled underpants provided. Except for these gullible freshmen, most kids realized it was a nocturnal lark and looked forward to when they could inflict the same sort of cruelty on their younger brothers and sisters.

Kenny Melhorne was one of the sceptics. He came from a long line of brothers and uncles who had wised him up about the Cemetery Moon festivities. The Wickesborough Police, he learned, kept a discreet eye on events to make sure no actual desecrations occurred. They would shut the whole thing down if it ever got out of hand. Knowing this, he determined to go along with the gag and be accepted in the fraternity of those that endured the hazing.

He had already passed the preliminary tests. He shook the disembodied hand made from a glove with hot dogs for fingers, ate some cold spaghetti that passed for the decaying guts of a not very convincing corpse, and drank the corn syrup and red dye concoction he was told was blood. Once past that, he received his assignment: to retrieve the hand of the long dead witch, Eleanor Barley.

Eleanor was always on the list of graves to be visited; her reputation had only grown in notoriety since her death a hundred years before. Kenny confidently expected the "hand" to be the remains of a recent chicken dinner, hot glued together, and stuffed into a woman's glove. He made off on his quest.

Mt Lazarus is a large place, set aside for its purpose at the very founding of the town because no one could imagine trying to farm it. It is a moraine, a hill containing the stony detritus of a vanished glacier that had broken the shovels, and backs, of many generations of cursing grave diggers.

Kenny had a vague idea of the location of Eleanor's grave and was inclined to make a beeline to her plot, but the cemetery's boulders and rocky outcroppings made any straight line traverse difficult. He'd stick to the drives and paths that meandered around them. Besides, he reasoned, it was part of the game.

He was on a switchback, keeping an eye out for seniors ready to ambush the unsuspecting, when he saw something that almost stopped his heart; as he rounded the corner, he nearly bumped into a girl sitting on a tombstone. She was out in the open, bathed in moonlight and obviously not a party to any of the teenage prankster nonsense. She giggled when she saw his surprise and apologized.

"I'm sorry if I scared you."

Normally Kenny would have denied he had been scared but instead he was instantly smitten. He just looked at the girl and said nothing.

"I figured if I sat out here in the open I wouldn't be mistaken as one of the ghosts and goblins."

She pointed at the collection of ghosts and goblins lurking in the shadows near the cemetery gatehouse.

Her name was Juliana Eldritch and she was beautiful by all the adjectives that describe girls on the cusp of their prime; Kenny stared at her until it made her uncomfortable and asked him if anything was wrong.

"Nothing... I mean no... What are you doing here?"

Kenny got the words out, but he nearly swallowed his tongue doing it.

"I heard about Cemetery Moon and wanted see what it was all about."

"Do you go to Wickesborough?"

"I'm a freshman."

That surprised Kenny, he thought he knew all the girls in his class and he knew he would have noticed someone like her.

"Why didn't you go through the hazing with the rest of us?"

"My father wouldn't allow it. He doesn't go for all the Halloween stuff, he says its pagan."

She told him her family had just moved back to Wickesborough, that her father was assistant pastor at Calvary Methodist Church and, despite his objections to this "pagan" holiday, she had snuck out to investigate.

"So far it seems pretty boring," she said. She cocked her head to one side and asked him if he had any other questions. He had a million, but didn't know where to start, so he just memorized her face.

She slid off the stone, brushed some dust off the seat of her dress, and wiggled her toes in the grass.

Everything she did fascinated Kenny, she noticed, and savored the attention.

"I better get home; I don't want Dad to know I snuck out. Can I walk with you?"

Kenny jumped at the chance. They walked together down the path, talking and making goofy smiles at each other. She was barefoot and her dress was white, almost a nightgown, unseasonably light but beautiful in the moon light. He saw she was shivering.

"Are you cold," he asked?

"A little... I thought it would be warmer."

"Take my jacket," he said draping it over her shoulders. "I've been running around."

"You made it nice and warm."

He took a chance and put an arm around her shoulder and she made no objection. She smelled of gardenias.

"What are you supposed to be looking for this evening?"

"The hand of Eleanor Barley."

He'd almost forgotten about Eleanor until Juliana asked. By now, they were near her grave.

"Gross, I'm pretty sure it's still attached to her. Do you have a shovel?"

"No...No... I'd never..."

Kenny started to protest and then realized she was playing with him.

"It's a joke... it's just some chicken bones in an old glove," he explained.

"I know exactly where she is, I visit her all the time."

"The witch?"

"Hey... Be nice...We never would have met if it weren't for Eleanor."

"What does that mean?"

"If you weren't looking for Eleanor, you never would have come down the path and well... The rest is history!"

Juliana grabbed him and spun him around, laughing and giggling at the same time. Kenny was in heaven, he was head over heels in love with this girl already. He wondered how she knew where Eleanor was buried, but she read his mind before he asked.

"I love a good ghost story, silly... And my mom claimed she's a distant cousin."

She cocked her head and asked, "Are you sure you don't have any other questions you want to ask me?"

She laughed and skipped ahead of him stopped and pointed at a lonely plot that was clearly untended and neglected even in the pale moon light. He found the expected filigree glove and showed it to Juliana.

"That's awful... And I doubt if Eleanor ever wore a glove like that in her life."

Kenny agreed and laughed with her, anything she said, wanted, or suggested was fine with him. By way of making amends, they took some flowers from a recent burial and put them in an urn on Eleanor's grave,

"Perfect… Eleanor loves flowers," Juliana pointed at the mound of dirt. "And he certainly won't miss them."

Kenny picked a single rose from a funeral basket and gave it to Juliana. She blushed and kissed him. Kenny was over the moon, cemetery or otherwise.

"Could I take you to a movie or something?" "I'd like that, but, you'll have to meet my father, he's old fashioned that way."

They walked hand in hand through the damp, ankle high grass toward the cemetery gate talking and making plans. Juliana got very serious and said she liked him a lot, but if they were going to see each other, she had to get home before her father noticed she was gone.

"He'd kill me if he found out I was gallivanting around with a strange boy."

When they got to the gate, she kissed him on the check and warned him not to tell her father where they met.

As expected, there were seniors at the gate, so he threw up his hands in mock terror when they jumped out. He didn't care, meeting Juliana was the most memorable experience of his life and all their spook and goblin play paled in comparison. He gave the glove to the Prince of Darkness and his court of demons, all popular athletes elected by their peers. They gave him a back slapping approval and welcomed him as a fully vested member of Wickesborough High family.

Kenny was still basking in the afterglow of the lovely Juliana, when one of the demons asked him who he had been talking to. Kenny looked around for Juliana but she was already gone.

"Just a girl I met. She had to go home."

"I was following you since you left the Barley grave, I didn't see you with anyone."

"Her name is Juliana; I bumped into her near Eleanor's grave."

"Either you were seeing things or you were talking to a ghost…"

Kenny turned around and looked back towards Eleanor's grave; the flowers Juliana had placed there were plainly visible. Moonlight lit the hill they'd walked down and his footprints were apparent in the grass. He looked, but there was only a single set of foot prints. Kenny felt a chill run down his spine, but dismissed it as the cool night air.

The next day Kenny looked for Juliana between classes. He inquired about her in the school office, but no one had heard of her. He wondered if she caught a cold in the graveyard and stayed home. Reverend Conrad was his scout master and rector of Calvary Methodist; he figured he could ask him about Juliana without it getting back to her old man.

The Reverend looked him up and down when he mentioned her name then asked him where he'd run into Juliana. Kenny hesitated and mentioned school, she was a new student, and he just wanted to say hello.

"Young man," the reverend began, "Juliana Eldritch died years ago."

"Well, who'd I talk to last night?"

"I don't know, but Juliana is dead. … She didn't get to live much of a life…"

"The girl I met was alive."

"Juliana Eldritch isn't. Her father was pastor here. The pastor before me knew him. He said when she died it killed him."

"I'm sorry."

"I've heard people claim she was poisoned by one of Eleanor Barley's concoctions."

"Really?"

"No! People are always making up ugly things about Eleanor. They're both buried up on Mt Lazarus if you want to pay your respects. I don't know what you heard about Juliana, but tell the rest of the Cemetery Moon hellions to have some respect for the dead. You'll get to live a life… She never did."

He was confused when he left, Kenny didn't believe Reverend Conrad. The Reverend was old, well into his seventies, and maybe his memory was faulty. Maybe Juliana was joking about her name, maybe it was a family name or maybe she had been named after the deceased Juliana. He convinced himself there were any number of innocent reasons for the Conrad's confusion by the time he arrived at the cemetery gatehouse.

There was a Juliana Eldritch buried at Mt. Lazarus, he took the section row and plot number and set out. His heart sank as rounded the familiar switchback, the name Eldritch was engraved on the stone Juliana sat on.

He had been set up; some senior had put the girl up to this to make him look like a fool. Feelings of anger and sorrow welled up in him; tears streaked his checks as he recalled the golden, perfect girl he had so briefly met. She, like everyone else was in on the joke but him.

He sat on the large granite marker as Juliana did the night before, nursing his feeling of betrayal and heartbreak until he kicked something with his toe. It was his jacket, neatly folded on the grass in front of the monument.

A year went by and no one brought up Juliana, no one sniggered or joked about his romance with a ghost. The school year ended, summer came and went; no one uttered a single word about Juliana. Reverend Conrad apologized for getting angry with him. The rumor that Juliana died after drinking one of Eleanor Barley's mixtures upset him. He hadn't heard it in years, but he was worried that the same lies blighting Eleanor Barley's memory might be fastening to Juliana's.

When the Cemetery Moon rolled around again Kenny didn't join the fun, instead he made his way to the Eldritch monument by the familiar switchback and waited for the moon to rise. Along the way he spruced up Eleanor's grave and placed a rose in the urn.

He brought along an extra cloak, some flowers for Juliana, and a question or two he wanted answered.

A Little Friend to See Me Home

The Clarion River Valley is an old place. It drains a valley north of Pittsburgh and winds like a snake through thickly wooded hills in western Pennsylvania. The hills are eroded stumps of mountains that were once as high as the Himalayas and for all that time a river or stream has run between them. Sometimes it's been a freshet fed by the spring runoff from the surrounding mountains, at other times it has been a river of ice, a glacial finger of the Laurentide Ice Sheet. Today it is a wide, shallow, slow moving stream between unremarkable ridges on the Appalachian plateau.

The valley has seen many species come and go, as witnessed by their fossilized remains in the seams of bituminous coal found in the region. The descendants of some of these creatures can still be found in the valley, but they are exceptions, most of the fossils are of long extinct species. Scientists agree that the valley once teemed with animals that left no trace in the fossil record. On the other hand, some people claim that there are creatures in the valley that were alive then, but left no trace and never died out at all.

The valley's history begins long before white men brought the benefits of their civilization to the region. The Lenape gave the Alleghenies, river and mountains, their name after its mysterious ancient inhabitants, the Allegewi. It was said the Clarion River got its name because the water from the spring at its source was as pure as the sound of Gabriel's trumpet on Judgment Day. They may have had second thoughts, the spring fed a creek that eventually became the Clarion, it was called Liars Creek.

No one knows what the Lenape called it.

By the beginning of the eighteenth century the Clarion was the dominion of the Seneca, the southernmost nation of the Iroquois. Despite its abundant fish and game, the Seneca believed the place was haunted by Otkan, fearfully evil spirits. The Seneca hunted there, but they never lived along its banks.

The Mingos, a remnant of the Lenape, ravaged by smallpox, internecine warfare and the relentless encroachment of white men, were less finicky. They drifted into the area just before the French and Indian War and tried to settle there, but, for whatever reason, they moved on as well. The story goes that they were pushed out by whites, but they may have gotten an inkling of what the Seneca were on to, and left. On still nights, it was said; you can still see their lights moving down the Clarion.

At any rate, the white man never got the word and settled in the forest along the river's banks. The town clung to a swatch of flatland between the river and the hills and flourished because of the abundance of lumber nearby. The town survived thanks to the lumber and pulp industry, coal mining and the discovery of oil in nearby Titusville.

When the resources ran out and the industries moved on, the town collapsed on itself like a desiccating corpse. Its skeleton and sinews remained intact under a fragile veneer of dry skin, but the town was no more than the shadow of dreams and broken hopes.

The ebbing continues, and the backwater is now a trap for anyone without the means or ambition to get away from the melancholy town. It's a common enough narrative, towns that become the haunts of played out dreams. In Wickesborough's case it started looking the part before the people left; it wasn't really a ghost town, but a ghost of a town.

Despair is a constant in the town of Wickesborough. The coal mines, pulp mills and oil wells are gone and no replacements loom on the horizon, so the residents might be excused a bit of noisy desperation. Drinking, fighting and suicide are popular recreations, and on hot summer nights a resident might wonder if the Seneca weren't right.

This evening, Wickesborough wasn't sleeping well, a shroud of heat and humidity was draped over the Clarion valley like a soaking wet blanket. Distant lightning promised relief in the form of thundershowers, but not now, and not soon. Overhead the tree tops rustled, even though there was no wind.

Families sweltered in front of box fans or huddled in air conditioned houses to keep the oppressive heat at bay. Old timers, lacking such conveniences, simply endured on porch gliders or screened breezeways, waiting for a gust of wind that never came. Strolling in the mall and going to the Cineplex out on 422 was popular with young adults and singles, who exchanged wasted hours for the cool refuge.

Some teenagers, to their parents despair, came up with other methods to move air over their sweaty bodies, pursuing sex and other hijinks on sultry evenings. Some drove their cars at high speed, down narrow backwoods roads, tempting the devil, although the devil seldom resists temptation.

Josh Morgan and Cindy Merdano were two kids intent on testing the limits that night. Their limits didn't extend to using drugs or other felonious behavior, but they did use bad language, and annoyed people by playing their music too loud. Tonight they were driving fast and laughing at inside jokes, behavior a local cop might caution them for, but not wreck their futures with an arrest. The trouble began as they were making their way home.

"Who is that?" asked Cindy.

They saw a lone figure dog- trotting beside the road. From a distance he looked like Spider, a friend from school. Spider drove his pickup everywhere, so it was a surprise to see him jogging at night on a back country road.

From behind, the running man was short and stocky, wearing jeans and a black T-shirt with a pack of cigarettes rolled up in the sleeve, a la James Dean. It was exactly the description you would give to the police if you had to describe Spider. Even though he wasn't hitch hiking, Josh stopped to offer him a lift; he was a friend after all.

"Hey… Spider… Need a lift?" Josh called out as he pulled up.

"A little friend to see me home…"

Neither Josh nor Cindy understood what that meant and they were shocked when they actually got a look at his face. It wasn't Spider; in fact, he bore little resemblance to Spider. He was taller, thinner, and almost weedy; he had a nervous little cough and eyes that seemed to glow with a jaundiced light.

"I'm sorry…. I thought you were someone else,"

Too late, the stranger scrambled into the car. Josh's parents had told him not to pick up strangers, and his first instinct was to turn him out, but the guy jumped in before he could say anything. Josh asked where he was headed.

"A little friend to see me home…"

Josh was reluctant to turn out a traveler in need, even one that looked infectious. Cindy, on the other hand, was wary and questioned him. The stranger didn't answer; he just stared at her and mumbled:

"A little friend to see me home..."

Cindy wondered what became of the pack of cigarettes he'd rolled-up in his sleeve.

"I guess he wants to go home."

Spider lived in Deer Park, a collection of tract houses nearby, so Josh turned onto to 422 and headed towards the development.

Sheriff Andrew Taylor knew he was in for a long evening. Hot summer nights always brought out the weirdness in folks. He shared a name with the character Andy Griffith created, but there was nothing avuncular about this Andy Taylor and nothing of Mayberry in Wickesborough.

His jail would be full tonight, packed with drunk, angry men looking to take it out on his deputies. They would be arrested for drunk driving, drunk and disorderly and just plain drunk and mean. Liquor, heat and economic distress could generate a shit storm of brutal behavior.

Taylor had become the county sheriff almost by accident. A recently retired military cop, when the previous sheriff died, he was appointed to fill out the remainder of the term and was re-elected ever after. Wickesborough had a small, lazy and flabby police department that was typical for small, lazy and flabby towns in backwoods counties.

Taylor's county sheriff's department was, by contrast, a professional outfit that frequently picked up the abundant slack left by Wickesborough PD.

Their incompetence irritated Taylor, but he did it anyway. Crime in Wickesborough was just as real as any big city, and the people's problems were just as urgent. Taylor meant to do his best by them. A radio call started the weirdness ball rolling.

"Possible injury-accident on Bonner Road, near mile marker seven."

"Unit 12 responding."

"EMT also responding."

Taylor recognized Spider's truck as he pulled up. The accident was called in by people returning from the mall who spotted it in a ditch. The truck was wrapped around a tree, but Spider wasn't in it.

At first, Taylor hoped Spider walked away from the wreck, but that hope quickly faded. What started out as an injury-accident call had escalated to an accident with fatalities. It would become a homicide investigation in short order.

Burton Himmeldeutsch was placing flares around the truck. He had been the last man to run against him for county sheriff, and on nights like this he wished Burt had won.

"It's bad, Andy… Really bad."

The scene had gotten to Burton, and that concerned Taylor. Burt was an old timer and as nerveless as they come.

"Show me."

They inspected the truck. Its door was open and the airbag had deployed. The bed was immaculate except for some muddy smears that looked like animal tracks. Burton showed him some foot impressions that led to where a struggle had ensued. Blood was splattered around and already attracting insects. Drag marks led them to where Spider's body was cached. He was under the washed out roots of a willow in a creek bed. His throat had been lacerated, accounting for the blood.

Wickesborough relied on the state to investigate this kind of thing, but Taylor knew what to look for. There were some footprints in fresh mud; the print was peculiar, like no creature Taylor had ever seen. It had five toes like a human foot, but they were small. The foot, however, was long, nearly fifteen inches from heel to toes. The animal that left the print walked up on its toes, it habitually loped or ran in pursuit of its prey. It was the footprint of a predator.

Taylor inspected the body of Clarence Wendenor, AKA Spider. Spider seemed to be staring back at Taylor. He had the startled expression of the abruptly deceased and appeared as puzzled by what had happened as Taylor. The wound to his neck was concave and jagged, like an animal bite. Spider had a hank of hair or fur in his fist, so he had struggled with whatever had done this.

"Get some tarps and cover everything,"

"I want this scene properly documented."

"I'll get some photographs first, before the rain starts."

"I think we should bag the hands too."

"Done… I'll flag the footprints so the technician can take a cast."

Taylor was glad Burton was there, everything he'd suggested had already occurred to him. He'd been policing the county for decades longer than Taylor and was well past mandatory retirement, but no one, least of all Taylor, was anxious to see him go. Burton would do the scene right.

The wind rustled the leaves in the canopy overhead, but Taylor felt no breeze. The front was breaking up which meant thunderstorms in the near future, Taylor wondered if there would be anything left to cast after the rain moved through.

"Keep an eye out... There might be a rabid dog or coyote lurking around."

"No dog did that... A wendigo maybe, but no dog."

Josh and Cindy weren't exactly sure what to make of their passenger; he didn't talk, volunteer any information or indicate where he was going. He smelled bad, like a dog that had rolled in a rotting carcass. Cindy noticed his yellowish eyes were still staring at her and it made her uneasy.

Around Wickesborough, it is considered ill- mannered to notice physical defects in people, but Cindy couldn't help but note that their passenger had a number of features that, in the past, could have gotten him a job in a sideshow. His head sloped back to a point and was covered with fine tawny colored hair, except for a bald patch where it looked like the hair had been pulled out. His teeth were pointed and protruded from an over-wide mouth. His hands were small and delicate but his fingers were long, with fingernails that curved down, almost like a dog's claws.

"Here, here...Now, now."

Their passenger shouted and pointed at Jensen's, a Sunoco convenience store on route 422. He grabbed Josh's arm and nearly flipped the car sliding into the filling station.

He mumbled something and bolted toward the entrance.

"Drive Josh... Drive."

Cindy was nearly hysterical.

"But Spider..."

"That isn't Spider!"

Cindy shouted, as she stretched over and slammed down the accelerator with her own foot. Josh barely missed a gas pump as they peeled out. Their passenger had creeped Cindy out and she wanted to put some miles between them. Josh abandoned any scruples he had about stranding wayfarers, and took the hint.

Taylor heard the call on his radio, a disturbance at Jensen's Sunoco, and since his other units were tied up with Spider's accident, he responded. A crowd was gathering as he pulled up and Taylor knew it was bad. It had to be, nothing got people away from cable TV and air- conditioning on a hot humid night except something horrific, something terrifying, something so ghastly it could frighten the grandchildren into behaving. It would be a hot topic on the Night Terrors Show tonight.

It got worse.

The crowd parted as Taylor approached, their curiosity sated and anxiety relieved by the arrival of responsible authority. Jensen's looked like an abattoir. Gareth Lambert, former clerk and current victim, had sprayed enough blood and gore on the walls for ten victims. His throat was ripped out, like Spider's, but his body was shredded as well, like an animal had tried to dig through it.

"I saw the whole thing sheriff," a man volunteered.

The man swayed slightly and had the fruity breath of someone who probably belonged in the drunk tank, but whatever he saw sobered him up.

"What happened?"

"I was getting gas when Josh Morgan ran into the store and bit Gareth on the neck… Then he started ripping him up."

"You're sure it was Josh Morgan?"

"It was Josh."

Taylor alerted his deputies about Josh, had his office put out an APB and called in his off-duty deputies early. The chief of the Wickesborough department was called so he could take over the crime scene.

The store had a security camera which recorded the assault in grainy black and white. The attack was quick and ferocious; Gareth had barely looked up before he was ripped to shreds. Taylor's professional demeanor was tested by the gruesome video, but he carried on.

"Is this the person you saw commit the assault?"

"No", he said. "It was Josh Morgan."

Taylor also knew Josh, he was a typical kid from Wickesborough not yet formed enough to tell if he was one of life's winners or losers. The person in the video wasn't him. Taylor left the convenience store, carefully avoiding the bloody prints the killer made as he got away. They were narrow, like the tracks he saw at Spider's truck.

Taylor now had two crime scenes to secure; he made some more calls and tried to get the curious to leave before they tainted any more evidence. Taylor noticed the trees were tossing like a tempest, but he felt no breeze to cut the heat.

Josh and Cindy were driving home; their encounter with the unsettling passenger had put them off further cruising. They were anxious to get off the road. A windstorm seemed to be following them, judging by the way the trees were tossing around.

The weather report predicted a line of thunder showers would be coming through with the possibility of tornadoes. Although Wickesborough didn't get many tornadoes, Josh and Cindy were savvy enough to avoid being caught out in one.

Josh turned down Branch Valley Road. The road left 28 a little south of where the Kittanning Pike joined it and led down to the Clarion. All roads to Wickesborough lead down to the river, but Branch Valley Road is a particularly winding route, Josh thought of it as a short cut, but, at that moment, he couldn't think of a reason why.

The road was gloomy and shrouded by the trees that grew up to its shoulder. Its switchbacks and hair pin turns had brought generations of Wickesborough motorists to grief during the day, let alone at night, with a downpour impending. Josh wished he had taken the well-lit, straight and wide route 28 instead of being entangled in the coils of Branch Valley Road.

Cindy was nervously giving Josh driving tips when the bough of a large oak crashed down on the road in front of them. Josh reluctantly got out to move the branch when something that looked like Gareth Lambert dropped out of a tree. Cindy recognized their former passenger for the demonic shape shifter he was, locked the doors of the Honda and called 911.

Unfortunately, she also locked Josh out.

Taylor turned the crime scene at Jensen's over to Baxter Dunkel from Wickesborough PD when the call came that they had located Josh Morgan near Mount Lazarus Cemetery. Taylor responded, Branch Valley Road was nearby.

He turned on his lights and siren as he drove, the road was a treacherous drive anytime and he didn't want to be surprised by a drunk coming up from Wickesborough.

What Burton said bothered him. He was familiar with the Wendigo legend. The Lenape said they were demons who lived in the wind and tree tops. They were shape shifters, malevolent spirits that took over desperate souls and turned them into cannibals. Desperate souls −that made half the people in Wickesborough potential candidates.

Burton was a fan of Stephen King and H.P. Lovecraft, and maybe their fictional worlds had dragged him in too deep. Taylor had read a few of their books on Burton's recommendation, but he never bought the premise. There might be monsters living in Boston or Maine, but there was enough man-made nasty stuff in Wickesborough to occupy his time.

Taylor dismissed the Wendigo idea, he was about to confront a suspected killer and he didn't need a spook tale clouding his judgment. He called Burton for back-up.

Josh and Gareth were engaged in a life or death game of tag when he arrived. Josh was being chased around the Honda by Gareth, who was surprisingly agile for a recently deceased murder victim. Cindy was hysterical and Taylor assumed she was screaming, although the superior sound proofing of the Honda made it impossible for him to be certain.

Taylor drew his gun.

"Put your hands up... Where I can see them... Walk towards me and lay on the ground... Face down..."

Everything stopped for a second. Josh put his hands up and was in the process of doing what he was told, when Gareth jumped him and delivered a killing bite. Taylor went into a Weaver stance and repeated his order. Gareth ignored him and sprang on Taylor before he could shoot.

Whatever had jumped him didn't look like Gareth Lambert anymore, all Taylor saw were yellow eyes and a mouth full of sharp teeth. Taylor felt hot breath closing on his wind pipe, his arms were pinned to his side and he was helpless to resist. Cindy was watching the whole thing, beating on the Honda's windows and screaming. She would be the sole witness to his death if she survived.

Taylor heard the shot just a he felt the teeth on his throat, the beast fell at his feet and looked around. Burton was behind him, he had taken the shot.

The creature lay there hissing, it was pale and sickly looking, too frail to have survived a .357 in the chest, but it had. It was wounded and crippled, but still struggling to get on its feet. Burton stood over it and emptied his gun into the creature, reloaded it and put the barrel in the beast's mouth and scattered the brains over Long Branch Road.

Taylor crawled to his feet and watched as Burton got Cindy and put her in his squad car, returned with a twelve gauge and dismembered the creature's carcass with aimed shots at its legs, arms and head.

"I think you got him,"

Taylor said as Burton chambered another round.

"They're hard to kill," Burton replied. "I wanted to impress his friends."

Burton shone his flash light into the canopy above them. The trees were soughing like a hurricane and Taylor saw pairs of jaundiced eyes reflecting back Burton's light. Taylor looked at the bloody pulp and wondered how he'd ever mistaken it for Gareth Lambert.

"They need to see what happens when they leave the trees," said Burton. "Sometimes the old timers need a reminder."

"Old timers?"

"He was at the end… He'd been taken a long time ago… When they know their time's up they want to go home to die… A place of memory… A place they knew before they became Wendigos ... He was looking for someone to take him home."

"Why kill Gareth, Josh and Spider?"

"It's what they do."

"What the hell were they before they were those things?"

"People… Hopeless people … They fight it, but eventually they change."

"Into a Wendigo… This happen often?"

"Too often."

Taylor got up and walked over to the Wendigo. The figure on the ground was gaunt and old; it had had an oddly shaped head and claw like hands. The sheriff didn't know what to make of it.

"You say he was a … citizen… Once?"

"Yeah… And a veteran…"

Taylor saw the GAR button pinned to some filthy remnant of clothing he'd thought was skin. He wanted to know who this man was, his story and why he had changed. There was no hope of that.

"You didn't leave much for coroner."

"Best not to involve him… He'll say we're crazy."

"I'd be inclined to agree."

"So would I."

"Josh… Spider… Lambert… Will they become Wendigos?"

"No… You've seen to many movies… They're just dead… Leave them for the coroner; he'll call it an animal attack."

"What about the Wendigo?"

"I'll see to him… He was my great grandfather... They used to talk about him in the old days."

Taylor helped Burton gather up the remains. They wrapped it in a tarp and put it in the trunk of Burton's car. After EMTs collected Cindy, they buried the Wendigo in a section of Mount Lazarus where they had reinterred remains from abandoned graveyards. Burton and Taylor were the only mourners.

Overhead the tree tops tossed as they finished the chore, but this time Taylor felt a breeze. Large drops of cooling rain fell on Taylor's windshield as he drove away.

The Sewing Circle

"It's not like you'll be there forever. It's only for three months."

"I don't know anything about looking after old people."

"You'll be getting her some groceries and looking after the house. Lilith has a visiting nurse that comes by every day who "looks after" her. You're only there to run errands and be around in case there's an emergency."

Scott didn't want to do this, but he needed the money and the work-study co-ed behind the desk was persuasive. They'd spent a couple of weeks in lust during the last term and though no serious relationship developed, they were friends with benefits, as the kids say. The possibility of more mad, passionate weekends made Scott amenable to her requests.

She, Marion Barley, had an elderly great aunt, or, more accurately an antique great-great-aunt, who needed some discreet minding. His duties would be minimal, the position came with a generous stipend and Scott dearly wanted to stay in the niece's good graces, but he was still uneasy.

"She's ninety-something. What if she dies?"

"That would be an emergency. You call 911 and move back to the dorm. Lilith's 'ninety-something,' it wouldn't be completely unexpected."

"I don't like it."

"I'd be really grateful."

A grateful Marion—his mind raced as he imagined what that might entail.

Lilith and Marion were strange names for women of their respective ages. Lilith was a trendy name, it was suddenly popular thanks to the eponymous music festival; at least he hoped that was why every other baby born recently was called that. Lilith was also the name of Adam's wife before Eve, and a demon that sucked the souls out of children.

Marion seemed, to him, like a name straight out of the nineteenth century, even though his Marion didn't subscribe to any ideas from that era. The oddness struck him, two women from the same family and, possibly, the only women of their respective generation given those names.

Scott resisted a little more, he didn't want to be a complete pushover. Marion leaned over, let her blouse fall open and clinched the deal. Scott got a memorable look at her familiar, but still fascinating body and agreed to take the job. They kissed and she painted the inside of his mouth with her tongue. He decided he'd be happy to look after an ancient aunt with a trendy name for the favors of young woman with an old fashioned name.

He was distracted by fantasies about Marion while he threw together an overnight bag. The job required that he spend the night at her house, but Aunt Lilith lived nearby and if he needed something he could just visit his dorm room. He had his own bedroom and laundry privileges, so he wouldn't bother carting over a load of extra crap, just the day-to-day necessities of life.

Lilith greeted him when he arrived. She was in a wheel chair and unbelievably frail. Her skin was transparent. It stretched over a lattice work of veins that moved her indifferently pulsing blood through her body. Her face was veiled and despite the clement weather, she was covered from neck to ankle in a floral print dress. Scott wondered if she covered up out of vanity or for warmth.

"You're so young," she said in a voice redolent with impending death. "Marion picked a good one for me."

Scott mumbled something about being older than he looked and was all the more responsible because of it. She laughed, actually cackled out something that sounded like a death rattle, and took his hand. He asked if she needed anything before he unpacked. She had nothing pressing and her sewing circle was meeting tonight, so he was completely free this evening.

Lilith patted his hand and said, "You'll see that I don't make too many demands."

Scott liked that.

Scott unpacked and, though it was not his habit, lay down and took a nap. It was the deepest rest he'd ever experienced. Fatigue rolled off of him and he fell into a deep sleep. His sleep experience was enhanced by a dream featuring the erotic antics he planned the next time he got together with Marion. He was awakened by voices downstairs.

There were about a dozen or so women in the living room, or, as Lilith styled it, parlor. They ranged in age from young to middle aged to very old, with Lilith taking pride of place in the very old division.

Scott couldn't help but think of the women deities in Robert Graves' The White Goddess; the maiden, the matron and the crone. He'd skimmed it during a mythology class and vaguely remembered it as claptrap about astrology, the lunar year and the ages of man. It was not the least bit applicable to the current situation.

Every head turned as he came downstairs, some quickly, some more deliberately, but no one paused in their labors. Scott caught a hint of Ben Gay in the air, not entirely unexpected. He didn't know exactly what to do or say until Lilith gestured for him to step in.

"Girls… This is Scott, the young man Marion got for me. I'll be living with him this summer."

"The girls" all tittered at Lilith's double entendre as she patted his hand. Scott noticed how much stronger her voice was. The frail old woman who he met earlier had definitely taken a step back from the grave—at least he wouldn't be making the 911 call tonight.

The ladies introduced themselves, but Scott managed to place a name only with every third face. All the younger faces seemed to be taking his measure and appraising his masculine qualities. He was flattered that they approved, he might even encourage them to stir things up in the hen house. It might sow a little discord and jealousy in their sewing circle, but c'est la vie.

The older ones openly stared at him with hungry eyes. One woman, Ethel, gave him a look that Scott could only regard as hunger. Another regarded him with unalloyed lust. Scott shuddered at the thought at those liver spotted hands on his body, but the image lingered like a premonition. Lilith got impatient with the attention the ladies were lavishing on him and brought it to an abrupt halt.

"He's a real cad, this one, he'll flit from flower to flower with never a second thought, but he's mine, so watch out," Lilith interjected, apropos of nothing.

More tittering ensued.

After a lengthy silence that informed him the social time was over, Scott excused himself and went out to a beer bar where Marion would be waitressing.

"Hey you," Marion said as she slid into the booth next to him.

"You were right, taking care of your aunt is going to be a piece of cake."

"I'm so glad."

"What time do you get off?"

"Not soon enough, I have a final at eight."

"I was hoping for some gratitude."

Marion gave him the look she reserved for things she found under rocks; apparently her gratitude was going to be more metaphorical than actual. Scott was kind of glad she begged off, he was feeling drained, more drained than he had ever felt in his brief life, drained enough to forgo sex with the nubile Marion. It astounded him, but right now nothing was more appealing than crawling into the sack and getting some shut-eye.

He never got any gratitude from Marion. A week or so later she went off to Europe, supposedly traveling with some girlfriends. He heard that some frat boys had a similar itinerary, put two and two together and realized there was no such thing as a sure thing.

His summer rolled out like that. He got paid every week; every other day Lilith gave him a short list of groceries she needed and reimbursed him for everything he bought. She usually turned in early, so Scott was free after she went to bed. Twice a week the sewing circle convened and Scott got the night off. He tried the local hangs to connect with a horny hotty, but his heart wasn't in it. After Marion, the local girls seemed pallid and dull. Truth be told, he felt too run down to make a play for them.

He felt old. Riding the glider on Lilith's porch had become his favorite occupation after he finished his chores and errands—and he barely had the energy for that. His reflection in the mirror didn't lie, it told a distressing tale. Scott looked older and he noticed more hair in the shower drain than normal. His eyesight was going, he had no energy and he was preoccupied with nostalgia. Worst of all, he was getting forgetful.

Lilith, by contrast, seemed to becoming more hale and hearty with every passing day. Her voice was stronger and the body under the floral print dresses appeared to be fleshier. Once or twice, he saw her standing, but she made an elaborate pantomime of getting back in her wheel chair when she noticed him.

Today, Lilith had asked him to drive her to Mount Lazarus Cemetery to visit "the boys." It raised some questions, but at least he could nap in the car. He brought the car around and wished he'd drunk another coffee this morning.

"Who are you going to see?" he asked, regretting the question instantly.

"Some lads I knew when I was younger. I put some flowers on their graves when I can."

"They passed?"

"I hope so, we buried them… But all before their time. I try to keep their memory alive."

Scott thought about the era Lilith lived through: World War II, Korea, Viet Nam, even World War I and the flu pandemic of 1918. She had had the opportunity to know a lot of men who had died before their time. Perhaps one of them, maybe several, had been potential husbands. Maybe Lilith was mourning her own dead past. Melancholia came over Scott as he considered Lilith's might-have-beens, the children and companions she might have had.

"Just drive me as close to the plot as you can and drop me off. I'll make my own way from there."

Scott wound his way down the sinuous gravel tracks that constituted roads in Mount Lazarus Cemetery. He was dubious of Lilith's ability to take more than three unassisted steps, but she had gathered the flowers she carried from the garden on her own, so he said nothing. He drove through the cemetery in silence.

He watched the old lady in the rear view mirror as they made the short trip. It was the first time he had seen her outside of her house. She relished the fresh air blowing in her face and seemed to absorb strength from being out.

Lilith looked remarkably better in the daylight. Her face was unlined, almost youthful, and the hair he remembered as thin and grey looked fuller and darker outside. He saw the resemblance to Marion for the first time; she must have been striking in her youth. Scott was glad she was doing so well; he liked the old lady and hoped he had something to do with her rejuvenation.

"It's a lovely day for it," he said finally.

"You don't think I'm being morbid?"

"No… I think it's nice. I hope someone will remember me when I pass away."

She let out one of her unearthly cackles which left Scott wondering what was so funny.

The plot was in the old section of Mount Lazarus where the graves went back two hundred years. It was indifferently tended and the headstones spanned the history of grave marker styles. She stopped and talked to a grounds keeper, probably to complain about the neglect. Scott watched as she lingered over each grave. He assumed it was a family plot and Lilith probably knew or was related to all the inhabitants.

She waved off his assistance when she returned and got into the back seat under her own steam.

"Home Jeeves… I have my sewing circle tonight."

Scott didn't like being called Jeeves, but knew she meant it as a joke. He was tired anyway, and was happy to head back to the barn.

"The girls" started showing up around seven and gathered in the parlor, waiting for Lilith to make her entrance.

"Well ladies, times a wasting… This thing won't sew itself."

Scott wondered what it was they were making. It was long and done with fine, tightly spun linen with some busy embroidery symbols down its length. They had been working on it since he arrived. Lilith was definitely the grand dame of the group; the others almost kowtowed to her when she came in.

"Are you going out?" Lilith asked.

"No… I'm worn out. I think I'll turn in.

"Good for you… I'll make you some cocoa."

Scott tried to beg off. Lilith's cocoa was awful, but she insisted and he complied. Diva behavior, thought Scott, as he sipped the bitter drink. Would some sugar be out of the question he wondered? He was free now, but all he wanted to do was hit the sack. Something was wrong; he would see a doctor next week.

It was a night of fitful sleep with a pleasant dream. He had an erotic dream about Marion, and it was the most realistic fantasy he ever experienced. Marion came to him, her body lush and firm. She indulged his every desire and did all the things modern women do these days to please their men.

It was wonderful, but it came with an odd twist ending. At some point Marion morphed into Lilith, but a younger Lilith, who straddled him and held his hands to her firm breasts. He became aware that the women from the sewing circle were watching their love making as he ejaculated. Never mind, his climax was thorough and he fell into a deep, deep sleep.

The next morning he awoke still sated from his dream adventure. He wanted to lounge around in bed and wallow in its pleasant afterglow, but Lilith knocked on his door and asked him to get her some things. His knees creaked as he got out of bed; he would need a cane if they got any worse. He caught a glimpse of himself in the mirror by the door and was startled by how old he looked; he really needed to see a doctor.

The sound of a shower running greeted him as he hobbled out of his bedroom. Lilith was in the bathroom, so he'd have to do the shopping unwashed and looking like he'd just rolled out of bed, which he had. The disheveled old man look—he'd seen it on numerous old codgers tottering around Wickesborough—he'd fit right in.

Lilith had left the bathroom door open again; years of living alone and advancing age had made her forgetful of things like privacy. Scott went to close the door, but couldn't help seeing how youthful and vigorous the body behind the shower's pebbled glass door was; he dismissed it as a trick of light. As he approached, the door swung open and there stood Lilith, naked, soaking wet and as young as she had been in his dream the night before.

There was no modesty about her; she stood there defiantly nude, looking at him as if to gauge his reaction to her body.

"Do you like what you see?"

"You left the door open… I was about to close it."

"Please, indulge an old woman's vanity. I think I look pretty good."

Scott backed away, contradictory emotions wracked his brain.

"I'll be going to get the things you wanted."

"You smell like sex."

"Really… I've got to go."

She began fiddling with Scott's pants. He realized that that Lilith wasn't going to stop short of repeating the fantasy in his dream. Terror and bewilderment wrapped icy fingers around his soul, and more contradictory emotions churned in his brain. If she continued he knew he would succumb and bad things would follow.

He had to get away.

Something drew him to Mount Lazarus. There had been activity at Lilith's family plot since his last visit. A new grave had been dug; the dirt was mounded neatly beside it and covered with a blue tarp. it seemed odd that Lilith hadn't mentioned any death in the family, almost as odd as him winding up in Mount Lazarus. He went to take a closer look, with the shambling gait of an old man.

The hole yawned before him; it filled him with even more contradictory emotions, calm and dread. On one hand, Mount Lazarus was beautiful, the perfect place for an eternity at rest. On the other hand it was an eternity that entailed nothing but decay and the end of everything.

His eye was drawn to the large granite marker that loomed over the graves. It was inscribed with men's names going back a hundred years. They were all in their twenties. As he scanned the list, he stopped at the bottom; his name was there with his dates recently carved in.

Confusion was replaced by doubt, and then understanding as he noticed "the girls" of the sewing circle approaching. They were carrying what they had been working on, a damask shroud covered with elaborately embroidered with arcane symbols. It was his shroud; they made it for him.

A pain shot down his arm and he felt a crushing hand grip his heart as darkness swirled around him.

The two young women stood out among a crowd of indifferent mourners, as they watched the grave being filled. Scotty had no family to mark his passing, so the ladies of the sewing circle were there in their stead. Lilith wore the youth she had recently acquired gloriously; any casual observer would have assumed that the two stunning young women were sisters, not aunt and niece.

"Poor Scotty… It's sad to see him go," said Marion as she wiped a non-existent tear from her clear eyes.

"I tried to make his last day memorable, but…"

"You did your best. I'll miss him too."

"He was sweet… So well meaning… Like all the rest… He was so full of life, I hated to take it."

"It had to be."

"We almost waited too long this time."

"Like Eleanor…"

"Poor Eleanor…"

"It was her decision…"

"She always went her own way…"

"And now she's buried at the bottom of the hill."

"Where I'd be if Scott hadn't turned up."

"It was close, but he came along in the nick of time."

"I never want to be that old again."

"Nor do I... Ethel is looking a long in the tooth. We should start looking for someone for her."

"With the two of us looking it shouldn't be much of a bother."

"I met a couple of fraternity boys in Europe that might be suitable."

Lilith bent down, tossed a clod of dirt into the grave, walked to her car and drove away from Mount Lazarus.

When Christina came out to play...

The woods were a place where children played, a bit of scrub land between Route 422 and a faded housing tract called Deer Park. The development had been a tree farm once; clear cut to feed the pulp mills on the Clarion River, then replanted with homes. An unnamed tributary once ran through the tract and into Buttermilk Creek, but it was diverted into pipes to control flooding when the houses went up. Its course was filled in with topsoil and houses were built on top of it.

The woods started where the pipes emerged from the land fill and released their constrained water into a creek amidst the trees. The water looked toxic, but it provided damp habitat for wildlife that flourished around humans. It was shallow enough to cross without getting your shoe tops wet and clean enough for minnows, salamanders, and raccoons.

Locals ignored the marshy remnant of the tree farm; to them it was just a wasteland of shrubby undergrowth between regularly spaced pines. It still flooded after heavy rains, but, excepting those occasions, it was a suitable place for kids to have unsupervised adventures away from killjoy adults.

The kids always played in groups; the woods weren't particularly dangerous, but they all had heard stories about kids turning up in abandoned refrigerators after being snatched by psychos. They were wary of strangers and less gullible than children protected from knowledge of evil. Every weekend they mustered and cadres of similar ages would team up to play in the woods. It had been happening that way for years and nobody had ever been bothered.

Playing in the woods meant playing soldiers, poking at things with sticks, or building dams from creek stones. Much of what they did was a throwback to simpler times. If not for the rumble of trucks on 422 a hundred yards away, it could have passed for an afternoon from Mark Twain's era. It was all very bucolic and peaceful, until four kids went in and only three came out.

The kids in Deer Park were no worse than kids anywhere. The ones with both parents around were usually better off, but that was no guarantee. If one or more parents had jobs, they might have more material benefits, but that didn't always turn out to be an advantage. It was impossible to generalize about the kids, but that didn't stop the adults, their opinions were usually based on the last kid they encountered. Doug, Jason and Damien were the kind of kids that left good impressions.

They were nice kids on the cusp of puberty, before the sullen charm of adolescence took over. Doug was quiet and sensitive; Jason and Damien were not. Whatever, they were clean, obedient and, above all, respectful; respectfulness toward adults earned a pass for a certain amount of truancy, idleness, and mediocre grades.

The three had been in and out of the woods a dozen times since spring and, by now, it was getting old. Doug insisted they invite a girl he liked, Christina, to join them and Jason and Damien didn't object. They liked having her along because she leavened their raucous games with creativity they lacked. She was a regular playmate despite being a girl.

"We're going to the woods," Doug announced as if that would surprise her. "You want to come?"

"I don't have time," she said. "I have chores."

"Come on... School starts next week and I won't see you after Labor Day."

"Why? I'll still be living here."

"It'll be different... You know."

Doug was right. Christina was a year ahead of the boys, having skipped a grade. She was going to a new school this year and her life would carom off on a different tangent once the school year started. Christina was a smart, artistic girl and more mature than the boys in other ways. She didn't understand why she was pleased that Doug asked her to join them, but it was curiously satisfying to her. At first, she resisted, but relented under Doug's wheedling and half-reluctantly agreed to come out and play.

Today, she brought her sketch book and wore a white sun dress with little embroidery bluebirds on each shoulder, which disappointed the boys because a dress reined in the amount of roughhousing Christina, would allow. Instead, she spent the time watching them and sketching, but not participating in their games. Jason noticed her preoccupied mood and taunted her about having a boyfriend.

"Geez Christina … Maybe you could hang with us? If that's okay with your boyfriend?"

"Wise up Jay… I just don't feel like dropping rocks on fish."

"Has he kissed you yet?"

Christina was flustered by the directness of Jason's question, but gave back as well as she could, saying she was getting too old for their antics, although she called it "kids' stuff."

"For your information, I'm going to a dance with a boy from West Wickesborough."

"I knew you had a boyfriend."

Jason was smugly triumphant and didn't notice Doug hanging on every word.

She didn't say who he was, and a junior high dance might as well have been a trip to the moon as far as the boys were concerned. Jason and Damien were genuinely indifferent; they had no interest in such things. Doug was silent.

Christina saw Doug was upset and regretted saying anything. The entertainments of youth were giving way to the rites of adulthood and Christina felt nostalgic.

"I wish we could always be just like we are now," she said. "I wish it could be like this forever."

The boys listened solemnly as she said it; instinctively they knew that this was a watershed moment of some kind, of what exactly, they couldn't say. The moment passed and Jason and Damien made jokes about where they'd get food or go to the bathroom if they got stuck in the woods forever. Christina got up, brushed some twigs and leaves from the back of her legs and sat next to Doug. He didn't say anything but stared straight ahead biting his lip.

Dusk brought the outing to an end and the gang made its way out of the woods bantering as they went. Doug was mostly quiet, looking at the ground and trying to sort out his emotions. Christina was tired of his sulking and tried to lighten his mood.

"You're jealous, aren't you?" She laughed, punched him in the arm and took off running.

Doug chased after the giggling girl. He wanted to catch her and hold her down, for what purpose he didn't know. He finally caught her and tried to wrestle her to the ground. The smell of her perspiration mingled with the scent of her shampoo, and filled Doug with strange feelings as she wriggled in his arms. Their eyes meet for a second and the intensity startled them both, then he tripped and she broke free. Her laughter filled the woods as she ran away, but by the time Doug looked up she was nowhere to be seen.

Jason and Damien were panting like dogs when they caught up; Doug was there but Christina had disappeared into the trees.

"Where'd Christina go?"

"I don't know."

"Disappeared?"

"I guess."

"Psycho or Alien abduction?"

"Probably both."

It meant nothing at the time. Their day was over, soon they'd be back in school and Christina would join them again sometime. They walked home talking about nothing as night settled on the forest. They left the woods, parted without words, and went their separate ways. It wasn't until after eight that Christina's mom called and all Hell broke loose.

She called the boys' parents desperately seeking her lost daughter. Everyone reassured her, but they suspected that terrible news awaited the frantic woman; the disappearance of Renay Dobler was a fresh memory. They knew all the stories and sent up prayers of gratitude that this cup, filled with a parent's nightmare, had passed them by.

Friends showed up at the mother's house and volunteered to look for Christina. Soon, the woods were full of people with lanterns and flashlights, poking in the bogs and calling her name. It was late at night before the Wickesborough police arrived; they had ignored the mother's calls, but did respond to an anonymous report of suspicious activity in the woods along the highway.

When dawn came, it cast long shadows across a forest floor that had been searched and re-searched by some parent; every square inch of that forlorn thicket had been scrutinized by a caring adult. By then, the crisis had drawn folks from Wickesborough who didn't know Christina, but wanted to help.

It was a grid search by then, with the police looking as much for clues as Christina. They knew with terrible certainty that if she didn't turn up within forty-eight hours, she was likely dead. Unfortunately, the search by concerned amateurs had destroyed any useful evidence they might have found.

Dogs caught Christina's transient scent; followed it from the last place the boys had seen her, to the edge of the woods. The dogs lost the scent there and milled around in bewildered circles trying to re-acquire it. A team walked up the culvert pipes as far as they could until a weir of number 8 rebar, blocked their way. Another group entered a manhole upstream and searched the stream back to its source and, again, found nothing.

Suspicion settled on the boys, especially Doug, who shared more than he should have about Christina's first date. It came as a surprise to Christina's mother, who questioned him closely about this mysterious boy her daughter was seeing. The police also questioned Doug and he told them everything he remembered again and again, eventually they believed him.

There was brief flurry of interest in the case on national television. The publicity generated some volunteer searchers with ground penetrating radar, cadaver dogs and a PI who turned up a baker's dozen of sex offenders in the immediate vicinity.

Nothing came of any of it. By the end of the summer, the search for Christina was no further along than when it began and the police decided she disappeared sometime after separating from the boys. Officially, they theorized she was taken by an unknown stranger, but privately they were suspicious of Christina's mom and her conveniently absent boyfriend.

Christina was remembered at a school assembly at the junior high school she never attended. No one knew her there; her friends were still in the primary school she went to. The state and town voted to install surveillance cameras along the stretch of highway that bordered the woods to stop future kidnappings that never occurred.

Christina's mother's boyfriend returned from Afghanistan, which cleared him of the vile accusations whispered about him. They married and moved away from suspicious police and neighbors. Soon, the memory of Christina faded and almost no one thought about her any more.

Time passed and the boys drifted apart, still friends, but with rapidly diverging interests. Doug never stopped missing Christina. His thoughts were conflicted, but over the years, he started to understand his feelings for her.

He fantasized about what he would say to her if she suddenly showed up. Mostly, what he wished he'd said on that last day in the woods. There were also questions he wanted to ask, but if she said she was okay he'd be happy to let them go. He'd stopped going into the woods after she disappeared, but since then, every time he passed them, he always looked for Christina among the trees.

Doug was the first to turn sixteen, and a driver's license opened up his world. High school presented him with other adventures, there were girls to investigate, cliques to navigate and the bonding rituals like Cemetery Moon to endure. New horizons beckoned for him to come and explore, which he did with the gusto of his age. It filled his life and gradually his thoughts turned less and less to Christina.

His parents were glad to see him finally get over his obsession with the "dead girl", and get on with his life. He loved to drive and was a reliable steady kid, so his parents were liberal about letting him have the car. They gave him errands to run, knowing he enjoyed any time behind the wheel. They trusted him and figured it kept his mind off Christina.

On one occasion, he had a heavy roster of shopping and chores that kept him out until late. It was dusk and he was headed home, as promised, before nightfall. He took the access road that went by the woods, which he usually avoided because it reminded him of Christina. Today, she wasn't in his thoughts, in fact he hadn't thought about her for a while, but where the road turned left, he slowed down and, out of habit, glanced into the trees.

He saw something in the dim light; the indistinct figure of a girl wearing a white sundress like Christina wore the day she vanished. He slammed on the brakes and got out of his car to look, but saw nothing. He wanted to investigate, but it was too spooky; even before Christina disappeared he'd stayed out of the woods after sundown. Instead, he stood behind the guard rail over the culvert and stared into the trees until the forest became undifferentiated darkness.

Back in the car, he caught his breath and let the adrenaline drain out of him. As he pulled away he saw the girl again in his rear view mirror illuminated by the blood red glow of his taillights. This time there was no mistaking the white sun dress with bluebirds on the shoulders. It looked like she was waiting for him to join her in the woods, but when he turned around, she was gone. Terrified, he made record time getting home.

The next day he came back and searched the woods for some sign of the girl, but found nothing. The woods weren't empty; there were indications that kids with darker interests had been using the woods since he'd been there last.

There was a shrine to Christina some Goths had made in the deepest part of the woods. It was full of symbolism and nonsense derived from a song by a moderately successful heavy metal band. It was about a heroine dissimilar enough from Christina to avoid litigation, but close enough to generate local notoriety. Doug found no trace of Christina in any of this.

Weeks went by and the memory of the figure in the white summer dress joined Doug's actual recollections of Christina. He convinced himself that what he saw was imaginary. No matter how real it seemed, there was no reason to believe that what he saw was anything more than a hallucination. He had almost moved on.

On Labor Day weekend, he was in the backseat of his parents' car, returning from a family gathering, when they turned down the access road. He was absently watching the woods drift by when he saw her again; the girl in the white sun dress with bluebirds on the shoulders was staring at him. It was Christina.

His parents saw nothing and Doug said nothing. He hadn't told them about his previous sightings of Christina either, but they were suspicious. It was near the anniversary of her disappearance and Doug was moody.

"Are you okay?" His father asked.

"Yeah… Thinking about school…"

He mumbled something about the upcoming Cemetery Moon party as he watched Christina recede in the distance. His parents took what comfort they could from teenage aloofness and dropped it. When they got home Doug called Damien and Jason.

Damien and Jason had stayed close. They hung out together at school and, to the distress of the authorities, insisted on wearing black trench coats to class. They were well known pranksters at Wickesborough High; their clowning around got them props from their contemporaries and watchful suspicion from the authorities.

They listened to Doug's tale and agreed to accompany him into the woods. They pretended it was all a lark based on Doug's well known fascination with Christina, but, despite their cynical posing, they were scared.

The three friends gathered at the culvert the next day and slid down the embankment less gracefully than they did as children. They went to the place where they'd last sat together, and retraced the path they took out.

Nervously they checked the full arc around them and kept an eye in the tree tops as well. They saw nothing and heard nothing except a breeze that briefly animated the canopy above. They were joking about being snatched by Wendigos or murdered by Mingos when they reached the edge of the woods. They were about to go their separate ways when Doug saw a figure hiding in the scant brush.

The jokes about Indian boogey men stopped and without saying a word the three split up and circled around to converge on the hiding person from three points. He was as startled as the three boys when they cornered him.

"What the Hell are you doing?" Doug asked. "I was looking for Christina."

"Who the Hell are you?"

"Arthur … Art Benoit."

He was, he said, Christina's date to the dance years before. The police had never learned his identity, but he freely admitted it to the boys. Arthur had lived under a shadow since Christina vanished. At first, it was the terror that the police would find out he was the mysterious boy that asked her out and would arrest him. Eventually, he realized that hiding was a mistake.

"I should have gone to the police… Now I look guilty."

"You're nuts," said Jason.

"Why are you looking for her?" asked Doug.

"She's back… I saw her… Here in the woods."

"So go to the police."

"They won't believe me. I've got to find her… It will prove she never died."

Arthur made the boys uneasy, there was no reason to doubt him, or believe him, but it felt like he wasn't telling them everything. Arthur looked in their faces and saw doubt. He wandered away begging for their help and proclaiming his innocence.

By now, it was dusk, which meant it would be best if they left the woods to whomever, or whatever, inhabited it after dark. Doug was silent as he drove, but Jason and Damien were speculating.

"It must have been a Goth dressed like Christina for some cos-play game."

Doug grasped at this explanation and hoped it was true.

A week or so later, Doug was passing the woods and saw a figure in a white sun dress with embroidery blue birds on the shoulders walking toward the site of their last rendezvous. He called Jason and Damien and they met by the culvert, it was well before dark so they made their way fearlessly into the woods. They all saw the figure this time, she was facing them and it was definitely Christina.

Damien ran towards her, past the surprised Doug, who ran after him. Jason laid back and shied to the left keeping an eye on the girl in case she tried to give them the slip. She ducked behind a thick stand of laurel, but Jason had a clear view of it. They could hear her laughing; the same laughter they heard long ago when she disappeared.

Whoever she was, she would have to emerge from hiding eventually and she wasn't going to get away this time. They had her boxed in. Jason worked his way toward the left side of the laurel as Damien drew abreast of the right and they converged on... nothing.

There was nothing behind the laurel, so they tore apart the bush to see if she was hiding underneath and found more nothing. This area of the woods was fairly open so there was no place for a girl in a white sun dress with embroidery bluebirds on the shoulders to hide. They searched anyway, but came up with nothing.

It was dark by the time a frustrated Jason and Damien got back to Doug's car. They were exhausted and felt foolish.

"We've been played man. Christina's gone."

"Doug played us…"

"And that Benoit dude too."

"Yeah, no more screwing around looking for ghosts."

"Doug must pay though."

"Totally."

They vowed never to go ghost hunting again. The incident was over and ready to be dismissed from their lives.

"Hey… Where is Doug?" Jason asked.

This time they went directly to the police and reported the whole story. About how they'd seen Christina and how Doug had disappeared when they went after her. They told the cops about Arthur, that he was the boy that invited Christina on her last date.

Braxton Dunkel looked blandly at two troublemakers he knew from false fire alarms at the high school. When Jason and Damien insisted that they search the woods for Doug and question Art Benoit, he stopped them and asked when they'd last seen Art.

"Just after Labor Day," Jason replied.

"So… about a week ago you spoke to Art Benoit." "Yeah."

"The same Arthur Benoit who lived in Homewood Estates in West Wickesborough?"

"Maybe…"

"Was this the same Art Benoit, who shot himself a year ago on the access road?"

The boys exchanged glances until Jason spoke.

"He said he was Art Benoit… and he knew about Christina… and you guys didn't believe him."

"The sheriff checked him out… Burt Himmeldeutsch questioned him about an attempted abduction of a girl in Saxonburg two years ago... Arthur told him about the dance with Christina and all… He kept saying he never hurt Christina, but Burt thought he was holding back…"

"That's what we thought when we talked to him."

"And you talked to him exactly a year after he killed himself. Arthur was pretty twisted … He might have done Christina, but he's dead, and you two jerk-offs better stop running your jokes into the ground."

"We aren't joking…We saw Art a week ago and now Doug's missing."

"Have it your way, but I know you two… I'm not going to chase ghosts to amuse you assholes."

"What about Doug?"

"You better tell him to go un-missing or I'll be up your asses so fast you won't know what hit you… Now get out before I throw you into lock-up for seventy two hours just on principle."

Jason and Damien left the police station knowing what they knew. In an hour or so, Doug's parents would start calling around, the police would be called in and a search would begin. It would go bad for them, what they told the police made them suspects or worse. Worse was the more likely outcome, because this time the police would find evidence connecting them to Doug's disappearance. Their only alibi was a ghost of a girl in a white sun dress with embroidery bluebirds on the shoulders, hiding in the trees.

They returned to the woods and stared into the dark, not knowing what they expected to see. Doug was there; maybe frozen in the moment of time Christina had wished they all could share.

Panicky and fearful, Jason and Damian turned their backs on the woods and headed home, where bad outcomes were the only possibilities. They were out of hope and facing bleak choices when they heard the laugh, a laugh they'd known since they were children; the high pitched laugh of a girl in a white sundress with embroidery bluebirds on the shoulders.

The boys looked at each other and decided. They slid down the embankment into the unknown and followed the laughter; the laughter they last heard when Christina came out to play.

The Comforter

Barnett heard the sirens in the distance and knew they were coming down Johnston Avenue. From the direction, sound and long experience he knew it was an ambulance. The sound filled Barnett with dread; it meant somewhere a personal catastrophe was unfolding and soon he'd have another funeral to attend.

He heard a lot of sirens in Wickesborough because Wickesborough had lots of elderly residents, whose personal catastrophes often required emergency services.

In fact, if you judged Wickesborough by its streetscape, you would assume it was inhabited by nothing but teenagers and the elderly. Walking around, you rarely saw anyone in-between, since almost everyone moved away as soon they could.

The teenagers were the children of people trapped in Wickesborough by bad decisions, teenage pregnancies or poverty of imagination; the kids of people who worked two jobs to survive and drank silently, privately, in poverty every night of their lives. When these kids grew up or their parent's prospects improved, they would move away too.

None, of the bitter remainder, ever went out, at least during the day.

The elderly you saw were the living remains of an era when Wickesborough had not been prosperous, but was at least less poor. They were everywhere. The old people were almost never to be found in their homes. They were always gardening, fixing their houses or walking somewhere, but they were never indoors. They were always waving and greeting each other, visiting and gossiping or running errands for a shut-in. They were energetic, cheerful and busy, at least until an ambulance carted them away on their last ride to glory.

There was a desperate hollowness in all the activity that led up to that point; it was as if the frenetic behavior was a way to ward off the inevitable. They were very conscious when one of their peers began to falter. If one of their fraternity went missing, a tremor of anxiety ran through the aging cadre and, after a discreet interval, someone would check on that person. From experience, they knew that the last act of many of their friends was to disappear into their homes and endure their last moments in solitude.

Barnett didn't bother going out much these days, not that he was embracing his own end of life. His late wife had been a believer in the energetic pre-mortem program until she fainted and fell off a ladder while washing windows. She never regained consciousness.

Her faith in these desperate gerontological rites of passing hadn't done her much good and may have hastened her death. Anyway, since she died he hadn't had the time for the waving, walking around and whatever to ward off the unavoidable. He doubted its efficacy any way and, frankly, he just didn't care anymore.

Whatever, his absence had been noted, and his neighbor Foster had been appointed to check up on him. After the usual banalities, they had coffee seated around his kitchen table.

"Boy if these walls could talk…"

Foster opened with the standard gambit for starting a pointless conversation in Wickesborough.

"Yeah… they'd repeat a lot of lies we told long ago."

"Some good times too…"

"Maybe so… I was thinking of taking the Butler Coach Atlantic City excursion… Why don't you and Nan come along…? We can blow a social security check or two."

"I'll ask her. It might be fun."

Barnett knew there was no chance of the bus trip happening. Foster was as tight as he was poor, every dime he had was going towards the impressive piece of granite he would lie under for eternity. He liked Foster, but he was prone to melancholy reminiscences about dead friends, relatives and spouses and was, generally, a drag.

Foster took his leave; satisfied that Barnett hadn't gone claws up or was likely to fall off a stool with a rope around his neck to break his fall. Barnett had talked about the future during his visit, a good sign, obsession with the past set off alarm bells among his elderly comrades. He wouldn't require scrutiny again for at least a week.

Barnett wondered why the watchers dispatched someone like Foster to check on him. Foster lived most of his waking hours walking in the shadows of the past and was constantly mingling with the shades of the departed. Barnett wondered if Foster would even notice the change of venue when his time was up.

Barnett was considered morbid by his peers because he attended a lot of funerals, even funerals of people he didn't know. That was a fair number of funerals since, as small as Wickesborough is, enough people died around town that Barnett couldn't be acquainted with all of them. Early on it was discovered he had a knack for comforting the bereaved widows, husbands, or friends with soothing words and aphorisms. Over the years he had helped drain the pain that accompanied loss from any number of anguished loved ones, so whenever a wake or funeral was scheduled Barnett got a call.

There was usually a meal involved.

This evening, he was going to the wake of a man he didn't know at one of Wickesborough's three funeral homes, all conveniently located near Mt. Lazarus Cemetery. It bothered Barnett that he couldn't' recall how he'd heard about the funeral. Since his wife died he had noticed a decline in his faculties, and forgetting which funeral home had called him was just one more example of it.

He dressed in his best suit which is to say the one that was only twenty years out of date. His wife made him buy it; she wanted him to look dignified out of respect for the dead. He humored her, but always knew that he was there for the survivors, the dead were beyond caring.

It was the suit he was going to be buried in, so he wore it often, he wanted to get some use out of it before he joined the danse macabre. It occurred to him, as he pulled up his tie, that he did spend a lot of time thinking and arranging his affairs around death; maybe his neighbors were right, maybe he was morbid.

Barnett thought that he might give this funeral a miss. He didn't know the person; he forgot which funeral home was hosting the viewing and, frankly, it didn't seem worth the effort. He had been to many funerals over the years and helped turn grief turn to acceptance with his strange talent, but when his wife died, all he got was Foster mumbling some trite BS about how she was in a better place.

Barnett harbored no romantic notions about the afterlife, when you're dead, you're dead, all the rigmarole connected with dying was about making the survivors feel better. All in all, he doubted the effort was justified for the little good it did.

He called Foster to see if he wanted to play cards or something; an evening with him would be preferable to hanging around with the depressed relatives of someone he didn't know. Foster didn't answer and there was no way to leave a message; Foster was the last person on earth who didn't have voicemail or an answering machine.

Resigned to his fate, Barnett pulled on his black wingtips and promptly broke a shoe lace. The stream of invective and cursing that followed was outsized for the dimension of the calamity, but it convinced him he wasn't in the mood to comfort anybody. He flipped off his shoes and leafed through the TV guide to see what shows he wanted to sleep through.

"Hey…! Get a move on… People are waiting… Put those shoes on," said a voice from outside.

A little girl was rattling his screen door and shouting at him. It took a second for Barnett to take it in. He didn't recognize the girl, but she obviously knew what he was up to. Maybe she was the daughter of the funeral director sent to get him to the right viewing. Maybe there were two funerals going on and the funeral director didn't want him comforting a competitors mourners.

"Hurry up… Everybody's waiting on you," she insisted.

"Listen… Tell your father I'm going to stay in tonight. I don't feel well."

"You were well enough to curse at your shoes… You're late…"

"Late… What's the hurry? Is somebody else scheduled to be turfed in the same grave?"

"We can't start without you."

"I'm sure the guest of honor will be just as stiff whenever I get there."

"Just tie a knot in the shoelace and follow me."

Barnett tied the knot, a granny, much to his disgust as a former sailor, and followed the little girl as she skipped down Johnston Ave. He followed with increasing dudgeon as she led with the exuberance of youth. She was wearing an old fashioned white dress with a hem that went well below her knees and had some flowers plaited in her hair. She looked far different from the usual slovenly kids in Wickesborough.

She stopped at the corner, Barnett thought it was to let him catch up, instead she took his hand.

"I'm not allowed to cross the street without a grownup."

"Then how'd you get…?"

"Hurry up… You'd be late for your own funeral."

Barnett was beginning to take a hearty dislike to the adorable little tyke, but he joined hands with her anyway and made his way to Himmeldeutsch's Mortuary.

Himmeldeutsch Mortuary was in either a faux Victorian or Queen Ann house; Barnett was never able to tell the styles apart. Like all people in Wickesborough, he was related to the vast Himmeldeutsch clan. He glanced at the little girl, he thought he knew all the Himmeldeutsches, at least the ones associated with the funeral trade, but he didn't remember seeing her before.

Barnett went to pay his respects to the guest of honor at this post-mortem shindig, but detoured to say hello to Garrett Himmeldeutsch and get a few details about the stiff-in-a-basket, it was nice to know who was who when you went about the job of comforting.

Garrett didn't even acknowledge him when he walked up, which was strange, but even stranger, he said nothing when Barnett said hello. The little girl pulled him away and into the knot of mourners around the casket.

The codger in the box had a bigger than usual turnout, people his age usually didn't have many friends left. He must have been a man of some prominence in Wickesborough and Barnett wondered why he didn't know him. He looked familiar; they undoubtedly passed each other on the street, probably accompanied by their franticly waving wives.

Barnett realized with a start that the old man was wearing the same out-of-date suit and tie he had on. He liked the presentation; he was a connoisseur of such things. The dead guy looked a little gaunt for Barnett's taste and he made a note to start eating richer foods when he felt the reaper was coming to call.

"I want to look that good when I shed my mortal coil," he said.

The little girl giggled and pulled him deeper into the crowd.

Barnett didn't recognize anyone at the wake until a woman, who looked exactly like his wife, walked up and looked over the corpse. He wasn't surprised; there were lots of women around Wickesborough that resembled his wife. He had noticed that, as they age, all women, start looking like Betty White. It was the same with infants; they all look like Eisenhower, Churchill or Don Rickles when they started out, depending on where they were born.

Barnett made his way through the crowd and was mobbed. He was surrounded by mourners who pressed his flesh and thanked him for comforting words he'd uttered at some other funeral. He couldn't believe so many people remembered what, to him, were passing expressions of sympathy. Finally a few people arrived who Barnett recognized, Foster for one. He stood over the casket and said loud enough to be heard:

"I guess you won't be going to Atlantic City after all..."

Foster was more bent out of shape about someone missing out on one of Butler Coach's Atlantic City excursions than anyone should be. He was no more than three feet from him, but when he glanced in Barnett's direction; he looked past him, almost through him, just like Garrett.

Something odd was happening here. Was he the victim of an elaborate practical joke? If so, they had gone to a lot of expense. Was the corpse going to sit up and yell: "Surprise!"

He hoped not. Would there be a balloon drop? He hated balloon drops. Barnett turned to the little girl who still held his hand.

"What's going on here?"

"We're here to thank you."

"I thought it was to send off that stiff in the fancy crate."

"Exactly!"

"I don't get it."

"Don't you remember...? A long time ago, my Daddy was so sad... And you said something to him that made him feel better."

"Better?"

"Not so sad... You said something that took away the hurt. I came here to thank you."

"So I made everyone here feel better?"

"Everyone here loved someone you made feel better... Excepting Foster..."

"Well I better get to work on Foster then."

"It's too late for that," the little girl pointed to the shoes of the man in coffin.

The deceased had on the same black wing tips he did and one of the shoelaces was tied together with a granny knot.

When he looked up, he saw his wife was standing next to him. Barnett took her hand and kissed her. Together they mingled with people he knew, but had never met before. It was the best funeral of his life.

Reveille For Revenants

This is an Account of the Wickesborough Zombie Outbreak by Olstee Pettigrew

Exclusively for The Wickesborough County Herald Examiner, Press Telegraph, Clarion and Evening Bulletin,

Every town has its traditions and Wickesborough is no different. In Wickesborough, like many other towns, the traditions usually mark an aspect of its season with a festival to herald the passage of time and succession of the year.

Spring, in this part of western Pennsylvania, is presaged by Ground Hog Day, but, unlike the weather forecasting dilettantes in Pauxatawny, in Wickesborough, it marks the time when woodchuck Billies are captured and fattened up in back-porch pens for meatloaf suppers later in the year. All groundhog pups are called Billies, although that seems a small consolation.

Summer has its high holidays like Memorial Day, Fourth of July and Armstrong Massacre Day, but any weekend provides an excuse to get out and swelter in the backyard during the unremitting humidity of the season.

Wickesborough has an autumn festival centered on Mount Lazarus Cemetery. It is the Cemetery Moon party, where high school seniors try to scare impressionable freshmen into incontinence. It's a popular night of hijinks on the nearest full moon to Halloween, if you are not a frosh.

The coming of winter is noted informally in Wickesborough County by an event that occurs occasionally, but never fails to involve the entire community.

Sporadically, but always shortly after the winter solstice, just in time for the Christmas break, a time when the natural world is fallow, things can begin to stir in the unnatural realm. On these occasions the long dead will relieve themselves of the restraints of the tomb, claw their way out of the earth and go forth on a hellish gambol among the living. Some years, most of the residents of Mt. Lazarus Cemetery are out and about, looking for brains to eat.

Now, brain-eating ghouls wandering around your neighborhood might be a bit disconcerting where you're from, but it's an old story around Wickesborough. From long experience we know that, if confronted by a confused looking dead person, you get your deer rifle, or other large- caliber weapon, and shoot it in the head.

The good people of Wickesborough had been rounding up revenants long before George Romero released his fictionalized version of it called <u>Night of the Living Dead</u>. They called it the Resurrection Rodeo and for decades they sorted things out when the ambulatory undead got restless.

It was unremarked on by anyone outside of Wickesborough, although a few soreheads wondered why they kept burying people in Mount Lazarus Cemetery if every few years the deceased got out of their sepulchers and went for a stroll. That sort of thing didn't happen in Butler County or in the Catholic cemetery that anyone knew of.

There was a kind of symmetry to it, rounding up the walking dead, dispatching them and getting them back into the approximate hole they dug their way out of, provided they still had the tag they got after a previous resurrection. The same soreheads who questioned the efficacy of continuing to use of Mount Lazarus Cemetery described it as "zombie catch, tag and release."

There was nothing special about this year's zombie outbreak and the locals were coping with it in the usual fashion. It was a standard, unremarkable zombie outbreak, until the Government got involved.

Until the fuss started, we hunted down the undead during the resurrection round-up, or any time when the deceased come back from the dead. It was a local solution to a local issue and the whole county was involved. No one ever figured out what made our Wickesborough dead so frisky, but it was something for locals to do after they bagged their limit of deer.

It was something a father and son might enjoy.

Zombies are slow, so even a youngster can pick them off, provided the ammo has the proper stopping power. You should see the look in their young eyes the first time they blow the brains out of one of the cannibal fiends. After a day of traipsing after zombies in the woods, a boy might be tired, but he'll be raring to go again after splattering some ghoul's brains.

With zombies, you can pick them off all day provided you don't run out of ammo or linger too long reflecting on the transitory nature of life. It's a "shoot and scoot" world when dealing with our undead friends.

Nothing attracts zombies like loud noise, gunfire for example, and if you get the attention of enough of them, they'll swarm you and eat your brains.

The penalty for reducing your rate of fire in a zombie swarm is worse than death. Once they bite you, you become a part of their soulless retinue, similarly looking for living brains to consume until someone blows your brains out and the county burns your body at a chamber of commerce sponsored bonfire.

Unpleasant as it seems the cleansing role of fire is the only guarantee that the dead won't be coming back. Some people suggested that we just burn everybody in Mt. Lazarus, but others objected that there didn't seem to be much point to have a cemetery with nobody buried in it.

They went back and forth about this for years.

The only thing everybody agrees on is the bite of a zombie invariably turns good, honest, church going folks into howling demons, although there was the case of a man in Ford City who was bitten and recovered fully, except that he drinks paint.

People unfamiliar with the undead are inclined to think zombies are stupid, but that isn't true. They can talk and do simple mechanical things depending on what parts have mouldered away. A ghoul whose hand has fallen off isn't likely to sit down and play the piano, but he might be able to swing an axe with his good hand.

Some still remembered when they were alive and could be cunning, even deceitful. Some are brighter than an average vo-tech graduate and could have had useful, productive deaths, if they could control themselves around living human brains.

A meal of living human brains is pretty much all zombies care about, and much time has been spent on what it is about human brains that makes them so darned irresistible. Cow and sheep brains are as repulsive to zombies as they are to any living person outside of France. The brains of other deceased people are even less appetizing to zombies, which makes sense considering they couldn't gang up on living people if they were simultaneously trying to devour each other.

The ones we interrogated said fresh brains relieved the pain of being dead, but while we might sympathize with their discomfort, no one was willing to join their hellish carnival by letting them eat our cerebellums. The zombies refused to understand our reticence to volunteer our grey matter, so to save time and aggravation, we shoot them.

There is no reasoning with them.

Over the years we have learned how to spot free ranging zombies and the yard of an abandoned house is a good place to start. They like to corner victims inside and bang on the outer walls. It's amazing how they remember what houses are, but forget what a doorknob is. The outlook for the people trapped within is pretty grim unless the proper authorities have been notified.

If done in time, the zombie-alert siren at the fire station sounds, the volunteers break out their weapons and the women fix sandwiches. In a remarkably short time the volunteers muster at the fairgrounds and fan out to surround the zombie cluster. The reduction of the first reported infestation is really the start of the Resurrection Round-up.

Thereafter high powered havoc is meted out on zombies from deer stands throughout the state game lands. Everybody is up in their favorite tree popping off trophy- sized zombies.

Please remember, every zombie we snuff was somebody's grandfather before becoming a cannibalistic ghoul, so trophy is just a figure of speech. You must be respectful of the feelings of the deceased's relatives.

Besides most zombies are too far gone to mount; frankly they stink. It is hard enough to get that smell out of your memory without some grinning souvenir giving you a refresher whiff every time you sit down to watch the game.

I blame society for what happened in Wickesborough, and liquor. Traditionally, a hunter will take a nip occasionally to steady the hand if a twelve point buck strolls by. Sometimes, there are too many occasions between bucks, and ugly accidents happen. It didn't occur to anyone that discretionary imbibing would be any more of a problem than it was during deer season; no one expected anything more serious than a few tumbles out of tree stands.

The VFW sponsored a Resurrection Round-up Contest and Barbecue which started it. The participants paid an entry fee and whoever bagged the most undead got a prize and a pulled pork sandwich. It was for charity, they wanted to put in wheelchair ramps at the VFW hall so the disabled could drink on Sunday. Wickesborough County still had Blue Laws at the time and only private clubs were allowed to serve alcohol on Sunday. Unfortunately, some participants forgot it was for charity and the competition got rowdy.

First, there were accusations that some of the bodies in the count were not technically zombies yet. There were arguments about whether a complete zombie body counted more than a partially disassembled one. Some enterprising contestants had just lopped off the heads of zombies as they drove by, threw them in the bed of their pick-up trucks and claimed a full zombie. Of course, that irked people, as the headless corpses were left wandering around the county, knocking over corn ricks and scaring children and dogs.

Things got nasty, and the hunters began fighting and making a racket, which, of course, attracted zombies and soon all concerned were rolling in the dust. It was an unholy mess. Fortunately, the sheriff kept his wits about him and got the explorer scouts to turn a flamethrower on the zombies. Afterwards they ran over the smoking remains with a truck and things quieted down.

Sadly, Burt Himmeldeutsch had to put down a couple of sportsmen because they might have been bitten by zombies.

In this era of cell phones, video of the event became an internet sensation and it caused an uproar. A TV station in Erie aired it, and people as far away as Latrobe saw it as well. Harrisburg said it was a bunch of trouble makers from Philadelphia. The Lieutenant Governor declared a moratorium on zombie hunting and had the State Police investigate.

People were pleased that the State Police carted away some bikers as well as rounding up some zombies, but there was a problem: the zombies kept coming.

Granted, the State Police got rid of some zombies but also created some by a process they called "normal wastage" —the people they killed in the course of maintaining the peace. People were divided as to whether the State Police were a net positive or negative regarding zombies, but most were impatient to get back to actively snuffing zombies.

Unfortunately, it was not to be.

Wickesborough County was taking a beating in the national press on account of MSNBC making such a big deal of the First Annual Resurrection Round-up and Barbecue disaster. The consensus on Chris Matthews' show was we were a bunch of dumbass crackers for killing already dead people.

News crews started following the zombies, and soon reported that they were being mistreated. They refused to see that we were simply restoring them to their previous state of deadness, and depositing them back in the same hole they were originally interred in. They started calling zombies "morbidity-challenged Americans," which spawned outrage across the nation.

There was a lot of press coverage, but it didn't amount to anything. Everybody on TV began to yell at each other like when Bush was President, but no one had any solutions, like when Bush was President.

When there was a late snow storm that year and more than the usual crop of zombies wondering along the highways, we knew there were going to be some bizarre traffic accidents and more outrage.

Harrisburg issued travel advisories that warned holiday travelers to avoid zombies, but they still managed to nab the random tourist or two. Some stray zombies caused a bus load of Adventists to go off a road near Schoolhouse Falls, which really confounded things, as the ones killed in the accident were in and out of the grave before the injured ones were out of the hospital.

That's how it was with the Adventists, the whole congregation would appear as dead as a post and next thing you know they're out of their sepulchers, praising Jesus and looking for brains to eat.

Some theologians think it's because they believe in bodily resurrection, but in Wickesborough it's believed that their healthy pre-mortem lifestyle and restraint from spirituous liquors makes them livelier than your average zombie. A larger round is required to bring down an Adventist, particularly if it's charging.

After that, some Evangelicals came to investigate whether zombies were a sign of the Second Coming, but, as we explained, it doesn't require a special occasion to get the restless undead up and around in Wickesborough.

By now, the debate about what to do with the zombies had stretched into February, and when zombies upset the Groundhog Day festivities, people got upset. We hoped maybe a judge or somebody would tell us how far we could go in suppressing zombies, but we waited in vain.

The government was hard at work though, and eventually they got down to the business of blaming the most expedient party. It turns out the undead are citizens just like us and them being dead did nothing to alter their basic rights and privileges as Americans, as long as they paid their taxes. Of course, since they're dead they aren't endangered, protected from any workplace hazards, or eligible for social security. No word yet on how this went over with the zombies since they ate everyone who got close enough to ask.

It finally dawned on the politicians that as much had been done as could be done, without actually doing something. We couldn't just shoot the zombies, as they were citizens who happened to eat human brains, so with the legislature gridlocked as to who to nominate as scapegoat, the President acted.

By executive order he appointed a zombie Czar, or Tsar, to deal with the outbreak. The Czar, or Tsar, created some terrific anti-zombie commercials and identified two leading causes of the outbreak: non-Muslim fanatics opposed to the American values and dead people that came back to life.

He set up shop in Wickesborough and there was a parade and barbecue in the Czar's, or Tsar's, honor which, of course, attracted zombies, who were shot to demonstrate how we dealt with zombies, sort of a lesson in zombie history. The chagrin was palpable when our new Czar, or Tsar, immediately halted the shooting and started profiling the residents to see who was the most likely to be a zombie and who was most likely to shoot a zombie.

Our explanation fell on deaf ears. We explained that the surest indicator of future zombie behavior was a current state of deadness and the likeliest candidate to shoot a zombie was any male in the county healthy enough to carry a gun.

Our Czar, or Tsar, did not agree. Later, it was discovered he had a theory about a worldwide zombie conspiracy that controlled the world through international banking. He wanted to uncover the evidence here in Wickesborough and then breed a race of super zombie clones that would battle their satanic overlords and defeat their empire of evil.

It seemed like a good idea at the time.

After our Czar, or Tsar, rounded up everybody who was shooting his evidence, he deployed Alpha Squad Zombie, a specially trained, highly motivated team of covert specialists that would get to the bottom of the zombie menace.

They slipped out of town at night and tracked the zombies to their lairs. Unfortunately, later that night, the entire cadre of highly trained undercover zombie infiltrators were eaten and turned into specially trained, highly motivated brain stalking fiends themselves.

The Czar, or Tsar, had a change of heart after that, and went back to Washington, DC, to concentrate on stamping out the zombie scourge from there. He declared the Wickesborough County outbreak contained and left a deputy Czar, or Tsar, in charge.

Unfortunately, the zombies didn't get the message and kept coming. It got so a person with a brain couldn't go anywhere in the county without trailing a string of hungry ghouls behind him. In certain neighborhoods you couldn't get a decent night sleep because of the endless banging on doors and windows. It was zombie Halloween every night.

As acute as their distress was, no aid was forthcoming for the citizens of Wickesborough since the security forces designated to protect them were deployed around the fortified communities where the Government people lived and worked.

When the folks in Wickesborough got up a petition to get the Government to actually protect them, the deputy Czar, or Tsar, called them fear mongers. To impress on us how safe we were, the deputy Czar, or Tsar, went for a walk in the new zombie proof park the Government built by the Clarion River. He was eaten, but they appointed a new, tougher deputy Czar, or Tsar, the next day.

Nothing attracts the vehement and complete authority of an ineffectual government agency as much as an accessible powerless person, and since they were unable to do anything about the zombies, the new deputy Czar, or Tsar, set about devising regulations for the living citizens of Wickesborough County.

Neighborhoods were declared Zombie-Free Zones, which impressed everybody but the zombies who wandered in and out as they pleased. The government concluded from this that people were smuggling zombies into Zombie-Free Zones, Conspiracy to aid and abet zombieness was outlawed, as was aiding and abetting zombies. These new laws were backed by the full power and authority of the State.

The new harsher penalties reflected how seriously the Government regarded these offenses. Soon, they had rounded up every suspicious citizen and placed them in camps. Meetings to discuss the zombie problem were discouraged, as they were a common source of misinformation. In the name of community safety, all guns were collected to prevent unauthorized zombie hunting.

Resistance was dealt with severely, as this was a national emergency.

A bounty was paid to whoever uncovered secret opposition to the government's program and miscreants were repeatedly re-educated by government counselors, but to no avail, the zombies continued wandering around Wickesborough. Literature was screened, broadcasts censored and the local newspapers were seized. When bleeding hearts for the first amendment objected, it was pointed out that only commercial speech was being regulated; free speech was not affected: you could say anything you wanted, as long as no one was willing to pay for it.

Eventually, all the zombies in the ground were out of the ground and all the living were concentrated in Government-run camps. With no meals of fresh brains harder to be had, the zombies drifted into Butler County where they were gunned down by citizens that weren't under the deputy Zombie Czar's, or Tsar's, supervision.

Although brain-eating ghouls stopped being a factor in Wickesborough County, the Zombie Czar, or Tsar, was now a cabinet-level position, so the supervision of Wickesborough County continued to be funded.

They water-boarded everyone about the location of secret zombie cells and zombie collaborators; some confessed several times, but were kept locked up anyway −it kept things orderly. Of course, the expense of the camps and nourishing the inmates threatened the solvency of the county, so they gave us jobs in manufacturing to offset the cost of incarceration.

If you worked hard enough, you could be set free, at least that's what the sign over the camp gate said, although no one heard of anyone that had been. We mostly made inexpensive electronic gadgets for the Chinese and eventually everyone signed papers agreeing not to sue the Government or talk to the press.

If we keep our noses clean, we could vote again in ten years.

That summer Scott Baio announced he was getting married and the media left to pursue the hot new story. The government abandoned Wickesborough for Washington when it was decided domestic Zombie abatement could be done in DC. They issued a statement thanking all the Government employees for their efforts during the battle against the zombie curse in Wickesborough County. A zombie special interest law firm sued immediately, saying that calling zombieism a curse was discriminatory.

There was some ambivalence in Wickesborough County about the statement as folks were grateful for the government's help, but, all in all, most preferred the zombies.

After that, things got back to normal, but things were never the same. We learned our lesson. Zombies still pop up, but we don't shoot them when anyone's looking. If we get a few more than our normal crop, we put them in the trunk and drop them off in New York City. So far no one has complained. We had a bumper crop this year, more than we thought Manhattan could handle, so we put them on Butler Coach Company buses. The first lot we sent to Washington, D.C. The Adventists will take turns spelling the driver. They should be arriving pretty soon.

A Design to Die For

"Ozzy Mandis here… Bringing you the Night Terrors Show on WCVR, your hometown station… It's Cemetery Moon tonight and we're broadcasting live from Mount Lazarus Cemetery where all the cool ghouls, spectacular spooks and glamorous goblins are partying tonight..."

On the last full moon before Halloween, or Cemetery Moon as the locals called it, the seniors from Wickesborough High got up to mild mischief in Mt. Lazarus Cemetery. Mostly it involved dressing up as zombies and ghouls to scare freshmen by jumping out from behind tombstones. They carried on like wild Indians, as their elders would have said in less politically correct times.

Cemetery Moon was an old tradition in Wickesborough and lately WCVR, the voice of the Clarion Valley, celebrated it by having their late night jock, Ozzy Mandis, do his show from the epicenter of the hijinks.

Fracking had brought prosperity to western Pennsylvania, and some of that prosperity had spilled into the Clarion Valley. With prosperity came new people, with different ideas about things and some of these folks didn't care for the Cemetery Moon tradition. They had a litany of complaints about the customs and traditions of the inbreed hillbillies and rednecks that lived in Wickesborough before they arrived. That didn't sit well with some locals, traditions die hard in Wickesborough, and some die harder than others.

The new people didn't like that at all; they wanted the Cemetery Moon tradition to die faster, once and for all.

"A Night Terrors public service announcement everyone… If you're out on the highway… drive carefully and be safe… We want all the supernatural sophomores and seniors, frightened freshmen and jumpy juniors to show up for class tomorrow … Dell from Elderton is on the line…"

Dell was a newcomer who thought the whole Cemetery Moon thing needed to die a whole lot faster.

Mary Alice Jordan was driving home from a gab fest and kid's party thrown by the same Dell in Elderton. The party was to distract his kids from what they were missing out on during Cemetery Moon weekend. Her son, Travis, was asleep in the back, exhausted by an evening of sugar driven play. Mary Alice was tired too and wished she could climb in the back as well; instead she tuned into Ozzy Mandis' Night Terrors radio show to stay awake.

Mary Alice had lived in Wickesborough all her life, except for college in Boston. She had deep roots in the Clarion Valley, roots so deep her folks joked about being "half injuns." She definitely wasn't one of the new people and thought Dell was being nutty on the subject of Cemetery Moon. She had participated in the Cemetery Moon parties when she was a kid and was just fine with it.

Her ex-husband would have agreed with Dell, but he'd left her after law school and was nowhere to be found. She was bitter he never bothered to send child support and knew growing up without a father would make Travis' life harder. But she was a mom and moms do their best.

Although some of the new comers resembled her ex more than she cared for, Mary Alice got lonely, so she nodded along with Dell's nonsense just to be polite.

Anyway, it made her feel less provincial by having some friends among the new comers.

"Go ahead Dell…"

Mary Alice turned up the radio, to hear Dell give Oz a piece of his mind. She smiled as Dell began his familiar rant about how the Cemetery Moon was racist, homophobic and promoted stereotypes about the mentally ill, when we should be focused on global climate change instead.

"You know Ozzy, this Cemetery Moon business is racist, sexist and ageist..."

Mary Alice acknowledged that Dell had a point, Cemetery Moon made a fetish of the legends that grew up about Eleanor Barley, formerly an elderly eccentric from Wickesborough and currently a resident of Mount Lazarus. Eleanor had been quirky, but was not the evil old crone she was made out to be this time of year.

Dell droned on and the familiar litany made Mary Alice drowsy. The road besides Rabbit Run winds a bit near Blanket Hill and thanks to Dell, Mary Alice's mind wandered. Her mind wandered far enough to miss a curve and go off the road.

The Prius came to a rest at the foot of a small embankment. Shaken, but not stirred, Travis continued slumbering in the back seat. As Mary Alice's eyes adjusted to the dark, she realized she was in a field adjacent to Rabbit Run. The car had some new dings, but was minimally damaged. The head lights were out, but the moon was full, so she could make it home if she kept the speed down and used the fog lamps.

She checked her cell, there was one bar. She left a message for Dell to tell him what happened.

"Dell... I was run off the road by some climate change deniers near Hester's place... Joking... We're okay... The car looks okay, I'll call if we break down ... I'm going home."

Dell wouldn't get it until morning, but at least he'd know where to send the search party. She bounced across the field and onto a dirt track she figured connected to Rabbit Run Road. If she got to Rascal's Emporium, nee Truman's Store, in Blanket Hill, she could get on the Kittanning Pike and from there to Wickesborough.

She drove past the rusted old Desoto where Old Mr. Harriger was murdered two generations ago. It was said he haunted the place. She'd wandered these woods as a teenager in search of supernatural thrills, but had never run into Harriger. Naturally, the locale attracted unsavory types, but at least she knew where she was and the lay of the land, here about.

She pulled out of a densely wooded patch and stumbled onto a biker conclave. It was the Sex Demons, bikers from Pittsburgh, and newcomers of the most unsavory type. They were an alternative lesbian, gay, bi- sexual, transgendered motor cycle club gone rogue. The male Sex Demons dressed like "Tom of Finland" and their "Old Ladies" dressed like Bikers, in order to make an ironic statement about their sexual identity. They originally came to Wickesborough because of the cheap rents, good schools, comparatively untapped crystal meth market and relaxed law enforcement.

They'd made quite an impression on the locals when they arrived.

They were torturing a man spread eagled over a motorcycle. Terrified, Mary Alice gunned the Prius to get away, but not before seeing the man's chest split open with a battle axe.

Tonight, the background music of the Sex Demons lives, like everyone else in the Clarion Valley, was Ozzy Mandis and The Night Terrors Show.

"We have Eric Odin of the Sex Demons; head Demon in charge, on the line… Do you agree or disagree with Dell, Eric…"

"Definitely disagree Ozzy…"

"Who's there with you Eric?"

Well… Scab… Screech… Lunger… Pick… The other Scab … Booger… Vinnie… Sleazy…Sneezy… Hopeless … and Doc.

"A big Night Terrors shout out to all the Demons."

Marshall, the man with the split chest, gestured to get Eric's attention.

"And Marshall."

"Come again Eric?"

"I forgot Marshall… he's a big fan."

Marshall started screaming until Eric hit him in the head with a wrench to calm him down.

"Sounds like Marshall's a tad distressed at being left out… A special Night Terror's shout out to Marshall at Demon headquarters."

"Thanks Ozzy, he'll be thrilled."

"How are you and the Demons celebrating this Cemetery Moon?"

"Thanks for asking Ozzy… We're initiating new members…"

Eric eyed Marshall.

"And retiring some old ones…"

"Sounds like a typical evening at the Demon clubhouse… Eh Eric?"

"Right you are Oz… And during the holidays we'll be going door to door raising awareness of the challenges At-Risk-Kids face."

"Terrific cause Eric… So you're hoping folks will contribute when a Demon shows up at their door?"

"Absolutely… We're working with Braxton Dunkel of the Wickesborough PD At-Risk-Children's task force… He told us about the financial difficulties he faces… And the club decided to see how it could help… We'll take anything…cars… jewelry… At-Risk-Kids… As well as cash…""I'm sure the people of the Greater Clarion Valley will be generous…"

"I hope so Oz… It's for the kid's future and their own."

A Prius is a quiet car, but not quite quiet enough for Mary Alice to escape Eric's notice.

"Stop her… I want that Bitch dead…"

"What's that Eric?"

"Nothing Oz… And uh … Oz… Ask your listeners to be generous this Holiday Season…"

"I sure will… I'll let you go Eric… It sounds like you're busy…

"Thanks for caring Oz…"

"Back with more Night Terrors in a sec…"

The Sex Demons pursued and had no trouble catching up to Mary Alice's slow accelerating Prius, but staying upright at the pace Mary Alice set was a different matter. Mary Alice swerved to avoid a deer and several bikers went down. Distracted, she never saw Eric pull in front of her and, due to one of its unconventional gear changes; her Prius accelerated and ran him over.

The bikers receded in her rear view mirror and Mary Alice figured she'd made good her escape. Just to be sure she pulled up to house of her friend, Hester Morris, to call the cops. Hester was another new comer, but less full of crap than the rest. The lights were on at the Morris house, but Mary Alice sensed something was wrong.

Gil, Hester's life partner, answered the door.

"Hi Gil, can I use your phone?

"Mary Alice… Come on in…"

Mary Alice realized how dreadfully wrong the something she sensed was wrong was, when she was grabbed and tied to an Ikea dining room set chair. Hester and the Morris' two girls were also tied to furniture and Gil had a gun to his head. As if to drive home the point about how wrong things were, everyone else in the room waved meat cleavers and gibbered like howler monkeys.

It was the dreaded People's Collective of the Communist Revolutionary Action Party. Gil was caviling shamelessly to Lapin, the head Anarchist in charge. They all wore Guy Fawkes masks, the disguise of choice for conformist anarchists everywhere. They believed it made them look edgier

"I'll do anything you want…"

"Of course you will capitalist insect filth."

"Take anything… Just don't hurt me… Or my family…"

"What about Mary Alice?"

"If you take her, is my family off the table?"

"No…"

"How about me?"

"We'll do whatever we want… we're the revolutionary vanguard."

With their bargaining positions clear, Gil continued to whimper.

Meanwhile, the Sex Demons nursed their wounds and Eric was taking abuse from Marshall. Eric was banged up, his bike was wrecked and he was in a very poor mood.

"That bitch trashed your bike, you pussy."

Marshall's disdain for the Sex Demons, despite his split chest and head wound had not decreased. He continued to needle and ridicule the bikers.

"All you Demons are pussies… Except the pussies… Your pussies are dicks…"

"How come you're still alive?"

"Because you can't do anything right… pussy."

Odin took the critique to heart, poured gasoline over Marshall and set him on fire. The remainder of his gang murmured their approval.

"Now find me that bitch in the Prius..."

Mary Alice's predicament was now much worse than bad. Gil offered Lapin his money, his family and Mary Alice to spare his own life. It was all a farce to the anarchists, but Lapin, made a pretense of considering his proposal.

"So we get your money, your wife, the kids and Mary Alice... To do with as we wish... If we let you go. Plus you'll refinance your house, give us the equity and not tell anyone?"

"And my 401-K... Anything... Just let me go..."

"We'll gang rape your wife."

"Go ahead, she's a bitch."

Gil's wife stared at him, he stared back.

"I'm sorry honey... What...? It's true... You were saying?"

"What about your daughters?"

"Sorry girls. Aleese, show Tish the ropes."

Lapin stared at Gil. The Morris girls, Tish and Aleese greeted the news with the sullen indifference of youth.

"I don't want anything from you... But I'm taking it anyway... and then I'll paint the inside of your house with your fascist pig guts."

After a pause that appeared longer, Aleese asked:

"The gang rape is before that though... right?"

Gil shot Hester a look, Hester only shrugs. The youngest Morris girl, Tish, decided to take the opportunity to speak truth to power.

"Lapin is a Trotskyite!"

"What did you call me?"

"Trotskyist swine, that's what my teacher, Mr. Bukharin calls you."

"Bukharin is a fascist tool."

"He also said you are a revolutionary dilettante and Bonapartist."

Mortally offended, Lapin ordered the Morris family dragged into their recreation room.

"Leave the new bitch where she is… I have a plan for her…"

Lapin turned on the radio and picked up the phone; Mary Alice had seen enough movies to know that nothing good happens after that.

"Thanks for that recipe for groundhog pot pie… Fresh ground groundhog is available at Rascal's Emporium and other fine stores. It's the Night Terrors Show with Ozzy Mandis coming to you from Mount Lazarus Cemetery… Lapin from Blanket Hill… you are on the air…"

There was a moment of awkward silence when it became obvious Lapin was unfamiliar dealing with the seven second delay during a live radio interview.

"Hi Oz… Am I on the air?"

"Lapin turn off your radio."

"Oh… that's better…Hi Oz… Love the show…"

"Thanks and what are you doing this Cemetery Moon weekend?"

"Well the People's Collective of the Communist Revolutionary Action Party…"

"That's the P.C.C.R.A.P…Right Lapin?"

"Exactly…

"Kudos on raising revolutionary consciousness with the Occupy Wickesborough action…"

"Thanks Oz… I'd like to give a special shout out to Komandiner's Sporting Goods where we liberated our tents and sleeping bags…"

"You put them out of business."

"We really stuck it to the man!"

"By the way, their "going out of business sale" continues all next week... Drop by for some real bargains."

"Great tip Oz... Death to capitalism... The People's Collective of the Communist Revolutionary Action Party ..."

"The P.C.C.R.A.P..."

"... In association with the Future Anarchist Club of Wickesborough High..."

"Go Ravens."

"Ravens Rule...We'll be smashing the tools of capitalist oppression in Blanket Hill."

"Will there be games and treats for the youngsters?" "You bet...every kid that comes dressed as a peasant or a worker will get to execute a Kulak, wrecker or enemy of the people, especially that punk Mr. Bukharin, who teaches social studies and likes to shoot his mouth..."

"At Wickesborough High."

"Right..."

"Go Ravens."

"Ravens Rule!"

"Sounds like fun, Lapin..."

"Yeah... sure... Whatever you say..."

Eric was still mourning his ride, when Screech, a respected Demon affiliate, reported the Prius parked in a cul-de-sac near Rascal's Emporium.

"You want I should grab her?"

"Yeah ... cover the exits and don't let anyone get away... I want them all."

The Morris house was still lit up and cheery when the Demons surrounded it. Whatever it was that didn't seem right to Mary Alice, escaped the Sex Demons notice because they had never been there before. With a tactical sophistication unusual for thugs, they peeked through the brightly lit windows to see what they were up against.

"It looks empty. The bitch is just sitting in the dining room."

Eric considers the depleted ranks of his gang; Mary Alice has done a number on them.

"She's tough... It might be trap... Got to trick her."

"You got it boss."

Screech grabbed his weapon, pulled a ski mask over his face, knocked on the door and yelled:

"Trick or Treat!"

Lapin was delighted that his call to the Night Terrors Show had paid off so quickly.

"Come in my little bourgeoisie scum!"

Instead of the adorable tykes dressed as hobgoblins or witches, he expected, or the more likely Buzz Lightyear and Disney Princess clones, a six foot, three hundred pound biker burst in and clocked him with a ball peen hammer. Eric and the rest of the bikers followed and fell on the surprised anarchists. Havoc ensued, and the dogs of war went at each other hammer and tongs, whatever that means.

Mary Alice watched as the brawl unfolded. Both sides took severe beatings, but that didn't slow them down. Eventually, Mary Alice got knocked to the floor by some flying bodies intent on killing each other. Simultaneously, darkness threw a cloak over the antagonists. Eric had shorted out the electrical box with his battle axe. Lapin and his anarchists, Eric Odin and his Bikers, took the opportunity and scurried away to regroup.

Mary Alice was forgotten and, when she woke up, she was free. Gil Morris, though a master of composing essays on the benefits of gun control and the evils of fracking, was less skilled at assembling Swedish furniture. Mary Alice's chair fell apart the second it tipped over.

Mary Alice needed help, the police, the sheriff, anybody, but her phone had no bars. She rushed to her car. Travis was in it, still asleep, but she had locked it.

Unlocking a Prius causes a distinctive series of attention attracting chirps and whistles, but getting into a Prius without disabling the security system makes more noise than an exploding calliope and would also attract attention. She needed a pay phone, but she didn't want to leave Travis. There were two pay phones left in Wickesborough County, one was located outside Rascal's Emporium and Mary Alice saw it from where she was. She decided to risk it.

"911... What is it you are reporting?"

"Bikers and some anarchists... I think it's the P.C.C.R.A.P.... are killing my friends in Blanket Hill!"

"In Blanket Hill? No one's been killed in Blanket Hill since 1763."

"What about Harriger?"

"Okay... Harriger... Blanket Hill adjacent... Thirty years ago. Hang- up now and tell everyone on Mt. Lazarus, that Devil's Night fun does not include pranking 911. Good Bye!"

"Please send someone..."

"You know it's a crime to make a false report to 911?"

"It's no joke... I'm serious!"

"So am I! The Sex Demons are initiating new members and the P.C.C.R.A.P. is hosting a children's party... I just heard it on Ozzy Mandis' show! Good Bye!"

Mary stares at the phone and remembered The Night Terrors Show and called Ozzy.

"Mary Alice Jordan from Blanket Hill… Go ahead…"

"Actually, I'm from Wickesborough…"

"Sorry my bad… What is going on, Mary Alice from Wickesborough?"

"Anarchists and Bikers are killing each other… call the police!"

"Where is that, Mary Alice?"

"On Mockingbird Lane in Blanket Hill… It's near the golf course."

Mockingbird Lane… Would that be next door to the Munsters?"

"Call the police… it's a riot."

"It may be a riot to you, but it might be less funny to someone who needs a paramedic and they're busy responding to a practical joke."

She hung up violently, breaking the hand set into jagged fragments. She was on her own.

Mary Alice needn't have been concerned; Linda and Phyllis, two "old ladies" of the Demons discovered Travis and were fussing over him, unconcerned with any attention they might attract by sitting on a livid Prius. They were also unaware that the first rule of parenting is to let sleeping children sleep.

"Look at the little guy…" "He's so cute…"

"I'm going to spoil the shit out of him…"

"And then we can sell him to that guy that teaches at the University."

"The one that goes to Thailand every summer…"

They talked about the future, their hopes and dreams until Eric, attracted by the noisy Prius, saw them.

"Get off their asses and cover the doors."

They pulled out their personal side arms and took up covering positions; Linda went to the front door while Phyllis carried a fretting Travis to the back door of the house.

Screech had just finished nailing an anarchist's head to the Morris's hardwood floors, when Phyllis walked in with Travis. He waved, but she didn't see him. He continued waving until Lapin did see him and cut off his hand with a machete. His screams lasted until Lapin also cut off his head and stuck it on a wrought iron candle holder from Pier One.

"Take that, enemy of the people,"

Moments later, Eric rounded the corner dragging Chip, another anarchist, by the hair. The look on Eric Odin's face was almost as surprised as the one on Screech's when he bumped into the grisly trophy.

"He'd just gotten his welder's certificate."

Eric vented his outrage at Chip, but to no effect, until the anarchist pulled his earbuds out.

"Dude… He was a fascist and class traitor…"

"What's your name…? Dude…?"

"Chip… What's yours?"

"Eric… Chip… I'm going to gut you like a cat fish and kick you out to the driveway so I can watch you bleed out on the gravel."

"Kind of harsh… Eric…"

True, but Eric was as good as his word, and did indeed gut Chip like a catfish then kick him, bowels in hand, out the front door.

"Don't shoot him Linda… it might attract the cops."

"I'll check him for smokes."

"Just don't shoot…"

Linda was searching the disemboweled radical for something menthol, when Mary Alice stabbed her with the jagged shard of the handset from the payphone. By now, the sound of the Prius, combined with the screaming and chainsaws coming from the house, convinced Mary Alice she could leave unnoticed. Just to make sure, she strangled Linda with the phone cord, but then noticed Travis was missing.

"He's gone."

"Who is?"

It was Chip. He had discovered his revolutionary principles did not preclude stealing cars to get medical attention. He grabbed Mary Alice's keys. Stealing the Prius, as he saw it, was a revolutionary solution to the rapid onset of shock. Mary Alice disagreed.

"Give me back my keys."

They struggled. Chip was doing about as well as a disemboweled social justice warrior tripping over his intestines could do, but juggling his guts while tangling with an enraged mother with an endangered child proved to be more than a full plate. Mary Alice kicked him in the nuts, which despite Chip's revolutionary principles, was still pretty disabling. He pushed her into the backseat and jumped into the driver's seat. Desperate to stall him, Mary Alice played for time.

"I'll drive you…"

"Fine… Take me to Clarion Valley General"

She finds a pair of knitting needles.

"After I get my son!"

"After nothing… I'm in pain and we're going to the hospital."

"Not without my son!"

Chip looked around to scream at Mary Alice and got a pair of knitting needles in the eyes for his trouble. Mary Alice pulled him from the Prius by his descending colon and tied the blind, disemboweled anarchist to the Morris's Caucasian lawn jockey with it.

Inside Eric was counting casualties. His Sex Demons had been reduced, but the ambulatory cases were still anxious to get back into action. Someone turned on the radio.

"Hey all you Ghouls and Ghoulettes… A word of caution from Ozzy Mandis… The Wickesborough PD… I know, I know, but they're still cops… They want me to warn you not to make prank calls to 911… Someone just did and I am told Mary Alice Jordan… A satisfied listener and caller to the Night Terrors program, is in a heap of trouble… Mary Alice… Call back and apologize… The Wickesborough PD may forget about the whole thing… or not. Go ahead, Dell from Elderton…"

"Mary Alice called me earlier… she had an accident or something."

"So you think she might be disoriented."

"Exactly… And combined with the effects of global climate change…"

"Right…Where was she calling from?"

"She said she was near the golf course… By now she's probably at a friend's house on Mockingbird Lane."

"Well the Wickesborough PD may want to talk to her. This Mocking Bird Lane…"

"Yes Oz?"

"Is that near The Munsters?"

Eric took this news badly. In all the excitement he'd forgotten the reason he invaded the house in the first place. Eric surveyed his survivors; either Scab or the other Scab had been hit in the face with a pasta maker and could barely see, Lunger had been nearly lobotomized with a meat thermometer, while Pick, Booger and Doc were disabled to a lesser degree. Still they were all he had.

"She's here... Find that woman and kill her."

The house was still dark when Mary Alice entered; she heard the Night Terrors program in the distance. She stumbled over a wispy blond girl in a Guy Fawkes mask trying to pry up her boyfriend's head from the floor where Screech had nailed it. Her boyfriend's predicament has momentarily distracted her from wreaking havoc on bourgeoisie enemies like Mary Alice.

"Have you seen my son? I really need to get him home."

"Those bastards nailed Scott's head to the floor."

"That's awful... Have you seen my son? I really need to get him home."

"He wants me to pull out the nail."

"Who...Wait... What? He's still alive?!!!"

"I think so... He's talking."

"How do you get your head nailed to the floor and survi...? "

"Do you think this will work?"

She shows Mary Alice the crowbar she found.

"How do you survive your head being...? Never mind... It'll do fine ... Did you see anyone with a baby come this way?"

"One of the biker's whore bags took him towards the back..."

"Thanks... Uhh..."

"Missy."

Suddenly, the crowbar was snatched from Missy's hands by a biker, either Scab or the other Scab, the half blinded one.

"That's my crowbar!"

"Give it back."

"Not on your life bitch."

Scab, or possibly the other Scab, it was too dark to tell, impaled Missy with the crowbar. Showing remarkable poise, for someone so young, Missy slid up the bar and emasculated Scab, or possibly the other Scab, with some Pottery Barn poultry shears. Missy shoved the severed phallus and testicles in the unlucky biker's mouth and watched as he bled out.

"Chew on that, bitch."

Missy recovered her composure enough and pulled the crowbar out. She turned to Mary Alice, and then stared in confusion at her wound.

"How bad does it look?"

"You might want to go with a one piece this summer."

"Damn…This really hurts…"

"I'll bet… Maybe you should have someone take a look at it?"

"Like one of your bourgeois Doctors, you racist pig?"

Missy swung the crowbar at Mary Alice's head, but blood loss made her whiff. Mary Alice grabbed it.

"Thanks for telling me where my son is… bitch,"

Mary Alice slipped on Missy's Guy Fawkes mask as Missy slipped into shock. Disguised as an anarchist, she unfortunately immediately bumped into a biker.

"Where do you think you're going?"

He slammed Mary Alice against the wall, but thanks to regular Pilates and yoga, she was only winded. But, she was now questioning her commitment to non- violent conflict resolution, her opposition to concealed carry permits and wishing she'd picked up Linda's 357 when she had the chance.

"I just want to get my kid and go."

"Not until I learn you some respect little lady…"

The biker started undoing his belt and Mary Alice realized what sort of education in respect he had in mind. She ran to the kitchen looking for some poultry shears of her own, closely followed by the biker. Mary Alice was trapped and the prospects were looking grim for her, until a Callaway 3 wood caved in the bikers head.

"Hi… I saw you were in trouble… I'm Jamie, are you Missy's friend?"

"Yeah… I guess… I'm Mary Alice… You really laid him out."

"I always had a good power game… I went to Stanford on a golf scholarship."

He hands her a cleaver and pointed her in Lapin's direction.

"You better see what Lapin is up to, but later… Would you like to grab a cup of…?"

Jamie's invitation was interrupted by the sound of a chainsaw being cranked.

"Hold that thought… I've got to take this."

A biker severed Jamie's hamstring before the chainsaw, like all chainsaws, stalled. The biker jacked it and re-started it, but Jamie, in the meantime, cut the biker's jugular vein and carotid artery with a Cuisinart cheese slicer.

Jamie watched the blood spurting from his thigh and the biker's neck.

"That is going to really going to screw with my back swing."

Jamie made good use of his final moments and cut the biker in half, length-wise with the chainsaw.

"He made the fuel mixture too rich. No wonder it stalled."

Mary Alice rushed to Jamie as he collapsed.

"It's been awhile since I dated… But a cup of coffee would be okay…"

Jamie gazed into Mary Alice's eyes as the blood gushes from his leg, splattering on her cashmere twinset.

How can I get in touch with you?"

"I'm dying…"

"You'll be fine."

"Grraghuh…"

"Mabe not."

Mary Alice realizes she's now talking to a corpse.

"We'll play it by ear."

Mary Alice was covered in blood, but, she grabbed a fireplace poker and headed off to rescue the Morris family and secure their dubious assistance in recovering Travis.

In the living room, she found an anarchist and biker rolling around and decided to be proactive. She hit the biker in the face with the heel of her hand as she'd learned in a self-defense course. It drove a meat thermometer protruding from his eye socket deep into his brain. He immediately sat down and smiled placidly. His internal temperature was nearly a hundred degrees.

She used the fire place poker to beat the anarchist's head and face to a pulp, then pushed him into a large fish tank full of hungry piranhas Gil had been trying to make vegan.

She watched with some satisfaction.

Mary Alice wandered around looking for the Morris family, or, at least their bodies. Instead, she encountered the dead or dying remains of Anarchists and bikers, impaled or bludgeoned by interior design accents she recognized from Architectural Digest.

She made a note to renew her subscription.

She figured that they must be running out of bikers and anarchists by now, so she took off her Guy Fawkes mask and headed to the rec room.

The Morris family was alive and unhurt, but still tied up. She started by untying Gil.

"Gil, can you call the cops … While I find Travis?"

Her question was never answered because Gil ran away as soon as he was free. She freed Hester, who freed the kids.

"Forget him… I'll help you find Travis and call the cops,"

Before they could do either, Lapin returned with Gil and Dell.

"Please don't kill me… Please don't kill me…"

Gil continued his spineless caviling, but Dell was determined to make his point.

"I don't understand how you can disagree with a consensus of 97% of scientist… Hey Gil, great party, but can you get this ass to put me down. I came by to check on Mary Alice."

Lapin responded with a whiplash machete counterpoint and Dell's head rolled up to Gil's feet. Gil urinated on himself.

"Always happy to meet someone who takes climate science seriously…"

Gil continued to beg for mercy until Eric Odin entered carrying his trusty battle axe.

Lapin and Eric circled each other over Dell's twitching, albeit headless, corpse. Lapin swung and Eric parried. Gil cried. They continued circling each other and it looked like a Biker /Anarchist Armageddon death match was about to commence, when Mary Alice asked Eric:

"Why do you guys fight? You share similar beliefs, values and a profound contempt for our civilization."

Eric paused; he had never considered the question from that vantage point.

"I don't know, we just always have."

Eric and Lapin eyed each other.

"I'm out of anarchists…"

"I'm just about out of bikers…"

"And we still have Mary Alice and the Morrises to kill…"

Eric and Lapin shook hands and were about to forge an historic Grand Anarchist-Biker alliance when they were skewered by a halberd wielding smoking man.

It was Marshall, the captive set alight by Eric. His lungs were hanging out, he'd suffered a head wound and he was still a little bit on fire, but he recognized Mary Alice.

"You saw them split my chest… You saw them light me on fire…and you drove away… You bitch… "

"I didn't see them set you on fire…"

"You heartless, self-involved, self-centered… self-righteous… Prius driver… I'll kill you."

Gil dodged as Marshall ran by him and let him have an unobstructed shot at Mary Alice. But Mary Alice had learned a few things over the course of the evening, mostly that the Morris house was filled with all sorts of lethal bric-a-brac. She spotted a likely weapon; a highly polished piece of sculpture prominently displayed in a lighted niche. She impaled Marshall with it and Marshall collapsed.

Gil screamed.

"You Philistine… That is an authentic copy of Brancusi's "Bird in Flight," … A nearly priceless replica of the classic sculpture I bought at a significant discount from a dealer in New York,"

Mary Alice looked around for another weapon, but was interrupted.

"Hey in there… anybody home?"

A dark figure with a flash light stood outlined in the doorway; Gil grabbed the stranger's knees and begged for his life. Everyone except Hester looked away as Gil embarrassed himself.

"Relax Gil… he's a cop… I'm the one you should be worried about."

It was Deputy Burton Himmeldeutsch, fresh from investigating reports of African American teenagers drinking near the Rabbit Dell's golf course. He found nothing and decided to check the Morris house instead. He had Phyllis and the still sleeping Travis in tow.

"Everything OK in here? Hi Mary Alice."

"Hi Burt."

He knew four generations of Mary Alice's family, and now Travis. The Wickesborough PD had requested the county sheriff arrest the scofflaw Mary Alice Jordan since they were too busy writing reports about non-existent African-Americans and napping. He was prepared to give a strong rebuke to anyone pranking 911 operators, but changed his mind.

"I caught this one rummaging around in your Prius… she claimed she was looking for a bottle… She didn't have ID so…"

"I asked her to get the bottle from my car, I know her."

Himmeldeutsch gave the heavily tatted Phyllis the once over, twice.

"Really, Mary Alice? I would have sworn she rode with the Demons."

Mary Alice grabbed Travis and pocketed Phyllis' 357. She'd be packing next time.

"Well you know how hard it is to find baby sitters."

"I guess."

Himmeldeutsch turned to Gil and family.

"I like your Cemetery Moon party decorations. It's nice to see newcomers adopting local customs. I really liked the moaning masked guy pretending his head was nailed to the floor. .. But... I think you should turn the lights up, I almost tripped over him."

"Thanks for the tip Burt... We'll take care of it... Don't want to keep you."

"Yeah... well safety first... It sure is nice to see new people following our Wickesborough traditions."

Deputy Himmeldeutsch excused himself and turned to leave. He didn't mention the nonsense about Negros drinking nearby; no need to upset anyone.

Presently, the other Morris girl, Aleese, not Tish, the troubled one who went to the Nicolai Tesla Military Academy for Girls, had figured out how to get the lights back on. Gil looked upon the horrors in his conversation pit and despaired. His home is littered with two dozen or so bodies in various stages of dismemberment, castration, impalement, exsanguination and evisceration.

"How will I pay for this?"

"Shut up Gil... I'm calling the cops."

"Don't call... they'll just ask questions. I'll hire some of McClusky's Mexicans to cart away the bodies."

Hester glared at her soon to be ex-life partner and picked up the phone.

"None of the children are yours," she told him.

Mary Alice left them to sort out their domestic issues and took the still sleeping Travis back to the Prius.

"I am taking your car."

It was the blinded Chip who had somehow unknotted his bowel from the lawn jockey and jumped Mary Alice, with murder and car theft still on his mind.

"Not now."

"Fuck you… I'm going to drive myself to the hospital."

"How? You're blind."

Chip considered this while Mary Alice emptied Phyllis's revolver into his chest, reserving the last round for his head.

Mary Alice strapped Travis in, who woke up and smiled pleasantly at his Mommy. She turned on the radio in time to hear Ozzy Mandis sign off.

"Another great Cemetery Moon celebration in Wickesborough, everybody play safe and be happy… until next year."

Mary Alice smiled and drove away slowly. Her headlights were still out.

The Ghost of Buttermilk Creek

"I don't get it… What's the hook?"

"Well, like you always say, every town in the Midwest has a serial killer… Maine has monsters…"

"And every southern town has a ghost… This is western Pennsylvania… You found zombies? … Zombies are gold."

"No zombies, just some ghosts …"

"So, is there a celebrity tie in…? Did Scot Baio see it?"

Tom Haas was arguing with his show runner about a segment for a show called "Weird but True" about ghosts in a town called Wickesborough. The series pretended to investigate paranormal events —interesting paranormal events— nothing mundane or dull about their paranormal stuff. If it was dull, they'd make it interesting by adding a celebrity.

"This Wickesborough isn't near Pittsburgh… Pittsburgh is pretty spooky."

"It's about fifty miles north and east."

"Outside Pittsburgh… Is there a Hell mouth in town? A lot of places out there have Hell Mouths."

"No Hell Mouth, just three lost boys."

Haas had heard a bit of doggerel around a camp fire, years ago and for some reason it stuck with him:

> It's a mystery the waters still keep,
>
> About three boys crossing Buttermilk Creek,
>
> Out in the middle the ice was thin,
>
> And one by one the boys fell in.
>
> All of them drowned,
>
> Only two were ever found,

And the youngest still abides in the deep,

It's a mystery the water still keeps.

The first time he heard it; it chilled his blood; he had a terror of drowning under ice. As a boy in Salem, New Hampshire, he had fallen through the ice of a frozen pond and never forgot the panic as the weight of his skates and soaked clothes pulled him under. His friends got him out in time, but the memory of watching the world of light and air recede as he sank haunted his dreams ever since.

The idea of looking up at the world through the ice, with its abundance of air inches away, as the icy water filled his lungs, terrified him. In college he traced the rhyme to a town called Wickesborough and thought about making a documentary about it. The recent fad of ghost story/ paranormal activity shows made him think there might be some interest in a real ghost tale. A shabby segment on a basic cable reality ghost show was the best he could manage for now.

The executive producer was sceptical and disabused him of his fantasies.

"Let's hope they're really dead."

"They're dead…"

The events described had happened a hundred years ago. The exec was unimpressed.

"If you can't stir up some ghosts, keep an eye out for a Hell Mouth… They're usually in houses the realtors unload on outsiders."

His executive producer's words rang in his ears as he left to book a crew.

In the first part of the twentieth century, Wickesborough educated its children in an elementary school on a hill above the banks of Buttermilk Creek. The name was ironic; no one would have called it that after the tannery up stream started doing business. It spoiled the water, and even livestock refused to drink it.

The owner deeded the parcel of waste land back to Wickesborough and the site was deemed suitable for a school, as long as the pupils didn't get thirsty.

The location had the added advantage of being equally inconvenient to all parts of Wickesborough; so long treks to school became part of the local lore. The spot was on a hill close to where the creek tumbled over a derelict, but picturesque, mill dam which became Schoolhouse Falls.

By now the locals had stopped naming anything associated with the creek's foul water with Buttermilk in the description.

The Branch Valley Road ran up the creek on the opposite bank from the school until it crossed the stream where the mill pond tapered into its natural bed, a more manageable span for local engineers to bridge. The school looked lovely, sited as it was above the pond, but the students had to walk upstream several hundred yards to get to the bridge, cross it and then double back downstream to get to school. In warmer, fairer weather this was no problem, but during winter the pond's frozen surface offered a tempting, but dangerous short-cut.

One unseasonably warm February as the students were coming back from a holiday for a now forgotten president, Miss Laura Cloud was ringing a bell on the school porch to alert everyone that the business of education was in session.

She was the teacher and looked the part. She was considered plain by the standards of the time, the prescribed look for an educator and future marmish spinster. A spare, lithe woman with high cheek bones, a sharp nose and auburn hair tied up in a severe bun, she dressed as plainly as she looked.

The pictures of her that exist contradict contemporary opinion. To a modern observer, her bones were spectacular and she had a slender, but well- proportioned figure. Her sensuous mouth and thick hair, would have appealed to modern tastes and if she wasn't a teacher, she could have worked in New York or LosAngeles, either modeling, acting, or in porn, but it was neither the time nor the place for such choices.

Her eyes were disturbing. They were penetrating and hinted at vehemence that might have bordered on madness. Then again, it's just some photographs.

The kids rushed past Miss Cloud and took their accustomed seats. She noticed that the three Berrigan boys were straggling down the road. They were frequently late which annoyed Laura. She gave the bell a vigorous ring to make sure they knew they were tardy.

It got their attention.

She called their names and threatened dire consequences for the tardiest Berrigan.

The straightest route to the school was across the water and the youngest boy, Luke, took it. He slid down the bank and onto the ice. The older boys knew that the water ran fast under the ice and he was taking a terrible risk. The eldest, Matthew, went after him, but the ice buckled and together they went under. Mark, the middle boy, watched his brothers get swept away, then, for whatever reason, he jumped in and likewise disappeared. Three Apostles swept away in a matter of seconds.

Miss Cloud watched in horror as the three boys went down and began calling their names. She crawled out onto the ice, ringing her bell and searching frantically, but they were gone. When she realized the finality of the tragedy, she straightened up and knelt mutely by the creek. She never spoke to a living soul again.

The citizens of Wickesborough said she was struck dumb, the modern diagnosis would probably be catatonic seizure. She was institutionalized and, although no responsibility was officially attributed to her, locally she was blamed for the deaths.

Years later, according to legend, she escaped and was seen wandering beside Buttermilk Creek looking for the lost boys. She later drowned, according to people obsessed with symmetrical irony, or was re-immured, according skeptics. In local legend she haunted Buttermilk Creek on wintery nights with a full moon, ringing her bell and calling for the lost boys.

Eventually she morphed into the Ghost of Buttermilk Creek, a legendary demon that lured unwary local tykes to a watery, frigid doom. The tale was debunked and ridiculed by every subsequent generation of adult Wickesboroughians, but, like Eleanor Barley, she planted hooks into every subsequent generation of adolescents.

Haas and crew arrived in Wickesborough in late February and checked into the Clarion Princess where they were the only guests. The groundhog, in nearby Punxsutawney, had promised a late spring, but the thaw was well along in Wickesborough. It was positively balmy for February that year. The crew, in shirt sleeves, unloaded a van's worth of rental equipment into the room Haas had designated for viewing and editing.

They shot B-roll on the way, shots of Buttermilk Creek, Schoolhouse Falls, Laura Cloud's old rooming house, and the like, to cover the scripted narrative Haas had written for the talent. The script was light, most of the show consisted of footage of the crew being startled by strange sounds they heard in the woods and saying "What was that?" Since all of them grew up in New York or Jersey, everything they heard in the woods either sounded strange or startled them.

The show practically shot itself.

Haas left to conduct "research" while they set up and discovered which piece of equipment wouldn't work because they had forgotten a vital cord or part.

He spoke to a local disc jockey, named Byron "Ozzy" Mandis who did a paranormal call-in radio show at night. Yes, he'd heard the tale and spoken with locals who claimed to have seen Laura. Haas wanted him to play a local historian and parrot the party line, or "Chamber of Commerce" version of events. Oz was willing, but Haas needed some juicy gossip to spice things up as well.

Ozzy's recommendation was to hit the bars until he found someone who knew, or at least claimed to know, something about the events.

What Haas needed was someone willing to say anything on camera, whether it was true or not. Oz was willing to do that too, for financial consideration. Haas thanked him and said he'd be in touch if he couldn't get someone cheaper.

Whatever God it is that watches over basic cable television was smiling, because Haas struck pay dirt at the first place he hit, the Clarion Marina. The Clarion Marina was a riverside bar and restaurant that justified the "Marina" part of its name by renting jet skis and canoes. It was said that they rented canoes because, unlike the customers, they occasionally tipped.

A collection of dead beats and drunks occupied barstools and turned their heads in unison when Haas came in. The entertainment value of the new guy ran out almost as fast as he came in and the regulars quickly returned to drinking. Ora, the bartender, pointed Haas in the direction of an ancient old man drinking quietly on the corner of the bar, who likely had a Laura Cloud story. He was alone, Haas liked that, solitary drinkers were always a rich vein of bullshit.

"What can you tell me about the three lost boys?"

"Just this:

It's a mystery the water still keeps,

About three boys and Buttermilk Creek,

Out in the middle the ice was thin,

And one by one the boys fell in.

All were drowned,

Two were found,

And the youngest still abides in the deep.

It's a mystery the water still keeps.

In winter, if the moon is bright,

Laura Cloud still haunts the night.

By Schoolhouse Falls she seeks,

The boys she drowned in Buttermilk Creek.

Year after year she walks the creek,
Looking for their souls she seeks,
The boys she drowned in Buttermilk Creek.

On winter nights she calls their names,
But every night is always the same.
The boys were drowned,
And will never be found,
By the banks of Buttermilk Creek."

On winter nights, when the moon is bright,
And you hear a bell ringing in the pale moonlight.
Beware the ghost of Buttermilk Creek.
If Laura Cloud ever calls your name,
Your fate and the boys will be the same.
The boys disappeared and never returned,
And where they've gone will never be known.
It's a mystery the water still keeps."

Haas was a little nonplused by this, but intrigued. He'd never heard these verses before. He had his local color.

His name was Mo, short for Moses, Pennypacker was his last name and he spelled it out to Haas. His mother had named him and his brother Aaron after the biblical heroes of Exodus.

"She said it was because she found me floating in the reeds… And Aaron because he played with snakes."

"What are you doing later tonight?"

"I got plans."

The eavesdropping regulars laughed into their drinks.

"I'd like you to find Laura."

"No… There's a curse…Nothing good ever comes from looking for her."

Haas was willing to take his chances; a curse would be a big plus.

"What about talking about the curse… on camera?"

"By Schoolhouse Falls?"

"Yeah… At midnight."

"No."

"What if I pay you a hundred?"

"I won't go looking for her."

"Just tell the story and recite the poem, I'll do the rest."

Mo was reluctant to say much more about the three lost boys or Laura, but after a few more cocktails he became more talkative. Soon Haas had the lost boys' tragedy in hand and Mo had enough Dutch courage in him to agree to meet at midnight by Schoolhouse Falls and talk on camera.

Haas arrived early to let his crew set up. It was nearly a full moon so the green tinged low-light camera would look good—good and spooky. By mid-night it was clear Mo was a no show, so Haas started throwing stones in the water and shaking bushes. Predictably, his crew, panicked, manufactured ghosts in their heads and headed for the van. The cameraman, Santiago, was moving faster than Haas had ever seen him move which guaranteed the shaky video gold that was the sine-qua-non of the genre.

'They aren't paying me enough,' thought Haas as he herded "the team" back to the first set-up.

"You can't just run away the first time you hear or see something. If I start to run then you can run."

Haas saw "The Team" was ignoring him and were looking at something in the moonlit pond. Haas followed their look up stream where three figures dressed in shrouds were wading towards them and hooting like banshees.

"It's the three lost boys," screamed an intern.

The stampede was on again.

Haas noticed that "The Three Lost Boys" coming towards him were well into their forties, had wet suits on under their shrouds which were clearly old bed sheets—one of which was fitted. Haas helped them up onto the bank and thanked them for their entertaining charade.

They explained that Oz had plugged the shoot on his Night Terrors Show and they'd decided to come down and prank the crew.

"We had you going there didn't we," the least intoxicated one asked?

"Yes you did... Very well done."

Haas said, meaning exactly the opposite.

"Mo ever show up?"

"No... Any idea where he is?"

They figured he was home sleeping his drunk off. He lived, they said, in a crazy house built on stilts, by the confluence of the Clarion and Buttermilk Creek.

Haas wished them well and told them he hoped they wouldn't be arrested for drunk driving or wrap their cars around trees on their way home. They assured him they frequently drove twice as drunk as they were now and said goodbye. Haas figured he knew what the curse was: any one drunk enough to be out on Buttermilk Creek this late, stood a good chance of missing one of the poorly marked curves on Branch Valley Road.

Nothing more would get done tonight. Haas told Santiago to pack up, his talent was coming in tomorrow and together they'd go in search of Laura and her three lost boys. He looked across the pond and thought he saw something moving in the trees. The crew was busy throwing equipment into the van so there was no one to confirm what he saw.

'Probably an animal,' he thought, 'If it was anything at all.'

He looked again, something definitely moved. He thought he heard a bell ringing in the distance.

'Superstitious nonsense,' he thought

He walked a little further along the bank and kept an eye on the opposite shore – nothing. The weather was chilly and Haas made his way back to the van.

The temperature plunged over night, there was a hard frost on the ground and glare ice on the highway, perfect conditions for an appearance by Laura Cloud.

Talent, in the form of reality TV star Burt Tate, arrived and Haas spent the early part of the day finding him some cold weather clothing he'd neglected to pack. Komandiner's Sporting Goods outfitted Burt appropriately. Haas spent the rest of the afternoon writing out Mo's recollections on cue cards for Burt to ad lib.

It got Haas wondering about Mo.

He walked down to the Marina, but Mo hadn't come in yet. The bartender, Ora, suggested he might be having trouble parting Buttermilk Creek.

Haas decided to find Mo and got directions to his "rundown house", which is how the locals identified it. The poem was still in his brain:

It's a mystery the water still keeps,

About three boys and Buttermilk Creek,

Out in the middle the ice was thin,

And one by one the boys fell in...

To Haas, Laura Cloud sounded like a conventional haunt, like any of a number he'd investigated and promoted, but the curse bothered Mo.

"If she calls your name, you drown... Like the Berrigans."

Mo explained, as he finished a tumbler of discount bourbon.

"...Like it says in the poem."

Haas got that, he had other questions.

"So, you drown... In the creek... Right after she calls your name?"

"Maybe."

"So who survived to tell everybody about the curse."

"I don't know... The Fish and Game posts notices..."

"According to the poem, she's looking for her boys... Why would she call somebody else's name?"

"Maybe the poem lies."

"How does she know the names of the people wandering around at night?"

"She's a ghost."

Haas realized this conversation was going nowhere.

"There's still a yard waiting for you if you show up tonight."

Mo didn't say anything. He just stared into his glass, like he was reading the tea leaves at the bottom of his whiskey.

Haas returned to the Clarion Princess and stared out the window. He tried to read the tea leaves that floated by on the part of the Clarion River he could see. Every time he thought about the three boys it chilled him. He stretched out to take a nap, knowing that the story would return to him while he slept.

Darkness fell with an abruptness characteristic of a late winter's evening and another TV production lived down to expectations. Burt read his ad-libs with the authentic insincerity of a real pro, Santiago framed each shot exactly how he had framed every other shot he'd ever made, the audio man asked if they were having fun yet.

Nobody laughed.

Burt and Santiago bush whacked in the lengthening shadows looking for Laura Cloud, as a pale moon rose to replace the wintery sun.

"This is exactly where… And exactly when, countless people have seen the Ghost of Buttermilk Creek…"

Burt had run out of script and, uninformed by any knowledge of Laura Cloud, the three lost boys or Buttermilk Creek, decided to fill the silence with his own thoughts.

"A bright moon … On a cold winter's night… The way Laura Cloud likes it… The way a witch likes it… A night as cold as her tits…"

Everyone looked at Haas, who shrugged and made the gesture of scissors cutting the air, and mouthed the word 'editing'.

"It's cold, dark and moonlit… Must be the season of the Witch… Laura Cloud, drowner of young boys…"

"It was on just such a night that Laura Cloud emerged from the icy depths to drag the Berrigan boys to their death."

Tate was spinning a tale much more interesting than the actual case. Haas had a painful insight, he knew, as much as he protested, Burton Tate's claptrap would wind up in the final cut.

"Like a Kelpie, the infamous Celtic water horse, Laura Cloud seduces the innocent with her beauty then carries them to their watery graves, never to be seen again."

Haas knew that any moment Big Foot, Moth man and the Yeti would soon tumble out of Tate's bag of analogies, so he wandered off in search of the real Laura Cloud.

"Consider if you will, the icy fingers of death clutching your throat as your last breath floats to the surface as you watch…"

Haas quickened his step; Burt was hitting close to home.

"Many the nights a brave man of Wickesborough would tie himself to a tree and wait for the Sirens' call of Laura Cloud, only to be found the next morning hopelessly insane… Or dead… I leave you to decide which was the better fate…"

Tate was spouting utter rubbish, it would undoubtedly win an Emmy and probably a Peabody, an award honoring Media excellence, presented each year by a talking dog and his young companion, Sherman, from their Way-Back Machine.

The last grey glimmers of sun light retreated into shadows and Tom Haas quickened his step. Instinctively he knew what his ancestors knew: the woods are no place to be alone at night. Logically he knew that he was unlikely to run into a serious predator in this part of Pennsylvania, the last panther was killed two hundred years ago, and commemorated only in Happy Valley. He knew he was more likely to injure himself tripping over a homeless encampment, but he retraced his steps briskly.

Or at least he thought he was retracing his steps.

He was headed towards a glow around a bend in the path that led down to Buttermilk Creek; he could hear the water tumbling over Schoolhouse Falls. He assumed the glow was Santiago loading his equipment into the van and counting heads before returning to the hotel. His heart sank when he realized he was relying on Santiago to remember to do that.

He was resigned to spending the night in the woods.

He was warm enough and he had abundant clean water since the EPA had cleaned up Buttermilk Creek so ferociously that no squirrel or raccoon would think twice about peeing in its pristine water. Briefly he thought they would miss him at breakfast and send a search party but realized he was living in a fool's paradise—They wouldn't miss him until they needed him to sign their vouchers and collect their per diem.

He had just pulled his collar up and settled up against a tree when he heard a bell ring. Unnerved he began to yell for the crew.

"I'm over here…"

"I know Tom."

The voice was nearby, but he didn't see the beams of light from the flashlights that any search party would sensibly equip themselves with. Once again: Santiago.

He stood up and yelled louder while waving his arms, thinking that his rescuers would see better if he waved.

"I'm here… I'm here…"

"We know… we hear you."

It was Mo, with a strange looking woman standing behind him.

"I brought you Laura Cloud."

Haas considered this for a second. The girl Mo presented was made up to look like a cross between the girl from The Ring movies and Alice Cooper. The girl gave him a halfhearted wave.

"This can't be Laura Cloud… Laura Cloud would be over 120 years old by now."

"She's a re-enactor… Her name's Aleese."

"What's up with clown white and black eyeliner? There's nothing in the legend about Laura being some kind of zombie."

The young woman gave Haas a withering look.

"While doing my research I discovered I could get a better feeling of verisimilitude with scary makeup."

"Research?"

"Laura was the subject of my Senior Thesis in Women's Studies… My counselor thought it was good enough to get me into Bennington ... But I'll be going to Indiana next semester.

"I don't think her being a woman was…"

"Laura's crime was being an assertive woman in a patriarchal world."

"She drowned three kids… She was never accused of…"

Mo was crestfallen.

"Ozzy Mandis suggested her… I was just trying to help… I told her you'd give her a c-note."

"I don't know who's crazier, you, Ozzy or the girl."

"I'd say the girl… she has a paper signed by the governor that says so."

Haas didn't know what to say, but Aleese was irate.

"C'mon Mo… This fascist is on the wrong side of history."

Mo and Aleese walked down the path and into the dark. He quickly rethought his position and went after them, knowing he could at least get back to civilization with their help.

Haas was right on their heels, but they had disappeared. Lost twice in one night, he was beginning to believe in curses. Something, a movement caught his attention out of the corner of his eye, and somewhere he could have sworn he heard a bell ringing.

"Are you looking for me Tom?"

The voice startled him. He stared hard at where he thought he'd seen something, but nothing.

"We're done here Mo… The party's over."

"I'm here Tom."

For a moment he thought Mo and Aleese had circled around behind him.

"Let's go home."

"Tom… Tom Haas… Where are you?"

The voice again… In front of him… Maybe his situation wasn't so hopeless.

"I'm here. I'll follow you back to the van."

"Tom… Tom… Step into the Moon light."

The voice was nearer, behind him now, there was something un- nerving about the voice, it wasn't Aleese, it sounded mature. The voice was thin and reedy like an older woman.

"This isn't funny Mo."

"Come to me Tom."

Haas started walking. His face was whipped by the undergrowth, but he pushed on, away from the voice. The woods seemed alive with things he couldn't quite get a look at.

"Tom Haas, why are you running?"

The voice was now in front of him.

"Stop Tom… You'll hurt yourself."

The voice, at once consoling and terrifying seemed to be all around him.

"Be still Tom… There's nothing to fear …"

Tom stood very still and felt a hand rest lightly on his shoulder.

It was Laura Cloud. He knew it was Laura Cloud.

Laura Cloud was behind him, he wanted to look but he couldn't. If he did she would drown him. He ran as fast as he could as far away from her as he could. He ran down hill and off the bank of Buttermilk Creek. He hit the ice and slid into the center where the ice was thin.

"Don't go out on the ice Tom, it isn't safe."

The voice cautioned him, and with good reason, everyone knew that warm weather and fast moving water made the ice weak. But Tom was sprawled on the ice and not thinking straight.

"Be still Tom, don't move… Wait for help."

Tom looked to see who giving him such good advice. Santiago was standing on the bank waving his arms frantically. When he raised his head to acknowledge him, he heard the ice crack. He tried to get back to shallow water, but as he shifted his weight he fell through, and the water swept him under.

He never got to take a deep enough breathe to struggle for survival. Buttermilk Creek took him quickly. Its cold water filled his lungs and the silhouette of a slender woman passed in front of the moon as his world of light and air receded.

His body drifted under the translucent ice and the current carried him away.

It's a mystery the water still keeps.

The House on Catamount Ridge

A cold dry wind blew through a broken window, strong enough to send a shiver down your spine, but too weak to blow the dust off the wainscoting. Despite portents and omens, Marion and Lilith were focused on the windfall the old house represented.

"The money is in escrow…"

"Even if it falls through we get the money."

"It's enough to support us in our declining years."

The women cackled unpleasantly.

They stood in the entry way of the empty house, as they had many years before, many, many years before…

"I can almost picture Eleanor standing here…" "She could be standing here now… stupid cow…" "She made her choice…"

"I wonder what she thinks of her choice now?"

The women let out another unpleasant cackle that was as cold as the wind they shivered in and as old as the home they were selling.

In old, backward towns, there are always haunted places, haunted by a consensus mostly, the common opinion that something supernatural is going on there. The reality is most are just run down properties too large or too derelict for the elderly owners to care for.

The rest of the haunted places usually carry some connection to a human catastrophe or a hearsay connection to the spirit realm. These associations rapidly disappear after encountering an interior decorator with a modern palette of colorful paints and the passage of time.

The old Eleanor Barley place was different.

The local kids never rode their bicycles up there to throw rocks at the windows, local lovers didn't use it as a place of assignation, punks and low lives didn't deface the walls with graffiti—the Barley House was as undisturbed as the day they carried Eleanor out.

It wasn't as if the locals were particularly well behaved; other dilapidated dwellings bore witness to the vibrancy of local vandal culture. The various owners over the years hadn't held title long enough to paint or change the house in any way, so down the decades it went, rotting in peace like Eleanor in Mt.Lazarus Cemetery.

There was no consensus about the Barley House. Eleanor, by all accounts, had led a blameless, if eccentric life, but there was a belief that whatever was in the house had best remain in the house.

The house had been built a long time ago, before Wickesborough even, in a clearing overlooking the Clarion River, midway between Wickesborough and Blanket Hill. When the area was clear cut during the lumber rush, it had stood out, visible for miles on its bald hilltop plateau. Now it was invisible, shrouded by gloomy secondary growth denser than the climax forest it replaced. Visible or not, it was locally famous for being the former residence of Eleanor Barley, the witch of Wickesborough.

She and her sisters, Lilith and Marion, had lived in it, concocting potions and generally doing witchy things. It had changed hands so many times in the intervening years that the association with the three witches had worn thin.

The latest owners, another pair of Marion and Liliths, were two young women distantly related to Eleanor. They inherited the house from a recently deceased aunt, but didn't care to do the work necessary to make it habitable.

People thought it a remarkable coincidence that the two modern owners had the same names as Eleanor Barley's sisters, after all it was impossible to be that young looking and be that old. Hell it was impossible just to be that old. Some names just ran in families.

"So many memories…"

"It's time to move on."

In Wickesborough most houses were built of yellow Kittanning Brick with asphalt shingles and bunched in narrow lots extending just a few blocks uphill from the river. The Barley House was located on Catamount Heights, named after the bobcats that once inhabited the area, but long since exterminated by civic minded hunters. It was situated away from town on a plateau with an artesian spring that contributed its flow to many local streams.

It was an old fieldstone farmhouse eccentrically expanded over the last two centuries; there were wings on either flank of the two story main house with porches and balconies added erratically over the years. Its ramshackle outbuildings were added during various eras and were scattered randomly around the property. None of it looked very promising to the casual eye.

It was situated up a road that used to go somewhere, but now led nowhere and ended in the tangle of brambles, saplings and secondary growth that clogged the land. Since it stopped being a way to anywhere, the road became the house's driveway. It debouched onto Kittanning Pike, so the quiet was rarely disturbed by passers-by.

No one ever developed the land around the Barley place, so whatever the state hadn't set aside as game land, Barley, her predecessors and successors acquired by adverse possession. The boundary lines were a nightmare for surveyors, but no one in Wickesborough wanted to stir things up by making inquiries.

It was said that Colonel Armstrong passed by the house on his way to the Blanket Hill massacre, following his slaughter of Captain Jacob's Indian town. Indians and Europeans had previously lived in comity before that, but Armstrong fixed that. Marion and Lilith looked down the road that soldiers from the French and Indian War had marched along.

"Too bad we can't fix it up… Grow herbs… Have the girls by…"

"The county would tax us to death."

"We have the place in West Wickesborough when we want to come back."

"I like the couple we sold it to."

"Yeah… They look like the perfect couple."

The girls let out another evil laugh that seemed to fill the house with dread. Lilith closed the front door behind her; Marion was already waiting in the car.

"Should we tell them about the cats?"

"Nah… I'm counting on Eleanor's damn cats…"

Marion and Lilith had unloaded their affordable fixer-upper on a couple new to Wickesborough who taught at the Indiana campus of Penn State. Walsh and Maeve had made some money thanks to a simulation game called Homestead, based on Homewood Estates, a failed real estate development in West Wickesborough. They dreamed of turning the old farmhouse into a tech campus similar to Apple's or Microsoft's, populated with the same bicycle riding, bearded millennials they hoped to nurture and exploit.

Despite Marion's and Lilith's opinion, the Barley House wasn't a total tear down; fieldstone is prone neither to termites nor dry rot. Walsh and Maeve wanted to use the original building as their headquarters and build a quad of aesthetically challenged offices around it, again, just like Apple and Microsoft.

Unfortunately they lacked the skill, vision and predatory business acumen of Jobs and Gates. They also lacked any talent as game developers—they stole the Homestead Game from a computer club at Wickesborough High. With nothing else in the development pipeline, their dream threatened to be as big a fiscal fiasco as Maeve's previous husband's efforts to make a go of Homewood Estates.

Their contractor had promised to meet them at this time and place, so they had time to kill. In the meantime they decided to poke around their rambling money pit.

"I want to look in that potting shed…"

"It's supposed to get knocked down today…"

"I don't see McClusky or his bulldozer…"

The potting shed was a tumbled down structure that once had windowed walls and an arched roof. Lately the windows were broken and the roof was collapsed. Maeve held back a dried vine and encouraged Walsh to join her.

"I don't like this place, it gives me the creeps."

"Relax."

A quick glance told Walsh that there was nothing worth retrieving, but Maeve was not deterred and yanked up a hatch in the floor.

"I wonder where this goes."

"Don't go down there…"

Walsh was showing rare common sense. Although not common, rattlesnakes den up in dark subterranean hollows such as Maeve was getting ready to explore.

Maeve was having second thoughts about descending into the cobwebby darkness, and was thinking of deferring to Walsh and letting him go first.

"I think you should take a look at this."

"Not on your life."

The next day, after the ensuing argument, another no-show by McClusky and another argument, a college student, who they hired to do the dirty work, showed up. Aleese Morris was studying Feminist Speleology/Archeology at Indiana State, which, along with a minor in local folklore, equipped her, with the required equipment and interest, to do what neither Walsh nor Maeve were willing to do. She was also an enthusiast for Wiccan ceremonies and Shamanistic nonsense.

Walsh and Maeve watched as Aleese burnt some sage, chanted and got "sky clad" or naked, which piqued Walsh's interest. She explained "sky clad" was how "old time" witches communed with the spirits of nature.

She then spoiled the effect for Walsh by slipping into a hazmat suit, hip-waders and respirator. Then, with more ropes, pitons, and carabiners than an Everest expedition would require, Aleese descended the eight steps into the cellar, and immediately returned because she forgot her flashlight.

"What did you see?"

"I don't know."

"Could you describe it?"

"It looks like someone has been canning cats."

Walsh had decided to investigate the rest of the shed after the interesting part of the program, the sky clad co-ed, ended. He threw a switch he'd found, and it illuminated the cellar nicely.

"Wow... This place is big!"

Aleese yelled this up to Maeve who hovered by the opening.

"How so?"

"Like a rec room, but smaller. With a lot of the cat things stacked on shelves."

Aleese cleaned the cobwebs and dust from the shelves and made sure any snakes had scattered. Walsh and Maeve came down a soon as Aleese sounded the all clear.

"What is this?"

Maeve grabbed a jar and immediately wished she had put gloves on before picking it up.

"It sort of looks like a bowling pin with a cats head... In a mason jar..."

Walsh accurately described the thing but was angling to get Aleese to use her special talents.

"Maybe getting sky-clad would help you identify
it?"

Aleese picked up a jar, opened it and sniffed, like a person who didn't believe the expiration date on a container of sour cream.

"Yeah, it's definitely Egyptian…"

Aleese turned the cat effigy in her hand; the effigy in turn began to twitch, like the contents were trying to get out. She ignored Walsh, but began stripping off again anyway. Maeve stopped her and smacked Walsh in the head.

"These look like hieroglyphics… But that's next semester so I can't be sure…The Egyptians used to mummify cats… it smells like natron… Yeah, somebody has been embalming cats. I better consult the coven."

"Is that really necessary? Isn't there some Federal agency we can call instead? Maybe someone sane?"

"By the sacred name of Bastet, Mihos, Sekhmet, Tefnut, Mafdet, Mekal and especially Pakhet… I must… powerful magic has been done here."

"Well, if you insist."

They explored some more and discovered a marble box in a niche, surrounded by candles melted down to solid puddles of wax.

It was inscribed with a bas relief that depicted a willful Persephone being escorted out of Hades by her stern, disappointed mother, the Goddess Demeter. Like all Goddesses, Demeter had hoped her daughter would aspire to more than being the girlfriend of the Lord of Hell.

Aleese looked at it and began speaking in tones that came straight from a bad horror film.

"In this tomb I sense a powerful spiritual force."

Aleese began taking off clothes again despite Maeve's efforts. To Walsh's distress, she also looked about to open the sarcophagus.

"I don't think we should open this… I've seen a lot of movies and nothing good happens after someone opens a coffin."

"Silence, unbeliever…"

Aleese waddled up to the cenotaph as well as a person wearing hip-waders could and slid back the lid.

"It's a kitty!"

Aleese scooped up a black cat from the casket and laid it on the floor. The cat, almost twice as large as a domestic feline, got up and staggered around; she looked like she had just escaped from the dryer a teenage boy had put her in. The cat was skeletal, sleep-drunk, with dead, sullen eyes. In short, she resembled any large cat that had been shut up in a box for an unknown number of years and then run through the cool cycle of a Maytag.

Aleese bent down to pet it, but the cat wanted none of that. The hip-waders protected her legs and feet, but her face, torso, arms and hands were, in her words, sky clad, and the cat carved angry divots into Aleese's exposed flesh.

"Bad kitty!"

Aleese yelled, as they watched the cat run up the stairs and into the surrounding woods.

"Well I hope that's a lesson for you, young lady… You don't play with unknown creatures from strange sepulchers without protective clothing and eyewear."

"Shut up Walsh," advised Maeve. "Are you okay?"

Aleese looked around the room and her eyes seemed to momentarily roll back in her eye sockets.

"I've felt better…"

Walsh and Maeve watched as Aleese stood up and checked her torn up arms.

"I've been marked to become an acolyte of Pakhet… Woe unto me… Cursed to wander the world as I am now, slave to the wishes of the 'one who scratches' until she releases me by devouring my soul in the fire of judgement."

"Are you sure?"

"Yeah, duh… Don't you guys know anything about third dynasty necromancy?"

Maeve and Walsh hung their heads and acknowledged their collective ignorance.

"So what's next…? Bactine… some moist towlettes… rabies vaccinations?"

"Silence… The power of your magic is as nothing before that of Pakhet! I must go. I am doomed to wander in the wilderness, living on what I can catch until Pakhet devours my soul."

"Well at least put on a coat it's freezing out there."

"No Pakhet's way is clear… I am to wander in nothing but my hip-waders."

"Okay then, we'll let your parents know."

"Great… And ask them to leave my dinner on the back porch, so I don't actually have to eat mice."

It was a melancholy scene, Aleese and Maeve climbed the steps, Walsh followed a step or so behind— a rear guard so to speak. In the shed they shared a lachrymose farewell with hugs, but Walsh spoiled the moment by lingering longer than was appropriate in the embrace. They waved good bye to Aleese as she walked away, Walsh tried to throw an arm around Maeve, but she shrugged him off.

Aleese threw a forlorn gaze back at them, lamented dismally at her fate, and then began stamping her feet and visibly shivering.

"Hey yeah, you know guys… It is <u>fricking</u> freezing out here… Maybe I should come in for a little bit… You know, warm up… I might be an indoor acolyte of Pakhet… Who knows?"

Maeve and Walsh wrapped the young girl in the dirty blanket they kept in the Prius. They discussed taking her home and dumping her on the Morris family's porch, but reconsidered. Hester, Aleese's mother, knew bikers and other unsavory types, so they took her to their condo in Blanket Hill while she recuperated and they came up with an alibi. Walsh tried to dab Aleese with Caladryl ointment, but she hissed and insisted on taking care of it herself.

After she licked herself clean and had a saucer of milk, Aleese lay down and took a forty-eight hour nap.

On the second day Walsh and Maeve were awakened by the terrifying presence of Pakhet, the oversized cat from the sarcophagus, resting on Walsh's chest, glowering at him with eyes that glowed like red hot coals. They heard the noises a sky-clad Aleese made chasing a terrified coyote that had a neighbor's cat in its mouth. Aleese delivered a killing bite to the back of the coyote's neck and freed the cat, which, in turn, did a strange kind of obeisance to Aleese.

Walsh and Maeve stared at the scene in horror as she then tore the coyote's head from its still shaking body.

"Hi guys!"

Aleese bounded in with all the energy a well-rested teenager can muster. Her appearance had subtly changed: her eyes had a slightly Asian look, her ears resembled those of someone who baked cookies in a tree and downy gray fur covered her body. In short, she resembled Olivia Munn, if someone rolled her in dryer lint, given her elf ears and then applied the gore of a mangled coyote to her chest.

Aleese saw they were surprised and attempted to explain.

"Just taking care of business around the casa."

Walsh ran away, but Maeve, driven by previously unknown maternal instincts, tried to counsel the unhinged girl.

"Aleese, playing with coyotes can be dangerous."

"Pssah… Dogs! Did you ever look into their eyes when you kill one? The green flame of life flickers briefly, and then drains away. Their eyes literally turn black! It's awesome."

"I'm glad your first time killing wild life was a good experience, but be careful. You must be starved, would you like some breakfast?"

"I got that covered too!"

Aleese showed Maeve several still twitching mice she had caught and began to eat them in the condos foyer.

"Do you want one? They're mighty tasty when they're still alive."

"Please God no."

"Yeah… I get it; it's an acquired taste… Just as well… I would have told you to paddle your own canoe and catch your own."

As a still struggling mouse went down Aleese's throat, Maeve fainted and Walsh returned with a shotgun.

"Don't make any sudden moves!"

"Really!?! It's me Aleese."

She rubbed up against Walsh in a seductive felinesque manner.

The face-off didn't last long, a linty, elf eared, Asian looking, naked Aleese was even more fetching than the other version.

"I must find a mate."

"Well okay, but Maeve can never know."

"Not you, you fool… I need a mate of royal blood, who can sire many kits to be the heirs of Mut."

"Mut… I thought you were some kind of cat."

"Uh… Mut is an older name for Pakhet, the one who scratches."

"Sorry…I forgot."

"Right… Read a book for once."

Over the next few days the trio settled into a routine: Pakhet still glowered at them with real hatred every morning, Aleese left each morning to wreak havoc on the local pets and wild life and Maeve and Walsh spent the day huddled and terrified, in Maeve's bedroom, the only room inside the condo that had a lock on the door.

Wistfully, Walsh watched from a window as Aleese licked herself clean after devouring the liver of a Labrador.

"Looks like Aleese got the Trumans's dog."

"Stop drooling, she's a cat demon."

"And a flexible one… I think she's growing a tail."

Maeve regarded her despised husband with refreshed loathing.

"We can't go on like this."

"Why? Amazon is still delivering."

"Really... Let's see what The Wickesborough County Herald Examiner, Press Telegraph, Clarion and Evening Bulletin has to say: Cat-like zombie girl spotted out of season… Coyote problem abated… Local cats even sassier… Aleese Morris still missing, At-Risk-Children's- Task-Force pleads for help… Ravens win opener."

"Go Ravens."

"Ravens rule. Don't you see, most of the headlines involve Aleese!"

"You'd think her parents would be more concerned. Isn't it weird Wickesborough still has a print newspaper?"

"We have to do something."

"Something! I think we've done enough"… "Oh Walsh, let's explore the mysterious potting shed"… "Oh Walsh, let's poke around in a dark spooky cellar"… "Oh Walsh, let's hire a colleague's nutsy nitwit daughter, who likes to get naked and hasn't got the good sense God gave an oyster"… "Oh Walsh, let's let said nitwit release the kitty spawn of Satan and bring the same nitwit home with us so she can free range on our neighbors' pets"… I suggest we lay low until this whole thing blows over."

"Blows over! We have to get her help… Counseling… Therapy… Spayed and neutered."

"I think it's one or the other."

"What is?"

"Either spayed or neutered, not both."

A knock on the door prevented the argument from erupting into violence, it was McClusky. There was something urgent about his knocking, Walsh and Maeve saw why when the opened the door.

"Well Mr. McClusky… Nice of you to finally show…"

"Yeah… I had some problems… Say, could you control your cat?"

Aleese was clawing at McClusky's leg and hissing.

How do you know it's our cat?"

"She told me."

Walsh and Maeve looked at each other, the specter of lengthy litigation peeked from behind McClusky's every word. Aleese stood up and brushed leaves from her now more abundant fur.

"I did. I also told him to tell you what he did to the temple of Pakhet."

"It was an accident."

"Blasphemer! You dropped your dozer on it."

"The blade bit and I got stuck in the hole."

"Then your minions broke every canopic jar disturbing the eternal slumber of Pakhet's acolytes."

For the next few minutes Aleese and McClusky argued about the facts, the blame and the responsibility for the catastrophe. Eventually, they agreed that McClusky's crew had caused most of the damage, and were either wandering around Blanket Hill serving Pakhet or headed back to Mexico. Either way, they agreed it was up to Walsh and Maeve to make restitution. Walsh spoke up first.

"That's a nice collar."

Aleese was sporting a rhinestone studded choker that read "Princess."

"Yeah I got it from a shepherd/collie mix that won't be needing it anymore."

"It looks really nice."

"You think so? Me too… I don't think I'm really the princess type though…"

"I could fix that."

"That would be so cool... Could you make it say Furry-Purry instead? I kinda like that name... 'Cause I purr and have fur."

"That can be done... But I'll need you to keep a low profile for a couple of days."

"Why?"

Walsh's plan was to change their names and flee before The Wickesborough County Herald Examiner, Press Telegraph, Clarion and Evening Bulletin connected them to events. He doubted that would fly with Maeve, but it would confuse Aleese enough to give him a few days head start before the heat came down.

"There have been reports of coyotes in Saxonburg."

"Where they have the wire rope museum?"

"The one and only."

"Well okay... I'll give it a look."

With Aleese gone it was easy to get rid of McClusky with a post-dated check they could stop. Walsh's first plan was carry out his first plan, but Maeve had a thought.

"Why don't we consult with Aleese's coven?"

Walsh regarded Maeve's suggestion as similar to jumping from a frying pan into a reactor core. Would their situation be improved by adding more necromancers? Even Aleese had cooled to the idea of involving more witches, although Walsh suspected she just liked being queen of the cat people.

"How do you suggest we find Aleese's coven?"

"The bulletin board in the candle shop."

The bulletin board in "Ye Olde Wick's Borough" was indeed a new age spiritualist playground and Maeve was surprisingly familiar with the contents. Many notes concerned helping women disaffected with their spouses. They offered spells and potions meant either to retrieve them or speed them on their way.

Walsh recalled one casserole Maeve cooked that caused his eyebrows to fall out; the recipe was on the board.

"Hey look it's that recipe for okra and groundhog au gratin."

"Give it a rest… We're looking for a witch."

"I'm a witch."

The young girl at the counter, Ethel, had overheard their conversation.

"We're looking for a serious witch."

Ethel couldn't have been more than eighteen and defined the expression "dewy young thing." She contrived to enhance the impression by wearing a flimsy white silk blouse that didn't conceal a lack of foundation garments, an equally flimsy skirt that draped, but revealed, the contours of her healthy young legs. As a finishing touch she coiffed her flowing blonde hair to frame her face with angelic exclamation points.

Walsh was beside himself, wondering how he missed all these spectacular babes in boring old Wickesborough.

"Oh, you must be the couple that uncovered the Temple of Mut and unleashed an Egyptian cat demon."

"How do you know that?"

"Well… It's the talk of the astral plane… It was foretold in the Akashic record… And I'm a witch, so I know these things."

"Can you help us?"

"Well I don't know, I'm not a serious witch."

"Sorry about that, can you help?"

"I'm just fuckin' with you… Of course I can help, it'll be a piece of cake."

"Thank God. When can you begin?"

"Sorry, I was fuckin' with you again. It will be extremely difficult and will require powerful magic."

"You're fucking with us again, right?"

"Nope, dead serious… Do either of you have a first born you're not fond of?"

"No."

"Well then it will cost a lot to deal with the cat situation. Cash deposit upfront."

"You guarantee the results?"

"Guaranteed!"

"Will this require you to be sky clad?"

"Most definitely… for hours on end, especially while I stretch and do my Pilates. Are you on board for that?"

Walsh was on board.

"You don't mind becoming a companion of Mut?"

Walsh was on board for that as well. The prospect of Ethel stretching and being "sky clad" got him on board for anything.

Marion and Lilith stood at the top of the cellar stairs and surveyed the scene of horror. Aleese was preparing to pull Maeve's heart from her chest while a pair of ravens pecked at the unfortunate woman's eyes. Ethel was dumping bags of natron onto a not quite deceased Walsh.

"Too bad about Maeve."

"Well no one really liked her…"

 "Ethel sure finished this fast,"

"Incredible, barely a week."

"She looks great."

"That frat boy really jumped Ethel's battery."

Ethel heard her name and gave a friendly wave to her mentors. She was otherwise occupied with wrapping a struggling Walsh in the bandages that would turn him into a proper mummy and fit companion for Mut.

"What's with wrapping Walsh up like a mummy?"

"It's Egyptian… Something Ethel came up with."

"Will it lift the curse of Pakhet?"

"How should I know? Do I look like a priestess of Ammit?"

"Ammit… That's funny… You're Vegan."

The two ravens began pecking at Walsh's eyes.

"Ravens sure like eyes. Where'd the Ravens come from? Go Ravens."

"Ravens rule…Ethel keeps them in the candle shop office."

"Nice touch."

Pakhet hissed and jumped on Walsh's chest and clawed at the parts of his face not wrapped in linen bandages.

"Seems like an awful lot to go through to make them fall out of escrow."

"They didn't strike Ethel as people that would walk away from equity."

"We'll get their escrow deposit and buy the house back when it goes into probate."

"What are we going to do with all the cats McClusky released?"

"I don't know, that was always Eleanor's thing."

"What the Hell do we do with Aleese?"

"I think her condition is mostly psychosomatic."

"She's grown a tail."

"I said mostly."

"The ears: Spock or Elf?"

"Elf… I think the ears and tail are a good look for her, but stopping her from rolling in dryer lint would be a good idea."

"Maybe we can find her a good home… Or we could trade her to some bikers to settle things with McClusky."

"They're good with animals."

"When summer comes… and she starts shedding… I do not want her in the house."

Aleese had finished playing with Maeve, clawed open her chest and threw her still beating heart to Pakhet, who devoured it in seconds. Walsh derived what comfort he could from his wife's final tableau, knowing his final destination as a companion of Mut, was to be buried alive in a coffin with his carved likeness on the lid. Ethel finished wrapping his head in bandages that muffled his protests.

"What the Hell are we going to do with that giant cat?"

Pakhet leapt on Walsh's chest and stared at him one last time with hate filled eyes. Walsh reached out with his bandaged arms and tried to strangle the menacing pussy cat. Ethel slammed the lid shut before Pakhet could get away and sealed the companions in their common sepulcher for the foreseeable eternity.

Marion and Lilith watched in stunned silence as the greatest of their concerns were resolved.

Ethel looked up at them and made a small curtsey.

"What's the matter? Cat got your tongue?"

Darkness Visible

Parts of the Clarion run deep which is odd since it also runs slow. Most rivers as old have cut their way down to bedrock and meander across generous floodplains creating sand bars and gravel beds, which menace the careless navigator.

Below Wickesborough that would be the case, but above its Buttermilk Creek tributary the Clarion is constrained by two granite batholiths that pushed their way up through the crust of the earth during the Appalachian orogeny, creating narrow headlands resistant to erosion.

Alternatively, the Lenape said that Wenotha, the punisher, split the rock with his tomahawk to wash away the man eating Ongweias and accidentally released Hadiades the great Black Snake of the river. Opinion is divided as to the veracity of both versions.

The granite is worn and cracked, every year the river carries a little more away, but today it still constrains the Clarion, and has since before the advent of man.

The source of the Clarion is a spring that flows down Liar's Run between Indian mounds while gathering water from various tributaries until it emerges from state land above Clarington and becomes the Clarion. The Lenape claim the area was inhabited years before by the Allegewi, a tribe unknown to the white man, the Eries, the Nanticokes, the Iroquois, or any other relative newcomers to the area. The Allegewi may have been the source of the legend about the Wenotha since Lenape tradition contains nothing else like it.

Today the Clarion drifts by Wickesborough in its inky black fastness. Wickesborough has a complex relationship with the stream; it offers recreation, but retains a sinister quality that discourages carefree splashing around.

The Clarion Marina was built on, and into, the River itself, regardless of how the locals felt. It rents a variety of water craft and otherwise does a brisk business at lunch time, dinner time, and at the bar. The bar in the Clarion Marina is the only area in the place where you cannot see the river. The regular clientele prefer it that way as all that slow moving water can make one bilious.

Ora Traynor was polishing glasses behind the bar and minding his morning customers, the lost souls who needed a bracer to face their drab lives, lives that mostly involved waiting until their empty husks were delivered to Mt. Lazarus.

Lined up next to the service bar, Ora called them murderer's row, a band brothers united in desperation, their favorite intoxicant conveniently nearby, a minimum of wasted time and motion between the pour and consumption. One of their number, Mo, was a no-show this morning; Ora would call him in about an hour, and then call the sheriff, if a welfare call was warranted. Ora never called the Wickesborough PD.

Within that time frame Mo was retrieved by Deputy Burt Himmeldeutsch and seated on his accustomed stool.

He guzzled well bourbon in tumbler sized shots and related his latest adventure to Ora, Burton and the assembled choir.

"I tell you its head was as big as a car..."

"Like Escalade large or a civic?"

"Closer to a Civic, but it was black, a giant black snake... And shiny... But you couldn't see it in the dark... But then I could... There was no light, but I could see it."

The congregation nodded solemnly. They had all seen snakes and other improbable animals in fevered dreams between drinks, but Mo's account was inspirational.

"Why'd you climb the tree?"

Burton wanted to know because he'd almost used a tranquilizer dart gun to get Mo down.

"Water snakes don't climb trees... It came out of the river."

Burton was unfamiliar with this bit of popular wisdom, but saw that Ora was listening attentively.

Mo was an amiable lunatic who stored large fragments of local lore and superstition in his otherwise alcohol addled brain. He was terrified of anyone related to Eleanor Barley. He believed he was a lost boy from a local legend who drowned on his way to school. He believed that phantom Indians stalked him carrying little lanterns. He said his mother named him Moses because she found him floating in the reeds and his brother Aaron because he played with snakes. He thought a limping Asian demon visited him while he slept. In short, Mo had a lot to drink about.

Burton and everyone else in Wickesborough dismissed Mo's ranting, but Burt saw Ora taking note and paid closer attention.

Burt heard the myth of Hadiades and Wenotha and figured that was where Mo was getting his ideas. He thought the myth came from the Seneca rather than the Lenape, but, still Ora looked serious and Burt respected Ora.

And that was why Burt staked out Mo's house that evening to see if there was anything to his claim. Sherriff Taylor had assigned Burt to a morning shift in deference to his age and length of service, but he had a feeling, and didn't mind losing a few hours of fitful sleep for a feeling.

Mo's house was on a spit of land where Buttermilk Creek flowed into the Clarion, at the very end of an undedicated road called Recluse Lane. The residents may have been normally social in every other respect, but they wanted nothing to do with their neighbors.

It was an odd, crazy house made of bricks but built on stilts, evidently to keep it above the spring thaw when water overtopped the dykes that surrounded the property. Burt could only marvel at the engineering the structure entailed. Burt parked on River Road and watched the Clarion roll on.

A loud guttural sound emerged from a second story window indicating Mo was down for the count. Burt felt sure that whatever Mo saw, it waited to hear the onset of Mo's severe sleep apnea before appearing.

Mo snored loudly, so loudly that neighbors complained and periodically banged pots and pans to make him turn over. Everyone knew it, and Burt suspected a neighbor wanted to make Mo appear more witless than usual.

It was a beautiful evening, a beautiful evening after a beautiful day, the only thing missing was moonlight dappling the occasional ripples on the Clarion. Burt watched the water, until he drifted into a hypnotic reverie. Lost in thought and holding an internal conversation on subjects lofty and low, he suddenly felt as if someone, or something, was watching him.

Himmeldeutsch stared intently at the water; it was inky and opaque, no light reflected off it. It was darkness so deep it reminded Burt of a black hole, blackness so dense no light could escape its gravity. He stared into the blackness until he became aware he was staring at two eyes, two eyes darker than the surrounding opaque blackness. Something beyond the event horizon was looking back at him.

Burt scrambled to start his prowl car as more of the creature emerged. It didn't come out of the dark; it was the dark, pure sensate evil, epitomizing darkness. Burton knew by now it was coiled around his car, a vast serpentine predator stalking its prey, him, toying with him until its cold dry essence was ready to strike. The smell of rotting corpses filled his nostrils, Burt un-holstered his weapon, and braced for action. He had no illusions about killing the beast, the gun was for self-offense, he would end things before the greater horror took control.

There was a rap on his window and Burt nearly blew the rapper away. It was the familiar figure of Ora standing in what had been, seconds before, the death dark coils of Mo's monster.

"You saw it."

"I think so… What was it?"

"You saw it alright… You saw Hadiades, the blacksnake."

"Where did it go?"

"It's still here, writhing around my feet."

A few minutes later they were in the Clarion Marina bar, Ora poured out two snifters of funny tasting brandy and the two men drank and talked.

"It's the Lenape version of the Lucifer story… The light bringer is cast down into Hell. The fallen angel creates his own world, next to ours, but he has to do it without light, without a firmament to separate… whatever… A counterfeit second creation, where evil is good, good is evil… Up is down… Dogs and cats living together…"

Burton smiled at the Ghostbusters reference; he needed it, his mind was still racing.

"I thought it was a Seneca myth…"

"The Seneca got it from the Lenape and the Lenape got it from the Allegewi. They never got along. Harriger thought the Seneca stole the story from the Lenape because they had an inferiority complex. Hadiades wars against any good he finds in Hell, their standards are higher than ours, but sometimes he wanders over here anyway."

"So he's real?"

"Hadiades? In a sense… You can't touch him or feel him, but you saw him, felt his weight, smelled his breath."

"And you used to discuss this with the guy that got killed out on Rabbit Run?"

"Harriger… Yes, it fascinated him. He taught psychology at Clark. When I was teaching comparative religions at Emerson."

"Emerson?"

"Yes… It helped being an atheist."

"I didn't know you were from New England."

"I'm not, but I move around a lot."

"Wait a minute… If you knew Harriger… and were teaching..."

"I was retired by then …"

"You'd be…"

Deputy Himmeldeutsch watched Ora's face resolve into an unfamiliar visage, that of an ancient Indian face, care worn and antique in its features.

"As near as I can figure, I was born in April of 1499… The Lenape didn't go in much for dates, what with living forever and all. I saw Verrazano enter New York harbor, it wasn't New York then, of course."

"You look pretty good."

"Thanks, I try to look after myself, but the smoking and drinking puts the years on."

"How did…?"

"A blessing or curse from an old aunt, who had the wisdom to die. I keep a low profile these days; there are only so many birthday greetings from weathermen you can stand. Drink up."

Burton took another swig from the snifter. It tasted like licorice and burned going down. Burt hated licorice. Ora gauged his progress and poured him some more.

"I'll need you to kill him."

Burton choked on his drink.

"Is that why you're feeding me the rot gut? This stuff is awful… Has it got magical Indian herbs to help me conquer Black-Snake-Zilla?"

"No this is some left over stuff the Dutch used to sell us. It's flavored with wormwood, the French call it Absinthe."

"I don't know about killing your snake… Any more of this and I might kill myself."

"That's the effect it had on the Lenape."

"Why don't you kill the thing?"

"It's an immortality thing… I'm so old my essence has become thin… in a few more centuries, a strong breeze will be able to knock me on my ass."

"Okay… Why me?"

"You're the bait."

"The bait?"

"We need a good man to attract Hadiades."

"I nominate Reverend Conrad."

"You don't know? You're a good man Burt… A lot better than that fraud Conrad… People respect you… You're the glue that holds this town together."

"I am?"

"Yes you Burt… You took out that Wendigo… Hell, you really put a dent in the drinking by golf courses after dark problem."

"I guess I have."

"You're the best we have. Hadiades only stalks people where the spirit of good runs strong."

"That's why we don't see him much."

"Exactly, Hitler… Stalin… Alan Thicke…"

"Alan Thicke?"

"Remember how he treated Gloria Loring?"

"Oh yeah… I see, the Hadiades ignores us because evil men so are common."

"Well yes… That's true… Of course Hitler and Stalin never visited Wickesborough."

"Tell me what to do…"

Ora painted Burt's face with signs meant to protect him, chanted an equally protective chant and gave him a stout branch of hickory, intricately carved with symbols.

"What do the words mean?"

"I don't know. I don't speak Allegewi."

"Are these engravings magic?"

"No, the last time I had to deal with Hadiades I got bored, so I started whittling."

"What do I do with it?"

"Hit him with it."

"Hit him?"

"YES, hit him… You're Irish…"

"German actually…"

"Six of one… Every German and Irishman knows instinctively what a hickory stick is for…"

Ora got Burt into a canoe, chanted some more and pushed Burt and canoe away. When Burt looked back, Ora had disappeared. Paddling out to mid-stream Burt sat and waited, and baled and waited some more, it was endless.

The canoe had a leak.

Burt kept at it, alternately baling and paddling until waiting for Hadiades slipped his mind. He sat down and considered paddling back to the Marina. It was three A.M. and Burt figured Hadiades was a no show.

The breath was the first thing he noticed; redolent with decay, the smell almost choked Burt. He next saw the head, and then the tail. He beat the creature, but it seemed to have no effect, in fact Hadiades seemed to be winning. The words Ora said came back to him; he was bait.

He thrashed all the harder, wind milling at the giant mouth that threatened to swallow him. Burt's gun was on shore, he had no choice but to resist.

Most of the Wickesborough PD's graveyard shift was watching Burt's antics from River Road. It was a popular place where the overnight crew could drink and ignore their radios. In the grey green images of their thermal night vision goggles it appeared that Burt was thrashing at some invisible demon. Their water rescue team was already in wet suits awaiting the inevitable.

Ora and Mo watched Burt tumble into the river from a vantage point behind the cops.

"Well that's that. He either drowns or he's rescued, and becomes the laughing stock of Wickesborough."

"We have a lot of candidates for that job. Do you really think he'll win it?"

"I think it will be a 237 way tie for second place. Never mind, Burt Himmeldeutsch is no longer a factor in Wickesborough, with him gone a fetid breeze of hopelessness and despair will blow through this town again. It will be like a breath of stale air."

Ora turned to Hadiades who was badly injured and wincing from Burt's beating.

"Back to Arkham, Cecil?"

Hadiades nodded a vigorous affirmative, as vigorous an affirmative a badly beaten river demon could manage. Mo bowed and saluted.

"Express my respect to the Old Ones."

Ora and Hadiades vanished into thin air and Mo walked back to his house

Deputy Himmeldeutsch stumbled out of the Clarion to raucous catcalls and laughter. Sheriff Andy Taylor was there to throw a blanket over his deputy and put him in the back of his car.

"Do you think they bought it?"

"Yeah… I saw the big black snake and Ora vanish together; I guess Mo will be hanging around."

"We should take him in for a 72 hour psychiatric hold then book him into 28 days of rehab…"

"Make him think twice about inviting his friends from New England to play. Think he'll take the hint?"

Burt fingered the hickory stick and carved a fresh notch in the handle.

"Maybe if I give him a more pointed suggestion next time."

Wickesborough Terminal

"Wickesborough Terminal… Butler Coach arriving…Wickesborough Terminal… Check your seat for personal belongings."

Milan woke and was abruptly pulled from an intensely realistic dream that she had no recollection of. It receded into the brightness of an unforgiving mid-morning, the kind of morning light that hurt the eyes and converted a cool, clammy dawn into a hot, humid afternoon. She had no memory of what happened in the dream, only a feeling as it became lost in the background clutter of her awakened reality.

It felt so real, as if it had really happened.

She looked around and realized she was in the waiting room of the Butler Coach Company Terminal, the only public transit company in or out of Wickesborough. The company had a long, if uneventful, history of carting people back and forth between Butler and Wickesborough, with the occasional chartered forays to Pittsburgh, Oil City and other fleshpots.

"You look lost, can I help?"

Milan heard a voice but couldn't immediately locate the source.

"If you are lost, I might be able to help."

"Lost" was the understated but accurate description of Milan's predicament, not that she shared that opinion.

Wandering without direction or purpose was how she had disposed of her life up to now; it was her "normal." She expected whatever deity that ruled her destiny to bless her with unwarranted favor, whatever else he did. Someone would provide for her, to set right whatever calamity that befell her. Soon, she confidently expected she would be prospering, enjoying more unearned bounty.

The voice came from a cheery young woman nested behind the information counter, surrounded with an extraordinary number of brochures for local tourist traps, extraordinary because Wickesborough was considered the blankest spot on the interesting-things-to-see map.

The girl didn't just smile, she beamed, and Milan could see this was a beautiful young girl.

The Butler Coach Terminal waiting room would be the waiting room in Hell if Jean-Paul Sartre had been from the Midwest. The building went up in the 1920's when the need arose for a place to keep people until they could be squired from Butler to Wickesborough and back. When it was new, it was painted in green and mustard toned paints, those tints were achieved with various ad-mixtures of lead, arsenic, and cadmium, all highly toxic, but popular colors of the time. Uranium glass was used in the windows, bathing its clientele with soothing, gamma radiation.

It was, of course, thoroughly insulated with asbestos.

By the nineteen eighties it had become a historically protected superfund site, and would have been of more concern if so many other things weren't killing the residents already.

One of which was Milan, or at least that was what she had been convicted of. Her crime was the kidnapping and murder of Rosemary Woodhouse. She had been in prison as late as this morning.

Her guilt was somewhat mitigated by the fact that Rosemary, a well-known lunatic and semi-pro drug user, showed up later, alive, according to reports, and definitely animated. In light of this her father had spent every bit of influence and every bit of stored up treasure he had to get her a retrial and out of prison. He struggled mightily and brought forth his dissolute daughter.

The effort ruined him and destroyed his life. A technicality got her sentence reduced, but he died before she was released. Her mother blamed her for his death and refused to speak to her. Now she was coming home to no one and nothing.

She retrieved a back pack which contained everything she had brought with her when they put her away. Mostly clothing from a few years past, not terribly dated, but from a different century and different person as far as Milan was concerned. She would be re-outfitted in due course, but for now her life would revolve around the halfway house, counseling, and manipulating her parole officer.

The pretty girl persisted.

"Give it a shot... Maybe I can help... What could it hurt?"

There was that voice again, Ethel, the extraordinarily perky concierge, attendant or whatever the drone seated at the information desk was calling, effulgent with good humor and optimism.

Milan had once been a pretty young thing like her, but age and prison had taken their toll on her. She caught a glimpse of her reflection, the grim, don't- fuck-with-me face she had adopted in prison had hardened into fleshy cement—the fresh faced girl of a few years back was gone beyond hope of redemption. The girl, who got what she wanted by flirting and making promises her body had no intention of keeping, had disappeared.

Apropos of nothing a fragment of unfamiliar poetry came to mind.

'One by one I tell my tales. One by one I tell my lies.'

It summed up her past, present and future, why not start her new life with the gullible little teenager behind the desk.

"If you think you can help, give it a shot. I'm ready for any assistance."

Ethel eyed her over a damn thick book, the sort of tome that had mostly disappeared since the advent of consumer electronics.

"Don't keep me hanging... Give me a clue... What are you here for?"

"You said you could help... Tell me."

Ethel looked at Milan, their banter pretended to be jocular, but it had an edge. Ethel accepted the challenge.

"Well fortunately I'm a witch, so I'll consult the caldron."

Ethel looked into an appliance on the desk beside her.

"That's a Crock Pot."

"Yeah, we also heat hot dogs in it... You are Milan Kumnacker and someone is meeting you to take you to take you to a halfway house."

"That's amazing... Are you really a witch?"

"That's what it says on my business card."

Ethel turned the business card holder on her desk towards Milan.

"It says you work at a candle shop."

"The other side."

"Okay, how did you know that?"

"I'm a Witch and Olstee Pettigrew wrote a story about you in the County Herald... And the caldron said so."

Ethel, like most residents used the short hand version of The Wickesborough County Herald Examiner, Press Telegraph, Clarion and Evening Bulletin's full masthead.

"The caldron..."

"Take a look."

Milan looked into the kitchen appliance and instead of seeing a ceramic tub half full of left over hot dogs, she saw a dark swirling mass of a molten grey something, something imperfectly mixing, a roiling kaleidoscope of shapes, fascinating and menacing at the same time."

"You cook hot dogs in that?"

"Around lunch time... They're better than you'd think."

"What else does the crock caldron say about me?"

"It seems you were a busy girl when you were younger."

"How so?"

"Take a look."

Milan again stared into the phantasmagorical appliance and this time saw her youthful antics replayed. In high school she had been breathtakingly promiscuous, the word as quaint as the sexual practices she indulged in then. It made her popular, but it was a wasting asset, she was never alone, but on the other hand she had no steady boyfriends, just guys that hung around for leftovers.

The Crock Pot made Milan uncomfortable; she didn't like others knowing her secrets. A lot of what got her through life had been based on the fiction she was an innocent girl, or at least not a round heeled mercenary slut.

Ethel raised an eyebrow and looked at Milan with new interest.

"Pretty naughty..."

Ethel read her mind.

"I guess you're looking to get the old band wagon rolling again. No shortage of men looking for companionship to bankroll your life style."

Milan thought about it. She had no skills; she was cunning rather than smart. She had always relied on the kindness of strangers—and her father—rather than her own devices. Living off credulous men had been her life and the career she intended to continue.

"That was a long time ago. I was young and stupid.

That's in my past."

"Stupid maybe, but not that long ago or in your past..."

She looked into the Crock Pot again. In prison she had used her looks to her advantage; going gay-for-the-stay and becoming the popular, fragile little white girl in a sea of hungry dark faces. The slow cooking marvel showed all of that in exquisite, excruciating detail.

"This is like watching one of those Penthouse Forum letters come to life. I can't wait to see what's next."

"Next?"

"Yeah it'll tell your future too."

Milan made a grab for the Crock Pot, but Ethel pulled it out of reach.

"I already know what's in store for me. The only thing I have to look forward to is a God awful present, and a depressing future."

"The future might hold some surprises… Let's go to the replay, shall we… Or in this case the foreplay… Although you never needed much of that."

Ethel chuckled at her own joke; something Milan had always thought was bad form. Ethel looked up from the caldron and made a sound like a train pulling a heavy load.

" Choo, Choo… Wow… I guess it's true, you can find a woman to do anything if you pay her enough."

Ethel stared into the vessel again, frowned, switched the dial on the front from on to off and back again, shook it vigorously and then rapped the appliance on its side.

"Damn it went blank."

"Does that mean my future's unwritten?"

"You mean after you pulled that train into the station?"

"Yes… After that."

"Perhaps, or it might have blown a fuse, it's hard to do anything in this place without blowing something… But then why am I telling you?"

Ethel's puns at her expense were beginning to wear on Milan, but she said nothing as Ethel controlled the fortune telling slow cooker.

"So, if it doesn't have anything to do with faulty wiring, I have hope?"

"Hope is the lie God tells us to keep us from committing suicide."

Milan began to cry, a unique experience for her.

She was crying for the first time not for the effect it would have on some guy, but because she was lamenting past behavior. It was her first experience with the truth.

In her hedonist youth she had manipulated and lied to get her way. It was a source of adventure and excitement for her and most of the time, save one, consequences free. Two young men, Leno and Bosco, had gone along with her on her last plan. They stole a car and inadvertently kidnapped the owner, Rosemary Woodhouse who was asleep in the backseat.

When they discovered Rosemary, Milan decided that the way to solve the witness problem was to kill her. She convinced the boys to go along and plotted how they would kill their victim. When the cops caught up with them, they believed that Rosemary had been murdered and deduced that Milan was the mastermind. Leno and Bosco rolled on her and she was convicted.

It had all gone badly.

The trio was convicted of murder. Convictions for kidnapping, arson and car theft followed. They were sent away for life and it looked like that was the end of it until, Rosemary showed up, after the trial, in the throes of DT's, and gibbering about her late son Andy.

A sentence reduction looked promising, but Leno and Bosco had been killed, in the meantime, by comrades of Rosemary's son. Milan only survived because she was in a woman's prison and beyond their retaliation.

Leno had been the last man to tumble into her snare and was stupid enough to think she cared.

Milan's game was old even then, it didn't take most people very long to catch on to Milan. She lied to stay in practice. Her CV was a litany of elaborations on fabrications. She lied to everyone, about everything, and everyone knew it. After brief experience women discounted what she said and never counted on her promises or anything else from her.

Men didn't care what she promised; it was the cut-rate word of a whore. As long as her gift for fiction came with the enthusiastic sexual gifts she was known for, it was all good.

She had been a toxic package in a beautiful wrapper. Now the exterior was looking the worse for wear and the men she got would demand more for less.

Ethel watched her sobbing to see if she faking, looking for the tell-tale tell, the sign Milan was subtly gauging her audiences reaction to the tears, Tolerant but impatient, Ethel patted her on her shoulder.

"Hey buck up soldier, it ain't over yet."

"It isn't all hopeless?"

Ethel fluffed her hair and gave her a mirror.

"I didn't say that, but some make-up, new clothes… maybe some exercise… You might make a living at a truck stop."

"You think?"

"Sure why not? Now go fix your face, I'll bet your luck's about to change."

"Did the caldron come back on?"

"No, but Olstee Pettigrew just parked in front."

"Who?"

"The guy who wrote the story in the Herald."

Milan was blank.

"Do I know him?"

"He was sweet on you in high school. He wrote all your book reports in freshman English"

Milan remained blank.

"No help I see… I'm guessing that was a large, not very exclusive club—friendly, but with a long line to get in."

"Maybe I'll recognize him when I see him."

"Not likely, he's wearing pants. He's here to drive you to the half-way house."

Olstee Pettigrew was a man, who had a sensibility in his use of language. He had grown up in Wickesborough which was regarded as a wasteland of low brow tastes. At least that's how the Mandarins of high culture at Indiana saw it. Olstee disagreed and labored at <u>The Wickesborough County Herald Examiner, Press Telegraph, Clarion and Evening Bulletin</u> trying to prove them wrong.

Milan appraised the sturdy example of north western Pennsylvanian manhood and decided he would do, not likely to spring for a vacation in Italy, but maybe worth a car and apartment for a minimum of effort.

"An apartment maybe, a car, not so likely.

Ethel was in her head again and it was getting crowded in there.

"A used car, maybe… And if you're lucky a semi- late model, but don't expect much chrome."

Ethel arched a brow by way of acknowledging she was indeed reading Milan's mind.

"Talk to him. See if you can turn him to your use."

Milan rose and met Olstee in mid terminal.

"Hi Olstee it's good to see you."

"Really, I wouldn't have thought so. I'm taking you to a half-way house. Not really up to your standard."

"I always liked you."

"Bull shit, I offered you an honorable companionship and you threw it back in my face like an unworthy offering laid on the altar of some two bit deity. Well look at you now, don't you wish you had that widow's farthing now?"

Ethel rolled her eyes. She hadn't heard a speech like that since she visited the Frank Capra exhibit at the Jimmy Stewart Museum in Indiana. Olstee was in high schadenfreude. Milan turned to Ethel.

"I thought you said he was sweet on me."

"You stood him up for the prom."

"I guess he holds a grudge."

Olstee looked confused.

"Who are you talking to?"

"Ethel."

"Ethel works at the candle shop."

Milan looked around and gestured in the direction of Ethel, but there was no one there, just a pot of old hot dogs.

"I'm sorry Olstee... I shouldn't have treated you so badly."

"Right, you don't even know who I am."

"You were sweet on me... You asked me to the prom... You wrote an article about me."

"About a criminal we were welcoming back into our midst."

"Is that all you can say about me? You used to like me... Remember?"

"Remember? The only thing people remember about you is you tried to kill somebody... And most people don't remember that."

"I'll bet some guys I know would disagree."

"Yeah, when they're fantasying... While they're fucking someone else... You're a masturbatory aide. You'll be remembered by what I wrote about you. Think about that when you're dying, people will only remember what I said about you. Whether you are consigned to nothingness or broken on the wheels of Hell, it is my judgment of you that will be carried forward."

"I'm sorry... I paid my debt."

"I'm sorry… The last recourse of the stubborn whore, I guess the town needs a new tramp now that Aleese grew a tail."

Milan looked around for Ethel, she needed an emergency extraction. Olstee was just getting wound up.

"Why should I forgive anything?"

"I don't know… I just got out of jail, everybody knows I'm a whore; I'll be on supervised parole for five years… My father died… So maybe I deserve a little slack."

"Slack… Do you know what Hell is?"

"I'd say I'm living in it."

Just for a second Milan thought she saw a flicker of satisfaction in Olstee's eyes.

"The Buddhists might call it a Bardo, the Bardo of bad decisions, the Hell of willful stupidity. You squandered an embarrassment of riches and consigned yourself to being a round heeled whore. Funny thing though, you despised being that, and were terrified someone, anyone, would pull your covers and reveal what a nothing example of humanity you are."

Milan began to cry again, broken by the judgment of a person she couldn't remember. It progressed from weeping to crying and finally to sobbing, as Milan bleated out her father's name.

"My Dad loved me."

"Yes, yes he did… I feel sorry for your father; I know nothing about him except what I learned from you, his daughter, a person who treated me like a bitch. I feel sorry that he labored to provide for an ungrateful whore. When he died the only thing you missed was the support he could no longer supply. Still, for appearances, I suppose you will have to look sad, but you will need someone to come up with the words of grief you can't think of."

"I tried to be a good person."

"Bull Shit!…You compensated for the growing evil in you by being a fraud. You're a nasty bit of work, and that truth keeps clawing its way from the back of your mind to the front."

A familiar voice chimed in from behind her.

"Hard to be jolly after that."

Ethel was back. She turned to look at Ethel and when she turned back to Olstee, he was gone.

"What's going on here?"

"I think you know… You said it yourself… You're in Hell."

"I want to look in the Crock Pot."

"Not a good idea. Not many happy endings for old whores."

"I don't care, I want to know."

Milan looked into the pot and watched the contents swirl and coalesce; she could see her reflection on the slick surface of the fluid. A face began to form underneath her image. It became by turns malignant, then malicious, malevolent and finally the most terrifying face Milan had ever seen. It spoke of the death of hope and an end to the conceits of humanity. It was a jesting horror, gibbering and mocking her, a harbinger, long expected, but always come too soon, to all men, in the fullness of time.

Milan began to scream.

The scream awoke Milan from her dream. She was abruptly pulled from an intensely realistic dream that she had no recollection of. She had no memory of what happened in the dream, only a feeling as it became lost in the background clutter of her awakened reality. It felt so real, as if it had really happened.

It reminded her of a short story she never read, something at Owl Creek something, a boy who always made moon eyes at her, had promised to write a paper about it for her freshman English class.

She was in terrible pain. Someone, someone in her cell block, was shoving a broom stick into her violently. She felt an awful tear inside herself and a spectrum of pain radiated from her core to her extremities.

Her blood drained out onto the floor around her she lay in it. It mingled dark grey and black metallic tones. She saw a dark swirling mass of a molten grey something, something imperfectly mixing, a roiling kaleidoscope of shapes, fascinating and menacing at the same time.